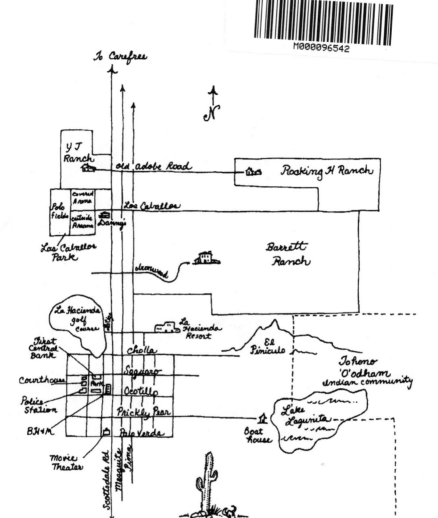

The Town of Pinnacle Peak

Heir Apparent
A Pinnacle Peak Mystery

by Twist Phelan

Published by SANDS Publishing, LLC
P.O. Box 92
Alpine, California 91903
Visit our Website: www.sandspublishing.com

HEIR APPARENT

Copyright © 2002 by Twist Phelan, Inc.

ISBN: 1 59025 017 6

First Edition

Cover design: Bob Paulson

Map: Erin Lynch Dover

Author page photo: David Stoecklein

Back cover photo: John Hall

Printed in the United States

0 9 8 7 6 5 4 3 2 1

Acknowledgments

Because I spend a lot of time in faraway places, the people who provided assistance in the writing of this book are few, but no less valuable. Thanks and gratitude are owed to:

The T brothers, who taught me ropin' (good luck in your next rodeo, boys);

Sandy and Diana, for making the book better;

Nancy B., for her enthusiasm and creativity;

E, the best *prima* anyone could have; and

J.

***

This is a work of fiction. The town of Pinnacle Peak does not exist, although I wish it did, somewhere in the desert north of Scottsdale, Arizona. Names, characters, places, and incidents either are the product of my imagination or are used fictitiously. Any resemblance to actual events, locales, organizations, persons or animals, is entirely coincidental – except in one instance. Any mistakes in the book are mine, of course.

Twist Phelan

for j:
oh, the days we've had ...

Prologue

The two bodies sprawled in the chairs, utterly still. Blood, dark and shiny, blotched their clothes. More pooled on the floor. A metallic sweetness permeated the air.

Averting his eyes but not his thoughts from the grisly discovery, Joe McGuinness took a step backward, then another. As he edged out of the room, a childhood memory came unbidden. When he was a kid he used to pretend he could undo something bad that had happened if he could repeat everything that preceded it, but in reverse. If he could take his jacket off the same way he had put it on and lay his mitt down where it had been, the ball would magically be called back to his hand and the shards of glass reformed into one piece reattached to the window frame.

Retracing his steps, he felt a momentary irrational hope that the horrible scene would correct itself. He raised his eyes to the clock on the wall, wistfully willing its hands to revolve the wrong way, from the six to the five to the four, backing up hours, then days, to the time when his only concern was keeping his job ...

Chapter 1

Friday, October 11

Atticus was dead. And because of it, Joe was waiting to be fired. It had happened a week ago. Driving back from a late night interview with a witness, Atticus Barclay was forced off the Beeline Highway. The big Mercedes rolled twice.

Joe sat at the far end of the small conference room table, its marble top cold under his fingertips. Through the open door he could see into the firm's reception area. An earth-colored Navajo blanket hung from an iron bar, undulating in the draft from the air conditioning. Below it was a low pinewood cabinet, its shelves crowded with Zuni pottery. A blackened branding iron bearing the firm's initials, the gift of a grateful client, leaned against the cabinet. The associates joked that all the firm's partners bore its mark, "Branded for life as a Barclay, Harrington & Merchant lawyer." I wish, Joe thought as he looked at the darn thing.

In the chair to his right slouched Katie Hewson, a second year lawyer. She sat without speaking, chunky arms folded on the table, her thin brown hair tied back with a spindly ribbon. Every minute or so she would reach down and tug at the skirt stretched over her thick thighs as though in rearranging the material she might somehow rearrange their shape, too. They shared a secretary, but Joe didn't know Katie well. She worked exclusively for Alistair Harrington, the firm's trusts and estates lawyer, while Joe reported to Atticus Barclay, firm senior partner and head of litigation.

On Joe's left, Jerry Dan Kovacs skimmed through advance sheets, humming a country western song under his breath. He was the other first year associate assigned to litigation. Joe knew Jerry Dan had nothing to worry about. A top graduate of Cornell and NYU Law, he had had his pick of offers in town.

Slightly plump, especially around the middle, Jerry Dan had brown curly hair and brown eyes surrounded by smile lines and round framed glasses. He didn't look like a lawyer and even less like a cowboy, despite his efforts to the contrary. This morning he wore a navy yoke-backed suit, a bolo tie instead of a strip of silk hanging down his shirtfront. As usual, black Tony Llama boots, their two-inch heels still not making him tall, completed his outfit. Their clumping heralded his comings and goings on the firm's wooden floors.

Unlike most of the litigation lawyers Joe knew, Jerry Dan didn't want to go anywhere near a courtroom. It was the fight on paper – not in front of the jury – that appealed to him. He lived to find the obscure case on point, the distinguishing fact. He could locate authority for any claim, the admission or suppression of any evidence. Atticus Barclay had described his appellate briefs as Supreme Court quality – United States, not Arizona – at the weekly lunch meeting. Every Thursday the attorneys met amid the clutter of deli sandwiches to review the firm's cases and projects and salute individual accomplishments. Joe had listened to the senior partner's praise, wondering if he would ever merit such singling out.

"Question of the day: How many attorneys are there in this room?"

The three occupants of the conference room looked toward the doorway. Standing there was a small woman, thin and angular, a sheaf of papers in her hand. Her hair, dyed a strawberry pink that looked as though it came out of a Kool-Aid packet, was pulled up into a lopsided ponytail, and her bangs were trimmed unevenly. Three silver hoops hung from one ear. Her face had a feline quality, more feral than domestic. Penciled-on brows arched like those of an old-time movie star, and her white skin was made paler by makeup. Her eyes and lips were rimmed in black, and only a pink slash on each cheek relieved the starkness of her visage. She wore ankle high boots with black pleated trousers and a matching man-style jacket, a lettered T-shirt underneath.

"Hi, Trudy," Jerry Dan said. "How's it going?"

Trudy Cummings worked as a paralegal for Stephen Merchant, the firm's real estate lawyer. She met with clients, returned phone calls, prepped her boss for zoning hearings, drafted subdivision documents, and found mislaid plot plans. The firm's highest-paid paralegal, she was rumored to make more than the new lawyers.

Ignoring Jerry Dan's greeting, Trudy snapped her gum and repeated in an impatient tone, "So, how many?"

"Three?" Joe ventured.

"Nope. Only one," she shot back. "Passing the exam ain't enough, guys. You gotta take the oath. And you're looking at the new person in charge of making sure baby lawyers get sworn in and everybody's bar dues get paid." She cracked her gum again and rolled her eyes. "Like I don't have enough to do."

She walked into the room, set the papers down on the table, and uncapped her pen with a flourish.

"Real names gotta go on these forms." She jabbed the fountain tip in Joe's direction. "Yours I know, Mr. Joseph Brendan McGuinness. It's Mr. OK Corral's I need." Her hand hovered above the paper.

"Jerry Dan Kovacs, ma'am," Jerry Dan replied, stretching *ma'am* an extra syllable or two. When he didn't want to sound fresh off Long Island, which he was, Jerry Dan's Southern drawl was sweet and thick enough to pour over pancakes.

"No, your full name." Trudy glared at him with eyes that glittered like a raven's. "What is it? Gerald? Jeremiah?"

"I told you, Jerry Dan Kovacs." *I told you* came out *Ah tol chew.* "I'm what you get when a nice Jewish boy from New York goes south and falls in love with a Mississippi Southern belle. Breakfast at our house is kosher grits." He smiled politely. "My father wanted to name me Jakob Daniel. You can put that down if you like."

With another roll of her eyes and a snort of exasperation, Trudy stomped out of the room, her boots making almost as much noise as Jerry Dan's.

"Did you catch today's slogan?" Jerry Dan asked when he was sure she was out of hearing.

Joe shook his head. "Her jacket was in the way." Trudy's outfit never varied: A dark trouser suit over a T-shirt printed with a politically incorrect message. "I don't know how she gets away with it."

"The firm tried to get her to stop last year. She claimed the messages on her shirts were free speech, guaranteed by the Constitution, and threatened to sue." Katie spoke for the first time, her voice flat and, to Joe's ears, hostile.

"'The Only Studs in My Life Are in My Earlobes' is protected speech?" Jerry Dan asked, more to himself than the others. Joe could see he was mentally reviewing the legal authorities for such an argument.

"I'm sure the fact her dad owns CelGen wasn't ignored by the partners either," Katie added. Definite hostility, Joe concluded. CelGen, a genetic research company, was one of the firm's biggest clients.

The intercom on the small ledge in the corner buzzed.

"Ms. Hewson, you may come in now," the disembodied male voice crackled.

A look of panic flashed across the woman's broad face.

I know just how you feel, Joe thought.

Lurching to her feet, Katie gave one last tug to the binding skirt, its snugness hobbling her walk across the room. Joe heard the door to the main conference room open. Over Katie's shoulder he saw a scowling Kemp Parrish stride across the reception area, hands clenched in fists at his side.

"Dammit!" Kemp muttered with every step.

Joe felt a stab of pain in his gut. "Kemp, they let Kemp go?" he whispered.

Jerry Dan looked at him with his eyebrows raised but didn't say anything. Kemp was the Harvard Law grad slated to be Merchant's right hand man. The ache in Joe's stomach got worse. What would he tell his mother? How would he pay off his student loans? He already knew none of the other firms in town would give him a job. His career as a lawyer was going to be over before it even started.

A door slammed.

"It's not fair. You can't do this!" A blotchy-faced Katie Hewson came into view, tears tracking down her cheeks.

"I'll make you sor –" She saw Joe and Jerry Dan staring at her and fled, her pantyhose making swishing noises as her thighs rubbed together.

"Mr. Kovacs, please," came the static-filled command from the intercom.

"Hey, why the serious face?" asked Riley Halliday as he sat in the chair vacated by Jerry Dan.

Joe shook his head. Leave it to his best friend to be cheerful in the face of a third of the firm being laid off. But then his place was assured. The only one of the three new associates to fail the bar exam, Riley had already been told he could stay on until he retook and passed the test.

"I'm not a paralegal and I'm not a lawyer, so I guess that makes me a parapalegal," Riley had quipped when he told Joe the news earlier that morning. "But I know I wouldn't be anything if I weren't a member of a protected species."

"What species is that?" Joe had asked.

"People who can't be fired because they've got a relative who's a big client of the firm. They can me and Aunt Cordelia ships all her legal work over to Woolcott & Jones within the hour." "Aunt Cordelia," as Joe and everyone else at the firm knew, was Cordelia Barrett, owner of one of Pinnacle Peak's largest ranches and one of the firm's original clients.

"More than a few other folks wouldn't be too happy either, American Express for starters. If I don't have a job, my dear aunt cuts me off like that." Even though Riley grinned as he spoke, his voice had an edge Joe hadn't heard before.

Joe considered what he knew of Riley's relationship with his aunt. She had raised him since his parents were killed in a car crash when he was a baby, supporting him through college and law school – rather nicely, if a BMW and a patio home in La Hacienda, Pinnacle Peak's five-star resort development, were any indication. Joe mentally shook his head. He didn't really believe Riley's lifestyle was at risk. Sympathetic commiseration, he concluded as he brought his mind back to his friend's question.

"It's Kemp." Hoarseness tinged Joe's voice. "They let him go. Katie, too."

"You know, I've always wondered what kind of name that was. Kemp? Who names their kid Kemp?"

"Riley, what I mean is if they were let go then ..." Joe's voice trailed off as Riley held up his hand.

"Katie was in trouble even while Atticus was on this side of the Pearly Gates," he said. "And Kemp isn't going anywhere."

"Then why was he so mad?"

"His mom told him if he got laid off he could stay at their house in Aspen while he looked for another job." Riley grinned. "Poor guy. Snow's supposed to be awesome this year."

Joe smiled back as much as his nervousness would allow and studied the face across from him, so different from his own. Riley's hazel eyes were flecked with green while his own were a dark blue. Joe's dark brown hair, wavy enough to look messy, ended above his collar and was already receding, making his forehead even taller. Riley's blond-brown thatch fell straight and was a bit too long for a young lawyer who was supposed to impress senior partners.

Riley absently tapped a finger against his thick lower lip. Joe noticed a recent addition of a few pounds had blurred his friend's sharp jawline and puffed cheeks. But the small cleft in his chin was noticeably more distinct than Joe's. Still, maybe that was why people often mistook them for brothers, Joe thought. But he hoped the reason was the way they got along with each other when together.

Staring at the grain of the tabletop until the whorls in the marble blurred, Joe's mind drifted back to when Riley and he first met. Friends since the first week of law school, after Riley guided him through a computer research project and they discovered a mutual interest in team roping, the pair roped and studied together the rest of the school year. Riley was better at both, even though he barely went through the motions when it came to academics.

When the other first year students started to look for summer law clerk jobs, Riley suggested instead the two work as cowboys at the Barrett Ranch. Joe had hoped to find a legal position; with his grades near the top of the class, Riley didn't need a job reference. Joe smiled at the memory of his friend's persuasiveness.

"C'mon, we'll be inside the rest of our lives. We gotta do this while we can," Riley had argued. So Joe spent three months on the range instead of in an office building. Somewhat to his surprise, when it came time to accept a permanent offer, Riley followed him to BH&M.

"Law firms are all alike," had been Riley's only comment. "I don't care where I work."

Riley looked at his watch. "Well, I'm out of here." He straightened his Armani tie and stood up. From what he had seen of Riley's work wardrobe, Joe guessed his friend could wear a different suit every day of the month. At the door Riley turned.

"Cowboy up, bro'. Remember, you can always work for Amber's dad." With a wink he was gone.

Joe winced. Amber Sulvane, the girl Joe had been dating since last September, taught aerobics at a local health club. She was short and blond with muscled arms and legs, and her obsession for spotless athletic footwear rivaled an urban teen's. Riley called her "Our Lady of Perpetual White Shoes," much to her fury. Five years younger than Joe, they had met in the law library his last year in school. She later told Joe she and her friend had been cruising for law students.

She had been ecstatic at the news Joe might lose his job.

"Yes!" she had squealed. "Now we can finally move to San Diego!"

Amber wanted to live at the beach. Her father, a doctor who had invented a special pacemaker, headquartered his company near Mission Bay. Amber had been after Joe since graduation to accept her father's offer to become in-house counsel for the company and, by implication, his son-in-law, too. So far, Joe had managed to duck both proposals.

Now at least the job offer was looking more attractive.

Left alone in the room, Joe swiveled his chair around to face the photographs on the wall behind him. His eyes lingered on the one on the left, its frame draped in black.

Atticus Barclay did not look like his movie namesake. Several inches under six feet, his round body resembled that of a medieval abbot, his burnished bald head crowned by a pair of snowy circumflex eyebrows. He had bulldog cheeks and ears that stuck out a little. A red bow tie was the only neckwear Joe had ever seen nestled under his chin.

While a student, during more than a few afternoons Joe had opted for the courtroom in lieu of the lecture hall, letting trial lawyers be his teachers. Barclay was the best. With a voice that sounded like tires on gravel and a wide, penetrating gaze that never wavered, he pulled truth from witnesses who wanted to lie and wove evidence into a tale compelling even to the most recalcitrant juror. Joe had found his exemplar.

An average student, Joe hadn't expected to win a place in Barclay's firm. His application for a summer clerkship his second year was based more on wishful thinking than reasonable belief. The senior lawyer himself was the interviewer. His handshake was firm but not bone-crushingly hormonal, and although Joe knew him to be over sixty, there was no stoop to his shoulders or bend in his spine.

Barclay's secretary had called two days later. Joe had a job. He wasn't told why and dared not ask. At the end of the summer the firm informed him he was under consideration for a permanent position. During Christmas break he received a written offer to join the litigation section as an associate. Joe breathed a sigh of relief and accepted it immediately. None of the other firms with whom he interviewed during the fall had shown any interest. He started in August, five days after taking the bar, working as a law clerk pending the exam results, which were mailed out last Friday. The same day Atticus Barclay died.

Jerry Dan appeared in the conference room doorway, banishing Joe's recollections.

"The good news is I'm still here. The bad news is I've got to work for Forrest until a new senior litigation partner is found."

"Way to go," Joe said weakly as his hopes sank. Forrest Whitford III was a partner in the firm, second in seniority to Atticus Barclay in the litigation section. There wouldn't be room for him in the firm's trial practice if Jerry Dan was staying.

The intercom crackled. "Mr. McGuinness, please."

Jerry Dan gave him a thumbs-up, and Joe pushed himself out of his chair.

One wall of the large conference room was glass. Joe could see past the small downtown of Pinnacle Peak to the saguaro-dotted slopes of El Piniculo, the thirty-four hundred-foot granite spire for which the town was named. The only other person in the room was Alistair D.W. Harrington. Co-founder of the firm eleven years ago with Atticus Barclay, he was seated at the far end of the polished wooden table. A large purple and orange hued painting of a cowboy on his horse hung on the wall behind him. The tallest lawyer in the firm, Harrington was dressed, as always, in a black suit. Prominent cheekbones and great hollow eyes gave him a skull's face atop a skeleton's frame. His complexion was the color of parchment, only a shade or two away from his bone-white hair. Joe thought he looked like an undertaker, which seemed appropriate given his area of practice.

"Please sit down, Mr. McGuinness." Harrington spoke slowly.

Joe pulled out one of the leather and wood chairs.

"As you know, the death of my partner ..." Harrington paused and looked out the window, staring for so long that Joe gave in to the impulse and swiveled his head to look, too. His movement seemed to bring the older man back to the conversation, and he picked up his sentence again, "... has necessitated a restructuring of the firm."

Joe felt knots bunching in his shoulders.

"Unfortunately, this means several employees, although otherwise qualified, must be dismissed."

Joe's palms became damp and his chest hurt. Harrington continued talking, but Joe couldn't hear what he was saying, his heart was beating so loudly in his ears.

"What? I mean, pardon?" he asked after Harrington stopped speaking and appeared to be waiting for a response.

"You have been reassigned to the Trusts & Estates department, Mr. McGuinness, as a replacement for Ms. Hewson. Unless, of course, you wish to seek employment elsewhere. If that is the case, you would receive a good recommendation from the firm. Atticus," again Harrington paused, "that is, Mr. Barclay, was pleased with your work."

Joe sat silently, his mouth in a small round "O." Relief coursed through him. He still had a job. Barclay liked his work! Elation quickly gave way to disappointment. Assigned to Harrington, he mentally grimaced. He hadn't even taken Trusts and Estates in law school. He wanted to go to court, not will readings.

Harrington cleared his throat, interrupting the thoughts swirling in Joe's head.

"I am aware you are interested in trial practice, Mr. McGuinness. Perhaps you can rejoin the litigation section once a new department head has been selected."

Joe made himself focus on reality. He knew getting another position was doubtful at this late date. Even if he had better credentials, all the local firms had already filled their entry litigation positions for the year.

"I appreciate the opportunity to stay, Mr. Harrington." Joe's muted voice reflected his mood.

"Good." Harrington's brisk tone signaled the meeting's end. "I will meet with you shortly about your assignments. Please prepare a status memorandum on the matters on which you were working with Mr. Barclay and deliver it to Mr. Kovacs."

Joe walked back to his office, unsure whether he should be happy or not. He stood behind his desk and started to gather case files. His secretary Lydia walked in carrying a glass of Coke.

"I understand I'm all yours now," she said as she set the glass on his desk, her small manicured fingers leaving prints on the frosty rim.

"You mean we're all Harrington's," Joe replied.

"Oh, Joe, I'm so sorry," she said. "I know what trial work means to you."

Joe smiled ruefully at the petite woman with delicate Chinese features standing across from him. She was dressed in a tailored skirt and high collar blouse, a jade brooch pinned at her throat. Her hair was swept back from her oval face into a black bun.

"Well, let's see how it works out," he said, trying to keep his voice light. He sat down in his chair. "And thanks for the drink."

"Amber called twice, and I've almost finished typing up your statute of limitations research. Is there anything else?"

"No, thanks. By the way, how did Annie like her lesson last night?"

Lydia's eyes brightened at the mention of her ten-year-old daughter. Annie was the proud owner of Peanuts, a chubby pinto pony. Joe had been giving Annie riding lessons.

"She loved it, of course. And I have another picture for you." Joe had refused Lydia's offers of payment, but that didn't stop Annie. His office wall and refrigerator at home were papered with gifts of her artwork. Lydia walked out to her desk, tucked behind a four foot partition across the hallway from Joe's office door, and returned with a crayon sketch of a barrel-shaped brown and white pony being ridden by a little girl with a pink bow in her cropped black hair. A tall thin man in a cowboy hat stood in the background.

Joe took the drawing. "It's great," he said, setting it on top of his desk.

"What's great?" Riley asked as he walked into Joe's office. "Certainly not your new assignment."

Joe wasn't surprised Riley had heard the news already. After Trudy, he was the best source of information on firm happenings. Lydia left unobtrusively, leaving the door ajar behind her.

"I'm going to see how it goes," Joe said.

"Are you kidding? Why didn't you quit? Firms in this town would be falling all over themselves to hire you as a litigator!"

"First of all, I can't afford to quit. I figure by the time I pay off my student loans my as-yet-unborn kid will be ready to start applying for them. I'm living paycheck to paycheck, my friend. Second, those other firms weren't exactly falling all over themselves to hire me six months ago. I don't know why they would be interested now."

"Well, they should be," Riley said, pushing aside Annie's drawing and perching on the corner of Joe's desk. "So I'm a parapalegal and you're a Deadhead," he said, swinging one foot like a metronome.

"Deadhead?"

"That's Trudy's name for T&E lawyers. She calls the people who inherit the Ungrateful Living. Get it? Grateful Dead? Ungrateful Living?" Riley laughed.

"Shhh, Harrington might hear you," Joe said, suddenly feeling annoyed. He began sorting the papers on his credenza into piles.

Riley pushed himself off the desk. "Merchant's waiting for me. I'll catch up with you later." He paused in the doorway. "One last piece of advice, amigo."

Joe looked up from a stack of pleadings.

Riley's expression was solemn. "Don't overcharge your clients for writing their wills," he intoned.

"Huh?" Joe's brows knitted together in bafflement.

"Otherwise you'll be a Croaker Soaker!"

Riley's laugh was louder this time. Joe was sure he could be heard in Harrington's office two doors away. Joe waved him down the hall.

"What's so funny?" Jerry Dan asked a moment later, sticking his head into Joe's office and confirming his fears about Riley's decibel level.

"Oh, Riley's giving me a bad time about working with Harrington," Joe replied.

Jerry Dan plopped himself into one of Joe's client chairs.

"Hang in there, guy. This will all work out." Joe was encouraged by his friend's smile.

"Besides," he continued, "maybe you'll be the one to find out what the D. W. is short for."

"What are you talking about?"

"Haven't you ever noticed how Harrington's name is printed on the firm letterhead? 'Alistair D. W. Harrington.' He signs all his letters that way, too. The thing is, no one knows what the D.W. stands for."

"I'll let you know if I find out. But now I've really got to –"

"Excuse me." Trudy reached past Jerry Dan and dropped a sheet of paper into Joe's in-basket.

"I've already heard this spiel, so I'll see you later." Jerry Dan touched two fingers to an imaginary hat brim and left.

Trudy raised her voice over the rumble of his boots in the hallway. "Listen up," she commanded. "Like I said before, you gotta be sworn in, even though the only Deadhead who goes to court around here is Harrington. Don't forget you're doing it twice; federal as well as state court. The paper tells you where to go and when you've got to be there. Don't look for any dues notices. The bills come directly to me so I can make sure they get paid. Got it?"

Joe nodded.

Trudy pointed a scarlet fingernail at him. "Screw up and you'll be sorry." She whirled to leave, her jacket swinging open. Across the chest of her T-shirt was printed "In Dog Years, I'm Dead."

Just like my career as a trial lawyer, Joe thought.

Chapter 2

Saturday, October 12

Joe was awake and down at the barn while the night shadows were still receding. With the change in his supervising partner, he had a rare weekend free from work. He wanted to be out riding early. Even in October the midday sun could be like a branding iron, scorching the desert flesh below.

He threw a fat flake of fragrant alfalfa into the manger and then opened the stall door. While the chestnut mare ate, he unbuckled and removed her blanket, first lifting a large longhaired cat off her back.

"Farley, I wish you'd told me you prefer sleeping on top of Cricket before I bought you that cat bed," Joe said to the furry creature, stroking his soft coat before setting him down in the barn aisle.

Farley put his nose up in the air and sniffed, as though to indicate his sleeping arrangements were nobody's business, least of all Joe's. The product of a show cat's one-night stand with a non-pedigreed suitor, Farley weighed almost twenty pounds. Light tan with chocolate brown face, ears, legs, and tail, he was lord of his manor, which included the stable and Joe's house. He refused to eat commercial cat food, existing obviously well on a diet of rodents who dared invade the hay barn. Farley liked only one manmade dish: oatmeal raisin cookies, preferably burnt, with a side of milk. About twice a month Joe bought the ready-made dough and after slicing off and eating a few chunks of it, baked the rest of the batch for Farley.

After checking Cricket's water, Joe walked back to his place to fix his own breakfast. He lived in a one-room adobe on the YJ Ranch, a four thousand-acre spread eleven miles north of town owned by Tess McGuinness Crawford, his mother's sister. The ranch had been founded by Tess's father-in-law, its name chosen to remind his rather bossy wife of what her husband claimed he spent half his day saying to her, "Yes, Julia." The YJ stock still wore the brand he designed; a Y connected to a J through the base of the Y becoming the shaft of the J.

Joe loved his house's stone floor, thick walls, and low ceiling crossed by wooden vigas; although, as Riley often teased him, "house" was probably too big a word for the place. Originally built for the ranch's foreman, its four mud walls had barely enough room for a bed, a desk, a narrow bookshelf, and a motor home-sized bathroom and kitchen. Instead of rent, Joe did odd jobs around the ranch, helping the foreman as needed. Also, since the loss of his horse in a riding accident the first week of August, he had the use of the ranch's horses. Cricket quickly became his favorite. A bright chestnut Quarter Horse, she was on the small side, but quick. Joe thought she was going to make a good team-roping mount.

Once he was finished eating, Joe pulled on a pair of Wranglers, his old boots and a T-shirt and walked back to the barn. He haltered Cricket and led her out of the stall, tying her next to the small tack room. He brushed the horse's coppery coat until it was glossy. Farley sauntered around the corner and sprawled in the sun to clean his fur, his tongue licks almost in time with Joe's brush strokes.

After picking out the mare's feet, Joe carefully arranged a worn Navajo patterned blanket on her back and then swung up his old roping saddle, adjusting it gently behind her withers. As he was cinching up, he heard footsteps on the gravel drive.

"Good morning, Joe."

Giving the leather a last tug, Joe unhooked the stirrup from the horn and turned to greet his aunt. Medium tall, Tess Crawford was solid and square shouldered, like a woman brought up on beef. She wore old cowboy boots under snug jeans and a man-sized shirt Joe knew used to belong to her husband. Under her sweat-rimmed Stetson were bright green eyes, the corners cross-hatched with razor fine slashes of innumerable wrinkles, a strong nose, and wide smiling lips on which Joe never saw lipstick. A hard built version of his mother, Joe thought not for the first time.

"Getting an early start?" she asked after hugging him with arms that were freckled and roped with muscle.

"Yes, I was going –"

The entrance of Java, Tess's rottweiler, interrupted Joe. She skittered around the corner and barreled straight for Farley, who continued his toilette unperturbed. The big dog braked to a stop in front of the cat and lowered her head, her nose inches from Farley's. A paw shot out and Java scrambled backward with a yelp of pain, a look of hurt on her face.

"Farley!" Joe scolded.

The cat ignored him and resumed his ablutions while Java stared on adoringly from a safe distance.

"Jeez, I'm sorry, Tess." Joe said. "You'd think he'd be more grateful – after all, it was Java who found him in that monsoon and brought him home."

"And now Farley plays with her toys, steals her table scraps, and otherwise bosses her around," Tess laughed. "There's no accounting for love."

"Love? Who's talking about love?" A grizzled man in jeans and a denim jacket, his face so lined it looked like an old boot, ambled toward them, his bow-legged gait rolling his body as though he were walking the deck of a ship.

"Morning, Hal," Joe said as he slipped the bit between Cricket's teeth and gently guided her ear through the slot in the headstall.

"Morning, Joe," the old man replied.

Hal Timmons had come to the YJ as a teenager more than four decades ago. Tess's husband was a toddler when he arrived. Hal watched Roy Crawford grow up, bring Tess home as his bride, and take over the ranch from his parents. After Roy's unexpected death, he became the ranch foreman. Hal was getting old and stiff, but Joe knew Tess would never turn him out, and his loyalty to Tess would never allow him to leave. Especially now that Tess was in danger of losing the ranch altogether.

"Where are you off to this morning?" Hal asked.

"I was going to practice a few throws and then take Cricket out on the trail."

"Would you mind riding the north fence line? I want to make sure there aren't any breaks. I came up short on the count again last night."

"No problem." Joe looped his rope over the saddle horn and slipped on a white roping glove.

Tess took off her hat and ran her fingers through brown hair bleached unevenly by the sun.

"We can't afford to lose any more." The tight expression under her eyes said more than her words. "With the price of beef down the way it is, I need every calf to make my loan payments."

Stock had been disappearing from the YJ during the last several months, a few head at a time. Weighing four to five hundred pounds each, the steer calves that were missing were the backbone of the ranch's economy.

"Dang it, I wish cattle-thieving was still a hanging offense in Arizona," Hal said, stamping his boot.

"Well, it comes close. At fifty cents a pound, you only have to steal one critter to be guilty of felony theft." Joe stepped into the stirrup and swung his leg over Cricket's back.

"Are you sure you should be throwing this soon? How's your shoulder?" Tess asked.

Joe moved his right arm forward and backward, trying not to grimace. "Not too bad for the first time out. Anyway, I can't put it off any longer. Riley wants us in the series."

"Just because Riley says something doesn't mean you have to do it. I swear, sometimes I think if that boy told you to jump off El Piniculo, you'd do that, too," Tess said.

"Aunt Tess –" Joe pleaded.

"Well, I'm worried about you. Don't rush that shoulder, hear? It's hardly been two months." She patted his knee.

"Yes, ma'am."

Joe nudged Cricket with his heels, and the horse started to walk down the barn hallway. He twisted around in the saddle.

"I'll be fine," he said, "Don't worry." He lifted his hand in a wave. "See you later."

Joe guided the chestnut mare to the arena in the front yard. Tess's husband had built it as a monument to his passion: team roping. Joe pulled open the gate, careful to avoid splinters. The thick wooden planks, originally painted bright white, had weathered to a light gray. Cricket shied at the shadow cast by one of the large lights mounted on poles around the perimeter.

"Easy, girl." Joe soothed Cricket as she pranced a few steps.

The mare relaxed and settled into a ground-eating walk. After a circuit of the good-sized oval, Joe urged her into a jog in front of the chutes, pens built to hold livestock waiting to be roped. Once kept dusty by cloven hooves, they were now full of weeds. The pair trotted by the small grandstand, Cricket's neck arched proudly. Joe noted with regret that another row of seats was broken, the victim of dry rot. He wished he had lived at the ranch when Roy Crawford was alive. Before he died, Tess's husband sponsored a winter roping series that often drew up to sixty contestants from as far away as Tolleson. Now only Riley and Joe, who spent many after work hours under the lights practicing their roping and riding skills, used the arena.

Joe cued the mare into a lope, guiding her into circles and figure eights with a light touch on the reins. Once a slight sweat broke out on the chestnut's shoulder, Joe steered toward the heading dummy in the center of the arena. He shook out his rope and made a few throws at the bale of hay with a plastic steer head and horns stuck into one end. He then moved Cricket nearer the fence and aimed for the heeling dummy, a sawhorse hooked on the side of the arena so that its back legs were raised.

With each toss Joe bit his lip at the searing pain. He hadn't told Tess the truth. His shoulder still hurt like hell. Ten weeks ago he had dislocated the joint and torn his rotator cuff; he'd been out of a sling only five days. But he was determined to be ready for the fall series starting this Tuesday night. He threw again, the ripple of pain bringing him back to the day of the accident.

Riley and Joe had trailered to a neighboring ranch for a team roping competition the weekend between the end of the bar exam and the Monday they were to report for work at the firm. Joe's horse, Ranger, a tall bay gelding he bought his last year of college and trained himself, was restless on the ride over. Telling Riley he was going to take a short ride away from the crowd to settle his horse, Joe headed toward a collection of corrals.

Opening the gate to what he thought was an empty enclosure, Joe started his nervous horse jogging along the fence. They went but a few steps when an explosive snort brought Ranger to a quivering halt. Out of the shadows of the shed in the corner trotted a large Brahma bull, one of the ranch's bucking stock bred for the rodeo circuit. The bull stopped about twenty feet away from the motionless horse and rider, close enough for Joe to see its red-edged eyes and flared nostrils trailing tendrils of mucous. The ebony-coated animal tossed his head, heavy with the weight of long horns that ended in lethal points, before dropping its nose for the charge. Joe tried to spur his mount out of the way, but Ranger sprang too late. The bull caught them broadside.

The two-thousand-pound impact felt as though a car had hit them. Ranger shuddered and squealed before collapsing onto the dirt. Joe was slammed into the rails of the corral, pinned there by his struggling horse, his right arm wrenched behind him at an angle nature never intended. He got a glimpse of the deadly horns now tipped in red before the bull backed away for another assault. He shut his eyes and waited for the second collision.

It never came.

After a long moment he opened his eyes again to see a group of cowboys gathered around him. Doc Lasher, the local vet, was injecting something into Ranger's neck while the others tried to keep the weight of the horse off him. After Ranger went limp, the cowboys slid Joe out from under the animal's body. When someone moved his right arm, Joe screamed and lost consciousness.

When he came to in the ambulance, he learned the bull had been stopped from goring him by Riley roping one of his hind legs and snubbing him to a corral post. Ranger had been put to sleep – in the first rush the bull's horns had ripped open his belly, shredding his insides. Joe's shoulder was crushed and wrenched when his horse was steamrollered into the fence.

Riley visited him in the hospital the day after the accident.

"Hey pardner," he said softly as he tiptoed into the room. "You awake?"

"Yeah," Joe rasped, still groggy from pain medicine.

"Amigo, next time pay attention to whose door you're knocking on before you go inviting yourself in." Riley's bantering tone was belied by the worry in his eyes.

"Simply my way of giving you a chance to see you'd make a better heeler than header." Joe tried to smile but winced instead.

"Forget that! Who won the winter series? Me heading and you heeling, that's who. And speaking of 'healing,' you better do some quick. We've got a title to defend."

Riley lapsed into silence, his fingers plucking at a button on his jacket as he surveyed the tubes running into Joe's arm below the thick bandage. After a moment, Joe asked the question that had been on his mind almost since he reached consciousness.

"Riley," Joe began, his voice still weak, "how did you know I was in trouble?"

"I don't know." Riley shrugged and looked away. "It was just a feeling, I guess. Almost as though –"

Before he could continue, a nurse walked in.

"How did you get in here? Visiting hours are over. You'll have to leave." She bustled across the room to check Joe's IV drip.

Joe reached out his left hand.

"Thanks, Riley," he said, "you saved –"

"Forget it. That's what brothers are for, right?" As the nurse advanced from around the bed with a stern look in her eye, he squeezed Joe's hand. "See you tomorrow."

"Tomorrow," Joe repeated sleepily, the medicine kicking in again.

While in the hospital, Joe thought a lot about Riley's "feeling." His mother had another name for it. Joe remembered the time he was playing in a neighbor's tool-shed as a kid and accidentally locked himself in. After he wore himself out crying and calling for help, she found him. When he asked her how she knew where to look for him she told him, "Intuition. All mothers have it." Bouncing Patrick on her hip, she added, "Brothers, too."

Two years after the tool-shed incident, Joe angrily questioned where this intuition had been when his little brother drowned in a neighbor's pool. Why didn't he or his mother know Patrick had wandered out of the yard and into the blue water, oblivious of danger as only a four-year-old can be? Sometimes Joe wondered if his devotion to the certainties of right and wrong didn't owe something to the unexplainable in his life. The death of his brother. The absence of his father, another subject his mother refused to discuss.

Even though he could barely remember him, Joe had felt something lacking in himself since Patrick's death. It was a void that remained empty until Riley stepped in and filled it, in return receiving the brotherly love Joe had pent up all those years. Before the attack by the bull, Joe sometimes imagined Riley was a long-lost brother, his second sibling. Now he knew whoever his real brother would have been, Joe couldn't have felt closer to him than he did to Riley.

Joe never talked to Riley about any of this. He tried to after he got out of the hospital, but Riley cut him off.

"Don't say anything, Joe. You don't need to."

A warm feeling of completeness had rushed through Joe. Riley was right. These things didn't have to be talked about between brothers.

A cloud of dust brought Joe out of his reverie. A dark blue and tan pickup truck bounced up the mile and a quarter dirt track that connected the ranch to Scottsdale Road. Joe recognized Jerry Dan's "cowboy car" – the nearly new Ford F-150 SuperCab XLT with trailer towing package, captain's chairs, chrome grille and hubcaps, aerostyle headlights, and a deluxe stereo radio tuned exclusively to country western stations.

Joe knew Jerry Dan had wanted to be a cowboy since his father took him for his eighth birthday to the rodeo at Madison Square Garden. Unfortunately, an allergy to horses stymied his plans. Undaunted, he opted instead to be what he viewed as an updated version of the town marshal; a trial lawyer in the desert, with Atticus Barclay cast as the modern day equivalent of Wyatt Earp.

To Jerry Dan, living the legend required all the trappings. He wore only cowboy jeans or Western cut suits over boots and went line dancing twice a week. Walking into his friend's office at the firm made Joe feel as though he had traveled to the beginning of the prior century. Framed "Wanted" posters and old guns were mounted on the walls, and a bronze Remington replica sculpture of a cowboy on a saddle bronc stood on the back credenza.

While Jerry Dan parked his pickup under a tree, Joe resumed his throwing practice, trying not to let the pain in his shoulder add a hitch to his toss. Jerry Dan walked to the arena and hooked his elbows over the top of the fence. Farley materialized and leapt to the upper rail, padding toward Jerry Dan like a tightrope walker on a high wire. Jerry Dan massaged the ruff around the big cat's neck and was rewarded with a rumbling purr.

"Hey, it's Jabba the Cat," he said as Farley turned around so his back could be scratched. Jerry Dan stroked along his spine, making his fur stand up with electrified static.

Joe walked Cricket over to the fence.

"What are you doing up so early?"

"On my way to a line dance and brunch in Carefree. Thought I'd stop by on my way. How's the shoulder? You looked pretty good when I drove up."

"It hurts, more than I expected it would."

"Do you really think you're going to be ready for Tuesday night?"

"I've stayed away long enough. Riley is set on winning the series again."

"Do what's right for you. I'll be there to make sure you have at least one fan in the stands."

Joe hoped Riley wouldn't mind. He had made it clear he didn't like Jerry Dan, despite the latter's overtures of friendship, and groused at his insistence on attending their roping competitions.

Farley, now on the ground, twined himself around Jerry Dan's dark denims. Jerry Dan looked down, then leaned over to brush the caramel-colored hair from his pants.

"Farley! You know better than that." Joe frowned at his cat, who was suddenly absorbed with a small bug on the ground.

"It's okay. Farley and I are buddies, aren't we, guy?" Farley butted his head into Jerry Dan's hand for a last rub behind the ears before strolling over to the shade to lie down.

"So, what does Forrest have you doing?" Joe asked, not sure if he wanted to hear the answer. He was aware of the firm gossip. Forrest was severe, demanding, and a stickler for the rules. Joe was assigned the parking place next to his in the garage. Every workday morning he carefully opened the door of his old Buick, afraid he would mark the creamy perfection of the Mercedes sedan invariably parked too close to the line. Now Joe wondered if enduring Forrest wasn't a small price to pay to get into court.

"Uh, he actually gave me a case to try next week," Jerry Dan said, avoiding Joe's eyes.

"Oh? That's great. What's it about?" Joe tried to ignore a pang of envy. Jerry Dan's the best of the new associates, he reminded himself. It's only logical he'd be the first out of the box to trial. But knowing it was true didn't make him feel better.

"Well, it's only traffic court," Jerry Dan said. "One of the head scientists from CelGen got a ticket for running a red light. He wants to fight it."

"So what's your defense?"

"The Doppler Effect."

"The Doppler Effect?" Joe frowned. "I don't remember that from school."

"We're talking science, not law. This guy explained it to me. You know what color you see is determined by the length and frequency of the light waves hitting your eye. Light hues range from infrared, which has long wavelength and low frequency, to ultraviolet, which has short wavelength and high frequency. Red light has a longer wavelength and lower frequency than green. As you drive toward a red light you're shortening the wavelength and increasing the apparent frequency. At some point it will look green, and at faster speeds blue, then purple. So I'm going to argue at the speed he was approaching the intersection, the red light was Doppler shifted so it appeared green."

"Are you sure about all this?" Joe asked.

"Absolutely. My client's an expert. The prosecutor won't even know what he's talking about."

"Well, good luck," and against the fence railing, jammed his hands into his pockets.

"Joe, you know going to court isn't what I want to do." Jerry

Dan's guileless gaze sought his friend's. "And working for Forrest is awful. The guy is hankering to be senior litigation partner so bad, he's worse than ever. Yesterday I wondered if they hadn't already promised it to him."

"What do you mean?" Joe asked.

"I overheard him dictating a letter to another firm about exploring a merger. He wouldn't be doing that unless he had the inside track, right?"

Joe knew mergers meant redundancies, and redundancies meant layoffs. He couldn't keep the anxiety out of his voice. "I barely kept my job at the firm as it is. I'd never make it at a new, bigger place."

"That's not true!" Jerry Dan protested. "In any event, Harrington told me they were going to look outside the firm for someone to replace Barclay. I probably didn't hear Forrest right, or maybe the letter was for a client."

Joe didn't think Jerry Dan sounded convinced. Neither was Joe. With effort, he pushed his concerns from his mind and changed the subject.

"Aren't you going to ask me if I found out what D. W. stands for?" he asked in an overly chipper voice.

"Well?" Jerry Dan prompted.

"No news yet," Joe admitted, eliciting an exaggerated scowl from Jerry Dan. "I even checked his diplomas and bar admissions." Joe recalled the memo he received his first week at the firm "encouraging" the attorneys to display their credentials. He had already hung his college and law school diplomas in his office, and had frames picked out for the certificates of membership he would receive from the Arizona and Federal District Court bars.

"Have you ever been in Forrest's office?" Jerry Dan asked. "Very weird – like a monk's cell. His desk never has any papers on it, and there's just a small stack on the corner of his credenza. No photos or personal stuff. He even took down the western paintings provided by the firm. His walls are empty except for his two Harvard diplomas." Jerry Dan shook his head. "It's peculiar, I'm telling you."

"You're one to talk about weirdness in office décor. Aren't you the guy who sits with the lights out in that shrine to the Wild

West?"

"I told you, it really works," Jerry Dan said. "You ought to try it."

Jerry Dan had described his work methods to Joe more than once. After he completed his library research, he waited until the firm closed for the day. When everyone was gone, he'd read through every note and every case one more time, then turn out his office lights, sit behind his desk in the dark, and think, often for hours. At some point, with the lights still off, he'd pick up his tape recorder and begin to dictate. In the morning his secretary would transcribe what was usually a flawless brief.

"Actually, I did," Joe confessed.

"How'd it go?"

"I did what you said. I waited until the office was empty for the evening, read all my research notes, and turned out the lights."

"And?"

"The cleaning crew woke me up a few hours later. When I hit the 'playback' button on my Dictaphone, all I heard was the hiss of empty tape."

Jerry Dan's laughter was cut short by the sight of a roadrunner breaking cover on the far side of the yard. Jerry Dan shaded his eyes with his hand, following the progress of the bird until it darted back into the bush.

"Darn!" he complained. "I've seen coyotes and I've seen roadrunners, but I've never seen a coyote chasing a roadrunner."

Joe chuckled. "Jerry Dan, I've got some more bad news for you. Roadrunners don't say, 'Beep! Beep!' and there's no listing for a company called Acme in the Pinnacle Peak phone book."

"Cartoons!" Jerry Dan grumbled. "I'm beginning to think you can't believe any of them." He looked at his watch. "Got to scoot," he said. "Or should I say boot scoot?"

He climbed into his truck, waving to Joe as he backed around and started down the drive, dust tendrils marking his exit.

Cricket had dozed while the two friends chatted. Joe tapped her awake with his heels and guided her out of the arena, heading north along the ranch's fence line. He loosened the reins and the chestnut mare eased into a comfortable walk, winding through the low-growing cholla with its fishhook spines. Ocotillos reached long fingers up to the sky where a red-tailed hawk circled. Joe caught a glimpse of a coyote, probably trailing them in the hope the mare's hoofbeats would startle a desert cottontail from its hiding place.

Joe sighed as his thoughts returned to the firm. He enjoyed his friends and loved the desert and the ranch. If Harrington didn't like his work or there was a merger, he knew he would probably have to move away and find a job elsewhere.

Several minutes passed before he realized it would mean leaving Amber, too.

Chapter 3

Monday, October 14

Joe stood outside Alistair Harrington's office, shifting his weight from one foot to another. Gertrude Slivens, Harrington's secretary, had called him there ten minutes ago but barred his entry.

"He'll be available shortly. Please wait," she said before returning to her paperwork.

Gertrude had worked for Harrington since the day the firm opened its doors. A spinster in her sixties, she was slavishly devoted to her boss, and ran his – she considered it their – practice section like a tyrant. When she decreed Mr. Harrington would see other lawyers only by appointment, they complied, even the ones who worked for him. When she summoned an attorney to Harrington's office, all work was dropped and the summonee hustled to the corner suite, knowing those deemed late faced the punishment of interminable waiting outside the closed door. She even maintained her post during the noon hour, eating her sandwich brought from home at her desk. And no one ever saw her go to the restroom. The only lawyer immune to her power had been Atticus Barclay. "Hi, Gerty," he would say as he knocked on and then opened Harrington's door, walking in only if his partner was alone.

Joe stifled a stretch and cleared his throat.

"Um, how about if I go back to my office until he's ready to see me?"

Gertrude looked up from her computer to stare at him for a moment before resuming her punching of the keys, jabbing them with such force Joe half-expected the machine to yelp in pain.

"I guess I'll wait here," he said to the top of Gertrude's head.

The intercom on her desk buzzed.

"Please send Mr. McGuinness in," sounded through the speaker.

Joe hesitated, waiting for a sign of permission from the iron-haired woman still bent over her work. When he didn't immediately move, she jerked up her head and glared.

"Don't keep him waiting!" she snapped.

Joe sprang for the door like a startled deer and opened it.

Alistair Harrington was sitting behind a large wooden desk with intricately carved legs. He waved Joe into a high-backed chair upholstered in emerald green with cushions so deep Joe felt as though he were in the jaws of some carnivorous plant that was swallowing him. He took his pen out of his pocket and balanced his legal pad on his knee.

"Have you had an opportunity to transfer your litigation work to Mr. Kovacs?"

"I'm finishing that up today, sir," Joe said, trying to keep the regret from his voice.

"Good. For your first assignment in this department, I would like you to –"

The intercom on his desk spit static and Gertrude's voice filled the room.

"I am sorry to disturb you, Mr. Harrington, but Mrs. Barrett is here, and she would like to see you immediately."

Harrington gave Joe a look of regret. "I am afraid we must reschedule our meeting, Mr. McGuinness. Clients take priority."

Especially this one, Joe thought, as the door opened to admit Riley's aunt. A trim silvered blonde in a taupe suit and ivory silk blouse, Cordelia Thatcher Barrett wore brown Italian-made pumps with low heels, even though she was only a few inches over five feet. A widow in her early sixties, she remained a strikingly attractive woman with delicate features and blue eyes. She still oversaw daily operations on the forty-six thousand acres to the southeast of the YJ that was the Barrett Ranch.

"Hello, Alistair. Thank you for seeing me on such short notice."

She extended a small hand, its wristbones encircled by a thick gold bangle, to the older lawyer. As Harrington rose to take it, her attention was drawn to Joe, who was struggling to extricate himself from the clutches of his chair.

"Oh, it's you, Joseph. I hope I'm not interrupting?" She looked again at Harrington, but it was Joe, finally making it to his feet, who answered.

"Not at all, ma'am. I was just leaving."

With a slight duck of his head, he started for the door, pausing halfway there as a thought occurred to him. "Congratulations on Sonny's latest win. The paper said he may make it to the Winston Cup next season."

A small frown creased Mrs. Barrett's otherwise unlined face. Joe couldn't tell if its smoothness was the product of nature or surgeon's skill.

"Thank you." She pinched her lips together as though to prevent any more words from coming out.

Joe saw Harrington's questioning look and began to explain. "Sonny, Mrs. Barrett's son, races stock cars in the Busch series. He's in the top five this year. The next step up is the real pros, the Winston Cup circuit."

Before he could continue, Cordelia Barrett broke in. "And now that he's spent all the money his grandfather left him, he wants me to finance this foolishness!" The tight lips couldn't contain her anger any longer.

Joe remembered the newspaper article on Sonny reported it cost at least a million dollars to field a stock car team for one season in the Busch Series. At the time Joe assumed Sonny was backed by sponsors, never imagining he used his own funds. Why didn't I keep my big mouth shut? Joe thought unhappily. My second day working for Harrington, and I've already upset one of his biggest clients.

"Anyway, it's nice to see you again, Mrs. Barrett," Joe mumbled, grabbing for the doorknob.

Behind him Harrington was settling Cordelia into the chair Joe had vacated. Her voice was still raised. "Today I want to do what I should have done a long time ago –" were the last words Joe heard before he shut the door.

He walked the ten steps down the hall to Lydia's cubicle.

"Word processing is almost finished with the latest draft of your memo to Jerry Dan," she said, referring to a summary of Joe's legal research on the cases he had been assigned by Atticus.

"Thanks. I'm going to get a cup of coffee," Joe said.

Lydia pursed her lips in disapproval. She had tried and failed to introduce Joe to the subtleties of oolong, jasmine, and Darjeeling tea, but he remained a confirmed java bean man.

Joe had the lunchroom to himself except for Trudy. She stood by the microwave, humming a song while watching a brown lump on a paper plate go around. "Phoenix" was spelled out in large turquoise script across her shirt front. Underneath in smaller letters were the words "It's Not the Heat, It's the Stupidity."

"Morning, Joe." Trudy was way too cheery. She smiled at him before resuming her vigil at the microwave.

Her greeting surprised Joe. When Trudy bothered to speak to him at all, at best whatever she said was followed by a derogatory term for a lawyer. More usually, it was a sharp remark delivered with a glower. A rare good mood, he thought. He didn't know much about Trudy other than her connection to CelGen and that she sang lead in a local band. Riley told him she was working at the firm because her father wouldn't give her the money to go to Los Angeles with her boyfriend to cut a demo record. "Better pay and beats flipping burgers, barely," had been Riley's comment.

The microwave dinged, and Trudy removed the plate. It held a large yam. Still humming under her breath, Trudy sliced the vegetable open, smashing her fork into its bright orange flesh. Joe didn't want to let the opportunity presented by her uncommon state of mind slip by.

His first day of work, Lydia had warned him. "This place is like a very small town. Watch what you do because there are few secrets." Joe had since concluded Lydia was wrong. There were *no* secrets when it came to Trudy. She seemed privy to everything worth knowing about the firm's lawyers and most of its clients.

"Trudy, could I ask you a question about somebody at the firm?"

She tensed her body and leaned slightly forward, like a game show contestant about to push the buzzer. "Go ahead."

"Do you know what Harrington's middle initials – you know, the D. W. – stands for?"

Trudy rocked back on her heels and slowly closed her eyes in concentration. The steam wafted up from her yam. Joe imagined he could hear the seconds tick by. Finally her lids flickered open.

"No." Her brows arched briefly in surprise before dropping into a scowl. She stabbed at her yam.

"Well, thanks anyway." Joe watched in fascination as she started to eat the pumpkin-colored pulp.

"What are you looking at?" she demanded between bites.

"Just thinking that's, uh, quite a breakfast," Joe replied quickly, taking refuge in a gulp of coffee. The hot liquid seared his tongue and made his eyes water.

"I eat one every morning," Trudy said. "You ought to try it." She pointed her fork in his direction. "Yams have a ton of progesterone. They'd bring out your feminine side."

"I'll keep it in mind." Joe swirled his spoon in his mug one final time. "See you."

"Not so fast." Trudy said, still chewing.

A variation on Popeye's refrain – "I yam what a yam" – popped into Joe's head. He decided it would be best if it stayed there.

"Was that Cordelia Barrett I saw going into Harrington's office?" Trudy asked.

"Uh-huh," Joe nodded.

"The Greedy Group will be nervous," she said knowingly, her voice muffled by a mouthful of vegetable.

"What do you mean?"

"Cordelia's got big bucks, plus the ranch. Why else would she be meeting with Harrington except to change her will?"

Joe tried not to stare as Trudy tore the yam's outer skin into strips with her fingers, tipped her head back, and dropped them into her mouth.

"So who's the Greedy Group?" he asked after an especially big piece had been consumed.

Trudy chewed for a moment, then swallowed with effort. "You know, the Ungrateful Living. All those folks who can hardly wait for her to off. It's like that sign Katie used to have in her office until Harrington made her get rid of it; 'Where There's a Will, There's A Relative.'" She wiped orange smudges off her chin. "Have to run – important meeting in two."

Joe looked at the clock. It read two minutes to ten.

"Want the rest of this?" she asked, gesturing to the disemboweled yam remains.

"No thanks. I need to be one-hundred percent masculine today."

Trudy shot him a look with narrowed eyes while Joe arranged his face into what he hoped was an innocent expression. He followed her out of the lunchroom, almost colliding with Riley.

"Hey." Riley stepped back to avoid the coffee sloshing from Joe's mug. "I thought you were cooped up with the old man all morning."

Joe bent over and dabbed ineffectually with his napkin at the spots he had made on the carpet. "I was until your aunt showed up. She's meeting with him now." He straightened up.

Riley raised his eyebrows.

"I opened my big mouth about Sonny, and she got pretty mad," Joe continued. "She said something about using up all your grandfather's money on car racing."

Riley's mouth twisted into a crooked smile. "I actually think Grandfather would have approved of what Sonny's doing. After all, he got his seed money for the ranch bootlegging in South Carolina. Heck, those booze runners were the founding fathers of stock car racing." Riley's smile twisted more. "Too bad ol' Wes isn't around to set things straight."

Joe knew this wasn't the only thing Riley wished his grandfather were still alive to fix. Weston Thatcher had sired two daughters. Cordelia married a wealthy businessman, while Claire – wrongly choosing love over money in her father's eyes – became the bride of one of the ranch cowboys. Thatcher had cut her out of his will and then followed his wife to the grave, never knowing Riley was to arrive seven months later. Cordelia refused to share the estate with her sister. Two years later Claire and her husband were killed in a car wreck. Cordelia became Riley's guardian and raised him with her only child, Sonny. Riley had told Joe many times he was certain if his grandfather had lived long enough to know about him, he would have changed his will again, and the Barrett Ranch would be half his now.

During the summer he worked there, Joe didn't see a lot of love or even warmth toward Riley from his aunt or his cousin. But he knew Cordelia had put Riley through school and paid for his patio home, clothes, and car. And Riley couldn't have afforded Sultan, his big black roping horse, or the truck and trailer they used to go to team roping events on his law firm salary.

Joe's thoughts were interrupted by the sound of a familiar voice. Riley heard it, too.

"Cowboy up," Riley grinned and slapped Joe on the back.

Joe walked around the corner to see Amber standing in front of Lydia's desk, her elbows resting on the partition. She wore a cropped red top – the color of her lipstick – that ended just below her breasts and black Lycra shorts that barely covered her bottom. White socks slouched around her ankles, and her athletic shoes were as clean as the day they came out of the box. She looked up as Joe approached.

"Hi, honey!" she squealed.

As he got closer, Joe could tell she had come directly from working out. Her bra top was wet at the neckline and under the arms. Tendrils of moist hair stuck to the edges of her face, and the tip of her blond ponytail was damp where it licked her back.

"Amber, what a surprise." Joe wondered why he sounded so stiff.

Amber hugged her elbows tightly, her breasts riding high in the cradle of her arms. "Darling, if you're not stuck here, you're off riding some horse. I figured if I didn't hunt you down, I'd never see you." Her lower lip stuck out, almost a pout.

Joe glanced down the hall toward Harrington's closed door. "Why don't we go into my office?" Joe didn't know what his new boss or Mrs. Barrett would think of Amber's outfit.

"I can only stay a minute. Daddy's going to be in town tomorrow night, and I wanted to go shopping for something nice to wear. You are coming to dinner with us, aren't you, sugar? I know he wants to talk to you about the job." She turned to Lydia. "Joe and I are moving to California."

"Mmmm," Lydia replied.

"Uh, Amber, don't you remember I'm supposed to start roping again tomorrow night? I was sort of hoping you would come cheer me on."

Amber wrinkled her nose, making her round cheeks even rounder. "Oh, sweetie, you know I can't stand rodeos. Everything and everyone is dusty, sweaty, and smells like horse's you-know-what." She lowered her voice to a whisper on the last three words. "I never did get my shoes clean after that last one you dragged me to." She looked down at her scuff-free toes and smiled before turning her attention back to Joe. "Well, I have to skedaddle. Call me, cutie. I'm sure we can work something out. You really can't miss seeing Daddy."

"I don't think –"

Amber stood on tiptoe, puckering up to give him a kiss. Joe stopped talking and bent down, letting her lips brush his cheek.

"'Bye, you guys." Amber waggled her fingers at Lydia before bouncing down the hall. Joe, holding his now cold mug of coffee, watched her go. Lydia raised her eyes to the ceiling and gave a slight side-to-side shake of her head, then went back to her typing.

"Is my memo for Jerry Dan back yet?" Joe asked when Amber was out of sight.

"The latest draft is on your desk," Lydia replied without slowing her fingers.

After locating the document, more than twenty pages long, Joe searched for the prior draft. He needed to compare it to the newer version to make sure all his corrections had been made. He flipped through the papers on his desktop and credenza, then buzzed Lydia.

"I don't think Word Processing gave me back my third draft."

"Is it in your in-basket?" Her voice sounded thin through the speaker.

Joe pushed aside some more papers, found the rectangular wooden box, and rifled through it. Halfway down was a draft of the memo. He flipped through the pages.

"This doesn't look like ..." he said in the direction of the speakerphone.

Moments later, Lydia walked into his office and plucked the

document he was holding from his fingers. She turned to the last page and scanned the string of numbers and letters at the bottom.

"No, this isn't it. Understand?"

She held the paper up for Joe to read, her finger pointing to the last line. Next to the trimmed oval topped with pink nail polish was the year, followed by a sequence of letters and numbers: "1013:1011:D2:R1/1:C1/1."

"Oh, I see," Joe said hesitantly.

Lydia put her hands on her hips in mock annoyance. "Joseph, you still don't know what these numbers mean, do you?"

"I remember there was a memo I meant to read ..." Joe stopped talking, a guilty look on his face.

"Okay, mister. Quick review." Lydia set the draft on his desktop, still opened to the last page.

"Now you know every document generated by Word Processing has its own individual code, right?"

Joe nodded.

"The code is always the last line on the last page of the document," Lydia continued.

"I'm with you so far," Joe said.

"Here's what all those numbers mean." Lydia pointed to the first six digits. "The first set refers to the date this particular document was produced. This document was printed out by Word Processing yesterday, October 13. The next set identifies the date the document was first created. Your first draft was done on October 11."

"How about the next group?" Joe asked.

"We're getting there. 'D2' means this is draft number two. The next two numbers identify the number of this document out of all documents printed in a particular Word Processing printing run. In this case, you can tell this was the only document printed. At the end is the copy number of the document out of all copies made. C1/1 tells you this was the only copy made. If you need more information, like the specific time something was printed, Word Processing has it in their computer records."

"Thanks, Lydia," Joe said. "I'll remember next time."

She picked up the document between two fingers. "So now we know this isn't your third draft, I'll go down to Word

Processing and see if I can find it."

After Lydia left, Joe sat in his desk chair and idly spun it from side to side. The silver frame on the credenza caught his eye. He picked up the picture of Amber and leaned back in his chair, studying it.

"Got a minute?" Jerry Dan's face, minus its customary smile, appeared in the doorway.

"Sure." Joe slid the photo into a drawer and waved his friend into a chair. "What's up?"

"I just got back from court," Jerry Dan said.

"How'd it go?" Joe leaned forward. He wondered when, if ever, he'd try his first case.

"At first it was great. The judge ruled my client could testify as an expert. He got up on the stand and explained all about the Doppler Effect. The judge ate it up. I could tell he was ready to dismiss the red light violation at the end of my direct examination."

"That's great! So why are you so down?"

"Of all the prosecutors there, I had to pull the one who used to be a high school physics teacher. On cross, he gets my client to admit he wouldn't have seen the red light as green unless he was traveling at a certain speed. Then he has him calculate how fast that would be."

"And the answer was?" Joe prompted.

"Approximately 16,740,000 miles per hour." Jerry Dan slumped in his chair. "Or, as my client so helpfully pointed out, a quarter the speed of light and 279,000 times the speed of sound."

"What did the judge do?"

"He fined him $167,355. A penny for every mile over the speed limit. His parting comment to me was to counsel my client on the penalties for perjury before considering an appeal."

Joe tried to swallow the laugh that rumbled up through him but failed, giving in to the convulsions until his sides ached and he was teary-eyed.

"Oh Jerry Dan, I'm sorry." Joe stifled a remaining chuckle.

Jerry Dan stood up, his face glum. "Well, I better go break the good news to Forrest."

Joe followed Jerry Dan out of his office to check Lydia's desk.

He wanted to see if the book on Arizona trusts and estates law he had ordered from the library last Friday had arrived. As he looked through the stack of mail and deliveries, the door of the office next door to his opened. Trudy appeared, looking smug, and marched down the hall without a backward glance. Left standing in the doorway was the office's occupant, Sydney Gardner.

Sydney had introduced herself to Joe the first week he started work, inviting him into her office for a cup of coffee. Classical music had played softly in the background. The coffee was strong and fresh. Joe guessed she was almost fifty. Her highlighted brown hair, cut in layers that skimmed her shoulders and framed her face, had wisps of gray amid the blond, and her neck was starting to wrinkle. Medium to tall, she favored boxy suits, shirts with bows at the neck, and plain pumps. Her large deep-set brown eyes seemed touched with sadness, and her smile didn't turn up at the corners. Joe heard she was divorced and didn't have any children.

Joe met Sydney's eyes. He thought they looked even sadder than usual. She backed into her office and shut the door firmly before he could say anything. *I wonder what that's about,* Joe mused as he found the book he was looking for.

Joe was still reading the T&E treatise in the late afternoon when Alistair Harrington knocked on his door. Joe buried the thick volume under some file folders in his in-basket and stood.

"Yes, sir?"

The tall man walked into the room, a manila envelope in his hand. Joe thought the seams in his face were sharper than the week before. *I'm not the only one who misses Atticus Barclay.*

"I'm sorry we didn't get to resume our meeting, Joe. Mrs. Barrett left me with quite an undertaking that was only just completed." He remained standing so Joe stayed on his feet, too.

"I understand, sir."

"I have a request, if it is not too much trouble," Harrington said. "This is a document Mrs. Barrett very much wanted to have today. The firm messenger is on another delivery and the commercial services are already booked for the evening. Would you be so kind as to deliver it to her ranch? I believe it is on your journey home."

"No problem, sir. I'll leave right now."

"Good." Harrington laid the envelope on Joe's desk. "She has an evening engagement, and I would not want you to miss her."

"Certainly, sir." Joe picked up the envelope and walked out from behind his desk, reaching for his coat on the hook behind the door. "I'll make sure this gets to Mrs. Barrett right away," he promised, stepping into the hall with one arm in a sleeve and the other searching for the armhole.

Once Joe was gone, Harrington lifted up the stack of folders, the corners of his mouth rising to form the barest approximation of a smile when he saw the title of the book that was hidden underneath them.

Chapter 4

Joe walked across the parking garage and climbed into his car. "Okay, Blind Buck, important mission," he said as he patted the cracked vinyl dash. He turned the key and prayed to the car god it would start.

Long seconds of clicking noises was the response.

Okay, okay. Joe tried again. *I absolutely promise to change your oil this weekend.*

With a cough like that of a three-pack-a-day Marlboro Man, the ignition caught and turned over.

"Extortionist," Joe muttered.

He backed out of his space, the white sedan backfiring once as though to remind him of his pledge, and drove up the garage ramp onto Ocotillo, turning left at the intersection with Scottsdale Road.

Joe thought Pinnacle Peak was a simple town to navigate. Built on a grid, the main streets were exactly a mile apart north to south and half a mile apart east to west. No structure in town was over three stories tall. Most commercial buildings were of the flat-roofed "Santa Fe" type: soft corners, deep window openings and wood accents, with the palette of a sunset splashed on their thick adobe-like walls. Here and there, in contrast but also in harmony, were turn-of-the-century Western-style wooden storefronts painted in bright primary hues.

Even though downtown was only five miles long, low speed limits and the beginning of winter traffic kept Joe to a crawl. From around Thanksgiving to just after Easter, Pinnacle Peak's population of approximately 3,000 tripled with the influx of tourists and winter residents, although it seemed to Joe each year the visitors were arriving earlier and leaving later.

Joe didn't expect the traffic situation to improve any time soon given the way the town was growing. La Hacienda, the golf course and dude ranch resort at the western base of El Piniculo, had just won its fifth star. The parking lot was always full at Latigo. A re-created western town built in the desert north of La Hacienda Golf Course, Latigo featured mock gunfights, old-time stores, rodeo demonstrations, and hayride steak dinners. Every year affluent visitors added to their multiple of getaway homes with a purchase in the desert town, or made it their primary residence. The patio homes and luxury lots developed in conjunction with La Hacienda were almost sold out, and developers were already looking north toward the cattle ranches.

Several miles from the office, past the turnoffs to La Hacienda and Latigo, the traffic abruptly thinned. Joe coaxed his car up closer to the speed limit. An old Buick Skylark, it had acquired its name when Joe bumped its nose into the law school parking lot wall, dislodging the "i" from the car company logo. Riley had stepped out to survey the damage.

"Look, it's a Buick with no eye. A Blind Buck!" he cracked.

The name Blind Buck stuck. A towel covered holes in the upholstery and the front bench seat showed a definite list to the driver's side. Despite several "$99 Special" paint jobs, stray streaks of rust radiated from its windows, the edges of which were duct-taped against leaks. Joe had had a choice: a nice car and no horse or the Blind Buck and Ranger. He didn't regret his decision, although he wondered if a horse wouldn't sometimes be a more reliable mode of transportation.

He headed down the highway, the pavement a patchwork quilt of heat damage stitched together with tar seal. The Sonoran desert rolled by his windows. Palo verde trees spread their low branches over creosote and sage, the tree's slender needles drooping downward. Sprays of ocotillos interspersed with rigid saguaros dotted the gray-brown sand, the latter's numbers fewer than a decade before as cactus rustling took its toll. Every new homebuyer wanted a talisman of the desert in the front yard. Now permits were required, and moving certain cacti without a "red tag" meant forfeiture and fines. Joe sometimes worried if the desert was tough enough to withstand the onslaught of asphalt and golf course greens and endless rows of patio homes.

Joe turned on the radio and a country western song filled the car, reminding him Jerry Dan had been his last passenger.

"She got the gold mine and I got the shaft" warbled out of the tinny speakers.

Divorce settlements set to music. Joe cringed and turned it off.

A Mack truck came up, its glittering chrome fender filling Joe's rear view mirror as it pulled around to pass. A few seconds after it disappeared over the next rise, the steering wheel twisted in Joe's hands. Joe coasted to a stop onto the shoulder, the newly acquired tilt of the car telling him what had happened before he got out. Walking around the trunk to the passenger side, he saw his decidedly flat rear tire.

"Damn!" Joe kicked the deflated rubber.

He looked at his watch and frowned. Riley was right; he should get a cell phone. He had resisted, not sure he wanted to be "connected" every moment of the day. Rolling up his sleeves, he opened the trunk, momentarily amused at the idea of owning a phone that would probably be worth more than his car. He wrestled out the spare and went to work.

Twenty-five minutes later he was back behind the wheel, the gas pedal pushed down as far as it would go. It was almost half past five when he turned left onto Ironwood, the road to the Barrett Ranch. He passed under two tall lodgepole pines supporting a crosspiece spelling out "Barrett Ranch" in hand-hammered iron letters.

Joe drove over a cattle guard, strips of rounded metal laid over a ditch in the road to prevent cattle but not cars from crossing, and followed the winding dirt track. Cattle clustered around silver water troughs, staying a respectful distance from the smooth strands of wire that flanked the road. The barbed variety scarred leather and sometimes severed arteries when an animal got tangled in it, so many fences were electrified now, something a cow needed only one encounter to learn.

From what Joe could see, every reddish brown left hip bore

the Barrett brand: the letters "RET" with a straight line or "bar" on top. He wondered if he was passing some of the calves he helped brand three summers ago.

Four miles from the main road, the ranch compound came into sight. On the right were cattle barns and corrals, places where stock could be doctored or penned until it was time for their trip to the slaughterhouse. Directly ahead was the oversized hay barn next to rows of metal horse stalls with connecting paddocks. To the left, on a small knoll and set apart from the other buildings, sat the ranch house, a Territorial two story. Behind it were smaller buildings that housed the permanent staff, seasonal workers and cowboys.

He parked in the circular drive and ran up the flagstone steps, not bothering to shut the car door behind him. Single level wings flanked the center of the house. Its low hipped roof sloped into a covered *portale* across the front of the house, supported by massive posts decorated with carved *zapatas*. The walls were exposed adobe and devoid of ornamentation save for the narrow inset windows topped with strips of wood. The emphasis was distinctly horizontal, evocative of the flat-topped mesas in the distance.

Joe dropped the knocker on the big wooden front door while struggling into his jacket, the envelope clenched in his teeth.

Please, he silently pleaded, let Mrs. Barrett still be here.

He was still tucking in his shirt when the door opened. Standing there was a young woman in her late twenties. She wore jeans and a white V-necked T-shirt that edged the base of her slim throat. On her feet were black ballerina flats. Full brows arched gently over brown-gold eyes tipped up at the outside corners, and her nose was small and straight. Two small gold rings hung from each ear. Joe's first thought was her cappuccino-colored skin would be warm to the touch.

"Yes?"

He snatched the envelope from his mouth. "My name is Joe McGuinness. I'm here to see Mrs. Barrett."

"Oh, you must be the lawyer. I'm sorry, she left about ten minutes ago."

Her voice was low-pitched and slightly accented. Joe found himself leaning forward slightly to hear her.

"Oh no," Joe groaned. "I was supposed to deliver this to her."
He held up the envelope, trying to cover his teeth marks on its
edge with his hand. "I was afraid I was going to be too late."

"But I see you have a good reason for your delay," the young
woman said.

"You do?" Joe asked, mystified.

She pointed to the grease stain on his shirt. "Car trouble, no?"

She had even white teeth and a slight overbite, causing her
plump upper lip to protrude over her even fuller lower one. A
small scar high on her forehead accented rather than diminished
the perfection of her skin. Joe couldn't stop looking at her.

"Mrs. Barrett said you could give the papers to me. Would
you like something to drink before you leave?" She tipped her head
to one side.

"That would be great," Joe said.

The girl turned and walked back into the cool house. Joe
followed, mesmerized by the braid of glossy black-brown hair that
swept across her back like a pendulum. The dimly lit hallway led
into a large kitchen, its tile counters bright and shiny. A large
wooden table was in front of the window on the left, the vase in its
center filled with yellow flowers Joe didn't recognize.

"Lemonade?"

"Fine, thanks."

She poured the pulpy pale liquid into two tall glasses,
handing him one before sitting on the edge of one of the table's
high-backed chairs. Joe leaned against the counter and took a sip.
Just how he liked it, more tang than sweet.

"What's your name?" Joe asked.

"Miguela Santiago Ortiz." Her eyes sparkled over the rim of
her glass.

"Miguelasanti ..."

"Mia, for short," she interrupted, her eyes dancing with
amusement. When she smiled he noticed for the first time the tiny
dark mole to the left of her bottom lip.

"Do you work for Mrs. Barrett?" Joe told himself he was
making sure she was the proper person to give the envelope to.

"Yes. I'm her personal assistant. I read to her, answer her mail,
do errands."

"How long have you worked for Mrs. Barrett?" Joe asked just to be saying something. He couldn't stop looking at her.

"Eight years."

Joe caught the defensiveness in her answer even while he was trying to figure out how he could have been so blind not to have seen her the summer he worked for the ranch.

"I attended ASU for a year," she said, her voice proud. "Before I had to drop out."

The look in her eyes stopped Joe from asking why. Still not wanting the conversation to end, he began talking about the three months Riley and he were Barrett Ranch cowboys.

"I know why we didn't meet then!" Mia broke in. "That was when I was staying in town, cataloging Mrs. Barrett's family papers."

Almost without his realizing it, the conversation shifted to Joe's passion for horses, roping, rodeo. Mia was an attentive listener. He was describing the rattlesnake that had slithered up through the hole in his car's floorboards when the clock on the wall chimed seven times. Mia looked up.

"I'm sorry, you'll have to go now," she said, rinsing out their empty glasses and setting them next to the sink. "I still have some things to do before Mrs. Barrett returns."

Mia walked him to the front door and opened it. Joe paused on the threshold.

"Do you like rodeo?" he asked impulsively.

"Some."

"Know anything about team roping?"

Mia cocked an eyebrow. "Is that where two cowboys chase after a cow, each trying to rope a different end?"

"Pretty close," Joe said. "What they're chasing, though, is a steer, not a cow, and he gets a head start. The first rider, the header, is aiming to rope the animal's horns or neck. If he makes it, then the second rider, the heeler, tries to loop the hind feet." Joe realized he was running on and felt his cheeks go warm. He paused to gather himself.

"Anyway, there's a team roping event tomorrow night at Los Caballos. Riley and I are competing. Would you like to come watch?" Joe leaned forward, hopeful for a yes answer.

Mia's eyes were unreadable in the shadows. Her pursed lips looked as though they had been sculpted.

"That would be nice," she finally replied.

Joe let out a breath.

"I'll pick you up around six. Where do you live?"

"Here."

"You live here?"

"I have a separate apartment in the back. But you don't need to come by. I'll catch a ride with one of the hands. I know a few plan to go." She tapped an imaginary watch on her wrist and shooed him down the steps.

"It was nice to meet you, Joe," she called from the *portale*. She clasped her hands behind her and leaned her hip against the edge of the thick front door.

"Nice to meet you, too. See you tomorrow." He climbed into his car, its interior dustier than ever from standing with the door open in the desert wind.

He was halfway down the drive before he thought of Amber and mentally flinched at how angry she would be when he told her he would have to miss dinner with her father.

"But it's not because I have a date," he said aloud, wondering as he spoke exactly whom he was trying to convince.

Returning to Scottsdale Road, Joe again headed north. The day's heat gone, he drove with the windows down, hoping to clear out some of the grit. Three miles later he slowed as he approached the cross street that led to Los Caballos Park, the largest horse-oriented public facility in the Southwest. Arenas, stalls, polo fields, and jump courses were spread out over six square miles. Joe ignored the twinge in his shoulder. He'd be there tomorrow night with Riley for the team roping series.

On the southeast corner of the intersection squatted a concrete block building. A wooden sign with "Danny's Cantina" hand-painted on it in now faded red letters was posted over the entrance. Joe turned into the gravel parking lot and nosed his car into a space.

He shucked off his jacket and walked toward the low-slung structure, its only decoration a row of Christmas lights hanging from its eaves. In front was a hitching rack, the eucalyptus bar showing the gnaw marks of many equine visitors. He pushed open the scarred metal door and walked to a table, taking a seat on a wooden chair with one leg shorter than the rest. He raised his voice over the hum of the evaporative cooler.

"Hiya, Danny!"

The rotund man behind the counter saluted him with a spatula. Although his hair had flecks of gray, his mustache still bristled coal black.

"*Hola, José! Quiere una cerveza?*"

"*No, gracias.* How about some fish tacos and a pitcher of water?" Joe held up two fingers.

"*No problema. Un momentito.*" Danny disappeared into the kitchen. Joe went over to the sideboard and filled paper containers with homemade pico de gallo, salsa, and fresh-chopped lettuce and tomato. Balancing the stack in one hand, he grabbed a small bottle of red sauce and returned to his table.

While waiting for his food to cook he looked around. The decor hadn't changed since his last visit. Or his first either. Red, white, and green streamers were pinned up near the ceiling, under which were hung photos of the Department of Public Safety and sheriff deputies who were frequent customers. Danny liked the *policia* to visit. "Keeps the bad guys out," he told Joe. Once, after too many *cervezas*, Riley asked why there weren't any photos of the local INS agents on the wall. Joe kicked him under the table, hoping Danny hadn't heard.

Joe met Danny when he was working on a small immigration matter for the firm last summer. The witness he needed to interview worked in the kitchen of the cantina. Joe had never eaten better seafood tacos; fresh mahi-mahi marinated in Danny's secret lime concoction grilled over mesquite and served in homemade tortillas. Besides, he liked talking to the owner. He made it a point to stop by at least once a week after roping, often with Riley tagging along.

Danny, dressed in his usual uniform of Guayabera shirt, sansabelt slacks, and *guaraches* with tire tread soles, brought the plate to the table and sat down across from Joe. Pulling the still steaming food toward him, Joe heaped on condiments while the older man fanned himself with a folded newspaper.

"*Como está, Señor Abogado?*"

"I'm Mister Errand-boy, not Mister Lawyer today," Joe mumbled through a mouthful of rice. "Mmmm, this is good."

Danny smiled, his brown button eyes disappearing into wrinkles of leathery skin.

"*Muchas gracias.*" He watched Joe inhale half a taco before speaking again. "What do you mean 'Errand-boy'?"

"I was just joking. I had to drop something by the Barretts'." Joe thought how much Danny was tied in to the Hispanic community. "I met someone there tonight. Do you happen to know Mia ..., Mia ..." Joe struggled to remember her last name.

"Mia Ortiz," Danny supplied, smiling so broadly Joe could see the gold edges of his teeth. "But of course. Mia's father and I were born in the same *barrio* in Nogales. After he died, I looked out for his family. It was I who recommended Mia to Señora Barrett."

"You know Cordelia Barrett?" Joe tried to hide his surprise.

"*Sí, sí.* She has employed many of my countrymen. She pays good wages, gives them decent places to live, and makes sure their children go to school." He dropped his voice to a hoarse whisper. "She does not look too hard for the green card either, you know what I mean? I myself have heard her say, 'If a man did not have the good fortune to be born north of the Thirtieth Parallel, who am I to deny him a job?' Maybe this view does not make her so popular with her *gringo* neighbors, but she is much regarded among my people." Danny leaned back in his chair and folded his arms. "Señora Barrett has eaten lunch here several times," he said proudly.

"Tell me about Mia," Joe asked while trying to imagine Cordelia Barrett eating tacos across the table from him, salsa dripping onto her silk blouse. He couldn't.

Danny's face softened. "A sad story for that little one. She had a year of the university. No one in the family had finished the high school before." He shook his head.

"Why did she quit?"

Danny scowled. "Jaime, her younger brother, was hit by a car.

He was little – six years old, I think. The driver, he disappeared. Jaime did not die, but his brain, it doesn't work right anymore, and all the time he is in the wheelchair. Mia's mother, she works hard as a maid at La Hacienda, but there is not enough money."

"How awful!" Joe said. "When did Jaime's accident happen?"

"Many years ago. Jaime, he is a teenager now."

That explains the eight years with Cordelia Barrett, Joe realized. "But can't Mia get a better job?"

"I ask her this myself. She tells me Señora Barrett pays her well and does not charge her for her room or her meals. She can arrange her work so she has time to help her mother with Jaime and she is permitted to use Señora Barrett's library – she has many books." Danny tapped the tabletop with his finger. "And I know Señora Barrett helps in other ways. When Jaime grew too big for his wheelchair last year, Señora Barrett bought him a new one. Mia was embarrassed, but it cost too much for her mother to pay."

Joe thought about the Cordelia Barrett Danny described; one he hadn't seen or heard about before. He wondered if Riley knew.

The bell over the front door jangled and two men walked in.

"Excuse me." Danny stood and went behind the counter.

Joe swallowed his last bite of taco, then waved at Danny with one hand while reaching with the other for a napkin to dab at the red sauce on his chin. He left some bills on the tabletop and walked outside, the evening breeze chilling the sweat on his forehead from the hot food.

He started the car and turned north once again onto Scottsdale Road. "Two more miles, Blind Buck, and we're home," he said, patting the steering wheel.

Still feeling the heat of the chilies he had consumed, he rolled up the windows and turned on the air conditioning, such as it was. He twisted the radio knob and twangy guitars blared. "Mommas, Don't Let Your Babies Grow Up to Be Cowboys." He sang along with Waylon, his career worries replaced with thoughts of Mia.

Chapter 5

Tuesday, October 15

None of the three research projects Harrington assigned him the next morning involved a legal issue Joe had ever heard of. *At least I won't have time to worry about tonight,* he thought as he carried an armful of case reports to a quiet corner in the library. He liked working there, surrounded by canyons of dark-grained book-filled shelves that ran from floor to ceiling, knowing that within his reach was every word of wisdom – and admittedly injustice, too – handed down by appellate judges since the ink was dry on John Hancock's signature.

The musty smell of the pages in the older treatises, and the way their leather bindings flaked away in his hand when touched, stirred unexpected emotions in Joe. He felt part of the fraternity – lawyers learning the law as it was and then contributing to its evolution.

But *I'm not really a member of the club,* he thought ruefully. Case books were just that; records of decisions in court cases. His name would never appear under Counsel of Record unless he made it to trial first.

Joe worked straight through the day, the wooden rungs of his chair leaving creases on his pants where his legs wrapped around them. He kept one eye on his watch as the afternoon wore on. At half past five he jogged across the parking lot to his car.

He was already waiting with Cricket in front of the barn

when Riley pulled into the YJ drive ten minutes early. Riley loaded Joe's gear into the dually's bed while Joe swung open one of the horse trailer doors. Sultan, Riley's big black gelding, twisted his head around in the narrow stall on the other side and whinnied. Cricket nickered back. Joe draped the leadrope over the mare's neck and lightly slapped her bottom. She stepped up into the compartment, her hooves ringing on the wooden floor. Joe latched the trailer door, picked up his rope, which was coiled in a protective carrier, and climbed in the passenger side.

"I'll see you at the arena," Hal shouted from across the yard where he was feeding the penned stock. Riley and Joe waved as they drove by.

Riley turned left onto Los Caballos road, passing Danny's parking lot, already half filled with pickups and older American cars. After a mile the pavement ended, and the truck and trailer bumped down the dirt track, twin plumes of dust in their wake. Riley braked to a stop on the field next to the rodeo arena.

Already parked at haphazard angles were at least fifteen other rigs. Some trucks were hitched to two-horse models like Riley's, while others pulled stock trailers that could hold ten head. Miniature lariats and Western saddles dangled from rearview mirrors. Most trailers still had horses tied to their sides, although a few riders warmed up in the small fenced oval next to the arena. The jean brand of choice was Wrangler, overwhelmingly blue with some women opting for bright colors, topped with pressed shirts and straw or cloth hats.

Opening the trailer's rear door, Joe clucked to Cricket. The chestnut backed out carefully and Joe knotted her leadrope to a metal ring welded to the side of the trailer. He brushed the already clean coat and combed out her thick mahogany mane and tail. The smell of dried hay mingled with the scent of horse sweat and manure in the still warmish air. Spurs chinked softly in the background.

Joe settled the saddle onto Cricket's back, cinching it loosely, and made sure the breast collar fit snugly against her chest before slipping the halter off her nose and hooking it around her neck. He guided the curb bit into the mare's mouth, careful not to hit her teeth, and pulled the headstall over her ears. He buckled the throatlatch and connected the tie-down, a strip of leather running from the noseband to the breast collar that worked as a brace for balance when the mare stopped or turned. After strapping protective rubber and leather boots around her fetlocks and shins, Joe refastened the halter over her head and went to check on Riley.

When Joe walked around to the other side of the trailer, Sultan, already tacked up, lunged at him with flattened ears and bared teeth. Joe dodged his charge, remembering how irritable the horse always was before a competition. Riley had a foot propped up on the corner of his truck's rear bumper, giving his round-toed, low-heeled roping boot a final wipe with a rag. He straightened up and grinned, tipping his Resistol straw hat back from his face.

"How's it going, pardner?"

Joe returned the smile, surprised at how stiff his face muscles felt. "It's good to be back."

"Hey, Joe, Riley!"

The two turned at the sound of their names. Walking toward them across the field as fast as he could was Jerry Dan, Mia at his side. For once, Jerry Dan's attire blended with the crowd's, save for the lack of wear on his inner jean seams that only hours in a saddle produced.

"That's that girl who works for Aunt Cordelia," Riley said as they watched the pair approach. "I wonder how she got hooked up with Jerry Dan."

Joe cleared his throat. "Actually, I invited her." Joe dug his boot toe into the dirt.

Riley cut his hazel eyes at him. "Really," he said. It wasn't a question.

Joe shifted his weight from one foot to another, wondering at the coolness that had descended between them. "I'm kinda surprised you never mentioned her."

Riley looked away. "I didn't think she was that important."

Jerry Dan skidded to a puffing stop in front of them, his round face pink from excitement or exertion, Joe couldn't tell.

"Look who I found in the parking lot!" he exclaimed. "She asked me where the contestants were, and I found out she was looking for you." Jerry Dan beamed at his new acquaintance.

"Hello, Joe." Her voice was more seductive than Joe

remembered.

"Hi, Mia," Joe said, searching for something more to say. "Uh, I see you've met Jerry Dan. This is Riley."

"We're already acquainted," Riley said curtly, turning and walking toward the truck cab.

"We're both nervous, and we have a lot to do." Joe apologized, wondering at his friend's behavior. Maybe it was a mistake to invite spectators their first time back.

"I understand," Mia murmured.

Her shimmering blue-black hair fell straight and heavy past her shoulders save for a few tendrils that caressed her face in the breeze. Joe wondered at the weight of it.

"Man, you really look like a rodeo cowboy." Jerry Dan gave Joe the once-over.

Joe protested with a smile. "I'm dressed the same as you are."

"Not quite." Jerry Dan shook his head. "I don't have one of those." He pointed at Joe's belt buckle, the twin of Riley's, a silver oval embellished with a gold pair of team ropers snaring a steer. Letters around its edge identified its wearer as the "Winter Series Champion."

"Girls can't resist them," Jerry Dan confided in a stage whisper to Mia. She smothered a smile.

Joe laughed. "Jerry Dan, that's ridiculous. How many buckle bunnies do you see hanging around here?"

"Just one." Riley slammed the truck door shut, his rope over his arm.

"Jerry Dan, why don't you buy a buckle?" Mia asked quickly. "I'm sure I've seen them in the Western wear stores."

Jerry Dan wrinkled his nose. "Those are for tourists and cowboys who don't rodeo. The only one worth wearing is one you've earned."

Their conversation was interrupted by the arrival of two riders, one mounted on a big buckskin mare, the other on a medium-sized bay. Out of the corner of his eye Joe saw Mia shrink back into the shadow of the trailer. Sultan gave the newcomers his usual welcome, squealing while letting fly with a kick from the rear, causing the bay to spook sideways. Its rider yanked on the reins then booted the reluctant horse forward next to his companion.

"Check out that silver dinner plate," Riley said under his breath. "How can he pull on his boots in the morning without that thing slicing him in half?"

The man on the buckskin doffed his hat and ran a hand through graying, close-cropped hair. The lines around his slate blue eyes were from the sun; the ones around his mouth the product of a lifetime of cigarettes. He had the thick chest and broad shoulders of a bulldogger and a belly that was starting to overfill an azure blue shirt with a Western yoke and snap pockets. Dark denim jeans were held up with a leather belt attached to a silver buckle almost five inches wide. "Rocking H Ranch" was spelled across its polished face above a picture of the spread's brand: a lower case h sitting on an arc that looked like a rocker on a chair.

"Welcome back, Joe." The man's voice sounded like rocks sloshing in the rinse cycle.

"Thank you, Mr. Healy." Joe didn't really know Chuck Healy, the owner of the Rocking H – dubbed the "Rocking Chair" after its brand – a nine thousand acre cattle operation on the north border of the Barrett Ranch, about six miles to the east across Scottsdale Road from the YJ. Joe heard Healy had moved to Arizona after he was forced to sell his big ranch in Colorado when his wife divorced him. His rate of expansion was a prime topic of conversation among Hal and other ranching locals. In only a few years Healy quadrupled the number of head he ran on his land and recently leased additional acreage from the county.

"How's yer bum wing?" Don Rogers had a high pitched voice with the undertone of a whine. Slight of build, he wore kelly green cowboy boots and a faded shirt over worn jeans. A wad of tobacco was tucked in his upper lip, leaving a bulge like a tumor. The squint in his left eye gave him a permanent leer.

"Fine." Joe didn't care too much for Healy's roping partner and ranch foreman.

Rogers' still nervous horse danced sideways. His rider raked him with a spur, his jeans hiking up to show a cloverleaf pattern – a long hooked stem extending from three leaves – embossed on his boot top that matched the brand on the gelding's quivering flanks.

"Dammit, Lucky, stand still," he snapped, smacking the gelding's neck with the ends of his reins.

Joe frowned. This was not the first time he had seen Don Rogers be hard on a horse.

"You boys ready to get used to second place again?" Riley asked. He was leaning against the side of the truck bed, arms and ankles loosely crossed. The zing of lariats and percussion of thudding hooves from other riders warming up sounded around them. Dust sifted through the air, its acrid taste and powdery feel unavoidable.

Joe inwardly winced at Riley's tone. Healy and Rogers had been the runner-up team to Joe and Riley in the winter series. The rivalry, at least from the Rocking H perspective, was bitter.

"Let's wait for the season to end before declaring a winner, shall we?" Healy fixed Riley with a flinty gaze.

"Speaking of winning, I heard you guys were in New Mexico last weekend for the summer regionals," Riley continued, unfazed. "How'd you go?"

Joe recognized the mocking glint in his friend's eye and wondered why he was baiting Healy.

The rancher's face darkened. "The old saying may be 'headers starve heelers to death,' but I never missed a steer. It was my partner who no-timed me every run," he rasped, his scowl deepening as he looked at Rogers for the first time since their arrival.

Rogers leaned over and spat a stream of tobacco juice, avoiding his boss's glare.

"No time – means he missed the steer," Joe heard Jerry Dan whisper to Mia, his head bent close to hers. Healy looked toward the voice.

"Why, Mia, I didn't notice you." Healy's blue eyes found Mia's dark ones.

Almost hesitantly she moved forward and dipped her chin in a single nod. "Hello, Mr. Healy."

"You know it's 'Chuck' to you." His voice dropped to an intimate tone. "I enjoyed our dinner at Patio de Piniculo. Perhaps you'd care to join me again this weekend?"

A wave of discouragement washed over Joe. He had never

eaten at the resort's famous steakhouse. The appetizers alone exceeded his food budget for a week.

"No thank you." A stilted cadence silenced the usual musicality of her tone. "I have other plans."

From his height on the horse's back, Healy swept his glance across the group standing next to Riley's trailer. "Looks like you do." He smiled wolfishly. Rogers sniggered. Joe clenched his fists as Riley straightened up.

"Hey," Jerry Dan said, "You can't –"

Healy half rose in his stirrups, his hand on his rope. Joe edged toward Mia, gauging how he could pull her to safety if things got ugly. A well-thrown lariat could cut like a bullwhip.

For a moment the riders and others on the ground didn't move. In the stillness, Joe heard the drum of boots hurrying up behind him.

"Chuck, how are ya?" Hal's voice boomed past Joe's shoulder.

"Fine, Hal." Healy relaxed back into his saddle. Rogers re-draped his lariat over his saddlehorn while Jerry Dan shepherded Mia closer to Riley's rig. Joe didn't miss the rigid set of her shoulders under the loose fabric of her shirt. He chewed on his lip. What exactly had gone on between her and Healy?

"Any luck finding your stock?" Healy asked.

"Nope." Hal looked grim. "And more head are missing since we talked."

"I'm sorry to hear that," Healy replied. "I had my man check my herds." He jerked his chin toward Rogers. "Other than the few he runs under his brand, the rest were Rocking H."

"I 'preciate the effort," Hal said. "Keep passing the word, will you?"

"I certainly will."

Healy looked at Mia and tipped his hat, then nodded to Riley and Joe.

"Good luck, gentlemen." He smoothly backed up his horse, then spurred it toward the warm-up arena. Rogers followed.

"Good timing, Mr. Timmons," Jerry Dan said. "Things were getting pretty tense there."

Unnecessarily provoked by Riley, Joe thought, wondering at his partner's mood. After Healy and Rogers rode away, Riley had disappeared without a word around the other side of the trailer.

"Don't you worry about those *hombres*." Hal's eyes twinkled like an Arizona night sky. "More importantly, tell me who your pretty new friend is here."

Joe introduced Mia. The old cowboy took off his hat.

"It's a pleasure, ma'am."

"Do you team rope, too?" Mia asked.

"'Fraid not, little lady. This stiff ol' body lets me climb onto a horse and throw a rope, but not both at the same time."

Joe said, "Hal used to be a rodeo bronc rider."

"Saddle or bareback?" Jerry Dan asked, unable to keep the wistfulness from his voice.

"Both. We didn't specialize back then like the fellas do today." He held up his scarred hands with their knobby knuckles. "Maybe it'd been better if we did."

"Hal's an example of what a big animal and a lot of nerve can do to you," Joe said, respect as well as affection in his voice. He thought all roughstock – broncs and bulls – riders were supremely skilled and ridiculously brave. Injuries were common and death not unexpected. "He even went the full eight seconds on Widowmaker." The big bay mare was the first locally bred bronc to be inducted into the Rodeo Hall of Fame.

"Wow." Jerry Dan let out a low whistle.

"I didn't mean to," Hal said, embarrassed at the attention. "I was trying to jump off of her but she kept jumping under me."

"Isn't bronc riding dangerous?" Mia asked. When she moved, her cropped shirt rose above the waistband of her jeans, exposing a narrow line of bare midriff. Joe forced himself not to stare.

"Thirty-five broken bones last count," Hal said. "But it was worth every second on those horses' backs."

"What about the seconds spent leaving them?" Joe quipped.

"I must admit, those were less pleasant," Hal said with a rueful grin.

"Did you ever ride a bull?" Mia asked. Her genuine interest in their conversation pleased Joe. She had already asked more questions about rodeo than Amber ever had.

"No, ma'am. A bullrider buddy once tol' me what it felt like sitting on El Toro. He said first you get shaken like a dirty ol' carpet and then a big fat sumo wrestler jumps on your stomach to finish you off. That didn't sound too appealing to me."

Riley appeared from the other side of the rig. He rested his tailbone against the truck's door and raised a boot heel to the running board. "I've ridden a bull."

Joe looked at him, surprised. He hadn't heard about this before.

"You have?" Jerry Dan regarded him with awe.

"It was my thirteenth birthday, and we were at a junior rodeo. Sonny and his friends entered me in the beginner bullriding. I didn't know about it until they called my name."

Joe knew Riley would have rather been gored than risk his cousin's ridicule by backing down.

"How long was your ride?" Jerry Dan asked.

"About two or three seconds – the time it took for me to come down after he tossed me up on the first jump."

Joe and Mia laughed, and Hal clapped Riley on the back. Jerry Dan's eyes widened. Obviously, he was impressed.

"Do many people make a living rodeoing?" Mia's words and movements were easier now, the effects of the encounter with Healy apparently dissipated.

"Sure," Jerry Dan responded eagerly.

Joe suppressed a smile, recognizing a "Jerry Dan Rodeo Lecture" was about to start. His friend's encyclopedic knowledge of the sport never ceased to amaze him. Jerry Dan knew facts and figures Joe was embarrassed to admit he'd never heard of, let alone memorized.

"A handful of teams, those at the top of the PRCA, Professional Rodeo Cowboys Association, make over a hundred thousand dollars a year," Jerry Dan began. Mia nodded encouragement. "They travel across the country and into Canada, doing nothing but rodeo. Another group of ropers is circuit cowboys. They work a forty-hour week and rope on the weekends, driving up to several hundred miles for competitions within their circuit. The pot at those rodeos might cover entry fees, travel expenses, with a new saddle or trailer to the big winner."

"So that's what Joe and Riley do?" Mia threw a quick smile in Joe's direction before focusing again on Jerry Dan. Joe's elation flickered through his chest.

Jerry Dan shook his head. "At Joe and Riley's level, it's informal ropings at ranches in the neighborhood and an occasional jackpot."

"Jackpot?"

"Entry fees pooled for prize money." Jerry Dan swept his hand toward the field of competitors. "These guys are in it because they enjoy working with a horse and a partner." He paused for a moment. "And I think some of them are motivated by more."

"More?" Mia repeated, puzzled.

"A feeling they're keeping something important alive," Jerry Dan said. "It's a reverence for a way of life they don't want to see disappear."

Riley straightened up from where he had been leaning against the truck.

"Sorry to interrupt this fascinating flow of information, rodeo fans," he said, "but my partner and I have to warm up our horses." He walked to where Sultan was tied.

"Good luck, you guys," Jerry Dan said. Hal touched two fingers to the rim of his hat.

"Be careful." Mia looked directly at Joe.

After the three had left to find seats in the bleachers, Joe led Cricket away from the trailer and tightened the cinch. He stepped into the stirrup and lifted his leg over the cantle, sitting down gently onto the seat. Picking up the reins, Joe waited for his partner while shaking out his rope the way Clem Smith, the handyman at his mother's café, had taught him.

The old cowboy kept an eye on Joe after school, and with his mother's reluctant permission, taught him to ride and rope. Joe took to Clem as though he were a favorite grandfather, and he felt as though he had lost a piece of his heart when Clem died during Joe's senior year of college.

Riley stood at Sultan's shoulder, facing backward, and loosened the reins. As the horse started to move forward, he grasped the saddlehorn with both hands and swung up into the saddle, the stirrup unnecessary. Joe watched with a bit of envy. He had never mastered the "cowboy mount," and his injured shoulder made it even less likely that he would.

That's the least of your worries tonight, he reminded himself as Cricket moved out at an easy pace beside Sultan toward the practice ring. He listened to the creak of his wooden saddletree and the squeak of leather, trying to let their rhythms lull his nervousness.

After a few circuits of the oval, Joe urged the mare into a lope and cautiously swung his loop. Tendrils of pain rippled through his shoulder. He pulled into the center of the ring and kneaded the muscle next to his collarbone.

Suddenly Cricket grunted and staggered a few steps forward. The chestnut had been hit from behind. Joe grabbed onto the horn to brace himself.

"What the –?" Joe exclaimed, twisting to see who had run into them.

"Sorry, I didn't see ya." Rogers backed his horse away, his malicious grin putting the lie to his apology. "Better be careful. It's easy to git hurt at a rodeo." He spurred Lucky's shoulder, and the bay wheeled around and loped away. Joe was still looking after him when Riley jogged by.

"How's it going?" he called.

"Great," Joe replied, trying to mask the pain in his shoulder.

Deciding to save his arm for their run, Joe coiled his rope and concentrated on loosening up Cricket. He urged the willing horse into a gallop, then signaled her to stop and back up a dozen strides, getting her ready for her role. Once he caught the steer, Cricket's obligation would be to keep the rope taut against the animal's struggles, usually by backpedaling quickly.

An air horn sounded from the main arena, signaling ten minutes to the start of the competition. Joe gave Cricket a quick pat.

"I need you to go well tonight, my friend," he whispered.

The mare's ears swiveled backward at the sound of his voice.

Riley trotted up next to him, and the two walked their horses over to where the other ropers were gathering outside the west entrance to the arena. Many of the competitors knew about Joe's accident, and more than a few hailed his return.

Joe scanned the stands, trying to pick out Mia from among

the tourists and locals. The former was either very pale or very sunburned and the latter usually wore cowboy hats or caps with the name of a farm equipment manufacturer printed across the front. Jerry Dan's windmilling arms finally caught Joe's eye. He and Hal were seated on either side of Mia, three rows up from the front on the left side of the arena. Joe waved and thought he saw Mia smile back at him, although the distance made it hard to tell. An elbow poked him in the ribs.

"What do you think?" Riley asked as the steers shouldered into the metal chute. Brown Corrientes from Mexico, all wore thick strips of leather wrapped under their jaws and around the top of their heads with holes cut out for their horns to guard against rope burns.

"Looks like they'll be a fast bunch," Joe said.

"Not the cattle, amigo. Our competition," Riley chided.

"Oh."

Joe regarded the twenty or so men surrounding them, all on horseback, partners near partners. He had always thought team ropers were different from other rodeo competitors. Generally a friendlier group, he found them to be less solitary than the cowboys who competed in the individual sports. Their get-ups were flashier, too. The big-chested quarter horses they rode were often bright-coated. In the group tonight, Joe counted six palominos, one paint, and one gray. More silver decorated their saddles and bridles, and most of their shirts came off the expensive rack at the western store Joe even saw a pink short-sleeved model with a polo pony galloping across the left chest.

Another difference, Joe had to admit, was fitness. More than a few bellies hung low over belt buckles, and many had never worked on ranches. Some hadn't even known how to ride before they took up the sport as adults. Team roping's been invaded by yuppies, Joe concluded as he recognized two other lawyers, an accountant, and his dentist in the gathering.

And an Indian. Joe stared at the dark-skinned man sitting bareback on a bay horse almost small enough to qualify as a pony. He wore a long-sleeved shirt, jeans, and running shoes. His coal black hair hung past his shoulders.

"Who's that?" Joe whispered to Riley.

Riley glanced over. "I've seen him on the news talking about the casino. I think his dad is the headman on the rez."

Joe had never been to "the rez," the Tohono 'O'odham Indian Community, a hundred thousand acre-plus reservation to the east of Pinnacle Peak. Non-tribe members needed a permit to access all but a few areas. He knew the word "Arizona" came from the Tohono 'O'odham "arizonac," meaning "small spring," and the law firm's cabinets displayed several of the intricately woven baskets for which the tribe, formerly known as the Papago, was noted. And, along with almost everybody else in town, Joe was aware of the 'O'odham's efforts to build a casino on their land at the base of El Piniculo, directly north of Lagunita, the area's only lake. Situated at the southeast end of town, the nine square miles of fresh water were much used by fishermen, water-skiers, and boardsailors. According to talk Joe heard around town, it seemed many didn't want the Vegas-style element and its concomitant problems in their backyard. The tribe saw no other way to raise funds urgently needed for education and health care.

"Why's he here?" Joe asked.

"Don't know. He's showed up at the last few ropings." Riley poked Joe in the ribs. "You better watch out. I remember something about him being the new 'bitter man.'"

Riley never did pass up a chance to tease someone thought Joe. "Who or what is a 'bitter man'?"

"The guy chosen to lead his people into war."

"Oh," Joe replied, nonplussed.

Joe looked back to where the man and his horse had been standing, but they had disappeared.

"We're up after Healy and Rogers," Riley said, tugging at the white cotton glove on his roping hand. "Second to last."

The air was filled with the high-pitched whine of twirling ropes. The horses appeared to be more relaxed than their riders, with the exception of Lucky. Standing apart from the others, the bay pranced in place, head bobbing, while Healy sawed on the reins. The cowboy caught Joe's eye and raised his hand as though it were a cocked gun. Aiming it at Joe, he pulled the "trigger," then threw back his head and laughed, making his horse skitter sideways.

The first pair got ready to go. The steer was loaded into the chute made of pipe fencing, a gate in front of him and a removable partition behind that prevented him from backing up. The riders readied their ropes, three small loops gathered in their rein hands and one big coil tucked under their throwing arms. The pair guided their horses into position, backing them into the far corners of the small fenced off areas on either side of the chute, header on the left side, heeler on the right. The horses waited, muscles bunching like coiled springs, their noses several yards behind the steer.

A thin elastic rope stretched from the chute door to the arena fence across the front of the box on the left, separating the header – the roper who would try for the steer's head – from the rest of the arena.

The header nodded. The gate man released the lever on the chute gate and the steer sprang free, galloping across the arena. Competitors as well as friends in the stands hollered encouragement. The header spurred his horse forward a heartbeat later, the animal's chest almost hitting the falling line. Ten seconds would have been added to their time if they had broken the barrier, designed to ensure the steer's head start.

The header's horse caught up to the running steer. Its rider made two quick circles over his head before letting his rope fly, the noose settling around the base of the sharp-tipped horns. He dallied the end of his rope around his saddlehorn, reinforced with strips of inner tube, and reined hard to the left, looking over his shoulder as his mount towed the balky longhorn like a tugboat pulling a barge.

The heeler, having moved into position but barred by the rules from throwing before his partner wrapped the rope around his saddlehorn and turned, now snaked his loop toward the steer's back legs. Snagging the right hind, he cued his horse to back up swiftly while he dallied his rope, making sure to keep his thumb clear. His partner spun his horse to face him, their tight ropes bringing the previously running steer to a stretched out halt lengthwise between them. The flagger called time and the riders shook their ropes loose, the newly freed steer scrambling away with a grunt. Recoiling their ropes as they went, the two ropers loped after their previous quarry, herding him through a gate at the other end of the arena. Joe sympathized with the disgusted look on the heeler's face as he followed the steer out the exit. Catching only one hind cost them a five-second penalty.

The announcer called out the time for the run and the names and handicap of the second team. The summoned pair loped quick circles in the arena, ropes singing overhead, while the next steer in line was prodded into the head of the chute. The gate banged open and the horses sped in pursuit, only to come to a confused stop a few seconds later. The crowd groaned. A few yards out of the gate, his pursuers about to close in on him, the steer abruptly halted, then ducked behind the header's horse, resulting in an unavoidable "no time" for the pair that drew him.

"Alpo Land for him," Riley remarked.

Joe knew it was probably true. Once rodeo stock became stale – cattle that wouldn't run or horses that wouldn't buck – they usually ended up in the can or on the grill without delay.

Joe watched as the other pairs took their turns. A few scored in the double digits, using up the three throws allowed per team. Some were penalized for roping only one horn or for letting the steer loose before it was "lined out" between the two riders. Others just missed altogether. One steer unexpectedly veered under the neck of the pursuing horse, bringing horse, rider, and steer crashing to the ground. The runs went quickly, each pair averaging about nine-and-a-half seconds, with some sevens and eights.

"The five teams with the best combined times from this round will qualify for the finals," the announcer reminded the crowd. "And the finals are where the money will be won."

Joe rolled his shoulders, trying to lengthen foreshortened muscles.

"Chuck Healy and Don Rogers," called the announcer.

Joe edged Cricket closer to the arena fence and watched the two men get set. Healy's big buckskin backed into the box without a problem while Rogers' bay, his eyes ringed white and his mouth dripping threads of white foam, jigged sideways, his neck arched against the reins.

Without warning, cattle started to stream into the arena

through the gate at the far end. Following them was a small band of Tohono 'O'odham on foot, many carrying placards. Joe looked for the "bitter man" he had seen earlier, but he didn't appear to be part of the group. The steers, spooked by the waving signs, galloped toward the chutes where the ropers were grouped. Lucky reared in fright, Healy clinging to his mane. With a curse, the cowboy yanked one rein savagely, and the horse dropped to the earth again.

The 'O'odham paraded in front of the grandstand, chanting and displaying their signs. Joe could see the words "Return Our Land" and "No to Governor's Illegal Law." He presumed the "illegal law" was the one recently enacted by the state legislature at the governor's urging that banned gambling near residential areas. Joe knew the 'O'odham already had sued to overturn the legislation, heightening the conflict by including demands for reclamation of or compensation for lands allegedly misappropriated by early settlers.

There was scattered applause from the grandstand, but the faces of the ropers were grim. Many owned the property that was being claimed or worked for those who did. Joe saw a few ropes swing free and turned to Riley.

"This could get nasty," he said worriedly, watching a few cowboys gallop toward their trucks. He knew the gun racks in range pick-ups were rarely there for decoration.

To his surprise, Riley looked unperturbed. "It's been a long time since Arizona cowboys have had a chance to take on the Indians." He folded his arms across his chest and leaned back in his saddle.

The 'O'odham continued their demonstration while loose cattle milled. A clatter of hooves above the din heralded the approach of a lone rider. His galloping horse was aimed straight at the arena fence. Joe watched transfixed and realized with horror that the horse and rider were not going to stop.

Stopping appeared to be the furthest intention from the horseman's mind. When his horse was but a few steps from the barrier, he dug in his heels and gave his mount its head. The horse collected himself and jumped, clearing the top rail and just missing a stray steer.

The rider pulled up in the center of the ring. It was the bitter man. He said something Joe couldn't hear and the group of 'O'odham grew quiet and faced him. He spoke again, and the group began to silently file out of the ring. The rider was the last to leave, never looking back. Two ropers shooed the remainder of the errant cattle out the gate behind them. Joe heard a few muttered oaths, but no one made a move to follow any of the protestors, who were getting into their vehicles and beginning to drive away.

Joe was relieved that nothing physical had come of the confrontation. "That was some jump."

"Too bad he showed up when he did." The rest of Riley's remark was drowned out when the announcer summoned Healy and Rogers into the arena.

Once he and his partner were in position for the second time, Healy called for his steer. The gate opened with a clang, and the animal ran straight for the other side of the arena. Healy's buckskin was on him in four strides, the steer caught around the neck before Joe realized the rope had been thrown. Rogers snared the back ankles a second later.

"Six and six," boomed the announcer.

"At least they've set the bar high." Riley seemed unperturbed as their names were called.

Six-six. We've done better than that, Joe reminded himself, rolling his shoulders under his brushpopper shirt, its tailoring generous enough to allow him freedom to throw. He briskly rubbed the section of rope he was holding, warming the dirty white nylon, as Riley maneuvered Sultan into his corner. The big gelding tossed his head, revealing the crown-shaped splash of white on his forehead that gave him his name.

"Cowboy up, bro'," Riley called.

"Advil up" is more like it. Joe's shoulder throbbed with every movement.

With effort, he pushed the ache from his mind, focusing instead on the basics Clem had drilled into him and the first real lesson he had taught Joe – Don't take your eyes off the steer. Ever.

Joe stared at the reddish brown back and curved horns as Cricket walked into the arena, her ears flicking forward and back. He stroked the mare's neck with the knuckles of his rein hand as he held her steady in the box.

Aim to lay the loop in front of the steer's hind feet, like setting a snare for him to step into. Clem's calm voice ran through Joe's mind.

Riley signaled and the steer leapt out. Joe waited until he sensed Riley starting to move before loosening the reins. Cricket gave chase, her powerful hindquarters propelling her through the loose dirt.

The hard-running steer broke left. Riley tracked him, balancing in the stirrups while leaning forward. He pulled even with the animal's left hip, the rope in his right hand twirling overhead and slightly in front of him. Riley's throw floated past the horns and landed around the thick neck, a legal catch that left the steer harder to handle. Sultan slid to a stop in the soft ground, his hooves leaving two parallel tracks, while Riley pulled the slack and dallied. The black gelding grunted and turned left, the steer twisting his head and bucking at the other end of the line like a hooked marlin.

The old cowboy's voice whispered in Joe's ear. *Throw in front of the steer's legs.* Focused on his target, Joe felt the heft of the nylon as he swung it counterclockwise over his head, elbow up, preparing to let it fly out of his swing. But as he released, an explosion of pain jerked his arm back, grounding his throw into the dirt. He grabbed his upper arm, blinking away tears, his body doubled over Cricket's neck. The mare circled in confusion. Dimly aware of Riley's approach, he gritted his teeth against the radiating burn in his shoulder and gathered up the reins. He guided Cricket to the far gate, accompanied by a smattering of applause, not looking at his partner.

Jerry Dan and Mia were waiting back at the trailer.

"Joe, are you okay?" Jerry Dan asked anxiously.

Mia stood next to him with her fingers twisted together, a distressed look in her eyes.

"I'm fine, thanks," Joe said, uncinching Cricket. The fire of agony had burnt down to dull embers of soreness.

Riley rode up on Sultan, with Hal walking up right behind him.

"How you feeling, pardner?" Riley asked.

"I'm sorry I let you down," Joe mumbled as he unstrapped the mare's boots one-handed.

"Now, Joe, it wasn't your fault. Your shoulder –" Hal began.

Forty-eight pounds of saddle crashed to the ground. Cricket shied away to the end of her leadrope as Joe stood rooted to the spot, his eyes filling and his right arm dangling uselessly.

"Here, let me take care of this," Hal said quietly, one hand soothing Cricket as the other reached for the fallen tack.

"Riley, could I talk to you for a minute?" Joe asked in a strangled voice.

He walked away from the trailer. Riley, still on Sultan, followed.

"Look, if you want to get a new partner, I understand." Joe couldn't hide his anguish and knew Riley could see it on his face.

"Forget it. You and I are a team. Don't say anything more."

Joe didn't believe Riley's apparent indifference to the night's results. His partner was usually the most ardent of competitors.

"I mean it," Joe said, his voice firmer. "I don't know how long this shoulder will take to heal." *If ever!* screamed in his head. "And it's still early in the season. With a new partner plus the points you already earned while I was out, you'd have a shot at the top. I don't –"

"Joe, I said drop it," Riley snapped.

Joe looked at Riley's stony face and stopped talking.

"I'm sorry, bro'," Riley said in a contrite voice, the set of his jaw softening. "Tonight wasn't important. These things happen. If I'm not roping with my best friend, I don't want to rope." He rubbed his hand over his face. "I'm worried about a project at work, and I'm taking it out on you. Sorry." He stared into the gathering dark, shoulders slumped from their usual erect carriage.

Joe wanted to kick himself. *Despite Riley's apparent nonchalance, he really is concerned about his job. And I've been blind to it because I've been thinking only about myself.*

"I'm the one who should be apologizing. Is it anything I can help with?" Joe asked.

Riley took a deep breath and straightened up in the saddle.

"Nah, I'm fine."

He picked the reins up off Sultan's neck and pointed a finger at Joe. "You know, there is one thing. There's this project I'd like to get started on early tomorrow. You wouldn't happen to have your access card on you, would you? You know I keep mine in my desk drawer." He grinned sheepishly. "I never thought there'd be a day when I might be the first guy in."

"Sure," Joe said, relieved things seemed to be back to normal between them.

Opening his wallet, Joe slipped out a white piece of plastic the size of a credit card. Not everyone at the firm was pleased with the new security system. Joe heard lawyers complain about long delays between the insertion of a card and the unlocking of the door, and some of the evening shift word processors had accused the firm of using the entry and exit records to crosscheck their timesheets.

"Do you mind driving Cricket back?" Riley asked. "I feel like riding home tonight. I'll pick up the truck and trailer from your place later in the week."

"No problem." Joe patted the big gelding's sweaty neck. "I still don't understand how you can ride this fella after dark without him spooking or running into things."

"I told you, Sultan is like Superman. He has x-ray vision." Riley laughed, his teeth gleaming in the dusk. Behind him the fallen sunset threw the dark mountains into stark relief.

They started back toward the others.

"Thanks, Riley," Joe said quietly just before they reached the group by the truck. He hoped his friend heard him.

Riley called out his good-byes to the group, then trotted the big black into the night, the pair seemingly morphing into a single phantom before becoming lost from sight among the darker saguaro silhouettes.

Joe walked up to Cricket, now untacked. Mia was standing next to her, stroking the white star in the middle of the mare's forehead. Jerry Dan and Hal chatted a few feet away.

Joe's mind raced, searching for the right thing to say. "I'm sorry I was so awful tonight," he finally blurted.

"Don't be silly." Her smile was as gentle as the Mona Lisa's. "I had a wonderful time. Your friends are very nice, and I enjoyed watching the roping." Mia smoothed the horse's forelock with long delicate fingers. "By the way, who's this?"

Joe patted the chestnut's shoulder, her coat stiff with dried sweat. "This is Cricket. She belongs to my aunt."

"What a nice horse." Cricket bumped Mia's elbow with her nose. "She agreed with me!"

"Actually, I think she's begging for a carrot," Joe said.

Mia lightly tickled the horse's velvety nose. Cricket twitched her upper lip in response.

"Um, would you like a ride home?" Joe asked, his voice tentative.

"No, thank you. Jerry Dan said he'd take me."

Joe felt his heart drop down to the vicinity of his boots.

"Mia, ready to go?" Jerry Dan called as though on cue.

"Maybe, I mean I hope, that is if you would like to, we can see each other again," Joe said in a rush.

Mia continued petting the mare. "That would be nice," she said.

A moment later she lifted her head and met Joe's eyes, holding his gaze for the barest length of time longer than necessary. His heart thumped hard in his chest. She leaned toward him, steadying herself with her fingertips pressed against his good arm. He felt the puff of her breath, then she pressed her lips against his cheek. She smelled like oranges: the sweetness of the blossoms, not the sharpness of the fruit.

Out of Mia's sight, Jerry Dan beamed at Joe, waggling his eyebrows like Groucho Marx. Jerry Dan and Hal helped Joe pack up his gear and load the tired mare into the trailer before beginning their walk with Mia across the field. Joe sat behind the steering wheel and watched them, waiting to turn the key in the ignition until he could no longer see them among the shadows.

His shoulder didn't hurt anymore.

Chapter 6

Wednesday, October 16

Joe couldn't breathe. A weight crushed his chest, and needles poked into his chin. A fetid odor gagged him while a dull buzzing sounded in his ears. Groggily, he opened his eyes. A pair of sapphire orbs stared back at him, black irises narrowed to vertical slits. With a yell, he thrashed upright, sheets entwined around his arms and legs.

"Farley! How many times have I told you ..."

The cat jumped off the bed and sauntered away, tail straight as a flagpole except for the crook at the end.

"You have to do something about that mouse breath of yours," he called to the retreating feline.

Joe pushed down on the alarm button and blinked the sleep from his eyes. He tried lifting his right arm and groaned. Despite a double dosage last night of cowboy Vitamin A – Advil – his right shoulder was still sore. Hope I haven't torn something new, he thought glumly as he untangled himself from the covers, got up, and walked to the kitchen. He replenished Farley's food and water dishes, then poured cereal into a bowl, mentally thanking Hal for volunteering to feed Cricket her breakfast. When Joe opened the refrigerator to reach for the milk, Farley reappeared, winding himself around Joe's ankles, his paws kneading the top of Joe's cloth slippers.

"Ouch!" Joe exclaimed, trying to free himself without ropping the carton or stepping on the cat. He gave up and looked down at the small pointed face.

"Okay, okay. Cookies tonight," he said.

Farley stood up on his two back legs and hooked his claws onto the hem of Joe's bathrobe.

"I promise!"

Apparently satisfied, Farley dropped to the ground with a small meow and exited through the cat door.

"Have a nice day to you, too," Joe called, trying to maneuver a spoonful of cereal with his left hand.

After breakfast, Joe pulled on jeans and a sweatshirt, then rooted in the back of his sock drawer, unearthing the sling they had given him at the hospital after his run-in with the bull. Slipping it over his head and under his elbow, he exhaled in relief as it cradled the weight of his arm, reducing the stress on his injured joint.

Joe shut the door at a little past six a.m. Dawn would arrive in another half-hour. Coyotes yipped to each other after a night of hunting, and the air smelled cold and clean. The gravel crunched under his feet as he walked toward the barn.

He quickly brushed the shavings off Cricket's coat and slipped an exercise bridle over her head. Not sure he could lift the heavy saddle, Joe led the mare outside to the corral fence. Climbing the rails like a ladder, he slid onto her bare back. The fiery pain in his shoulder had abated, although it still flared with any abrupt movement. Despite Hal's nagging, Joe had refused to go to the doctor. He didn't want to know how long it would be – if ever – before he roped again.

He headed toward the northern boundary of the YJ, planning an easy ride, just enough to prevent Cricket from stiffening up after last night's effort. Following the curves of a sandy wash, the chestnut moved along at a relaxed walk. Her hooves sank into the soft soil with a swishing sound, like silt being swirled in a miner's pan. Joe gave her her head, the reins swinging loosely from side to side.

The tension ebbed from Joe's muscles as his body moved with the rhythm of the mare's gait. He loved trail riding by himself. In his view, the saw-toothed mountains covered with weird foliage that seemed leftover from some prehistoric age were better appreciated from horseback, with its advantages of viewpoint and slow time.

But there was more to riding than beautiful scenery. At times he imagined himself a centaur, melded into his mount, or a true cowboy, living in a less complicated era. And sometimes, like now, riding seemed to be the only thing in his life that was predictable and certain.

At that moment a small band of javelinas trundled across their path. Cricket snorted and jumped, almost dumping Joe, who grabbed a handful of mane to stay on, grimacing as his shoulder twisted. Even his seat on the horse is tenuous, he thought wryly as he settled himself back behind the withers and watched the bristly-backed desert pigs disappear into the bush.

Cricket resumed her walk, Joe guiding her out of the wash to a narrow path that threaded through the cactus, taking special care to avoid the teddy bear cholla. He knew from prior encounters that barely brushing against the plant was all it took for the harmless looking thistle-white needles to attach. Sometimes a whole section broke loose, adding to the misery. According to Jerry Dan, the broken piece, once on the ground again, could take root and grow in its new surroundings. Joe wished there were a less painful way for the plant to propagate.

The mare circled around a stand of palo verde and mesquite trees and halted, her way blocked by a metal gate set into a fence of tightly strung barbed wire. They had reached the ranch's northern border. County land that was open to horseback riders, mountain bikers, and other non-motorized sports enthusiasts began on the other side of the fence.

A padlocked chain was wrapped around the gate and nearest fence post. Joe urged Cricket up to the gate, bumping her with his right heel until she was parallel to it. He leaned over and opened the lock with the key Hal had given him, then clucked to Cricket. She walked forward and sideways, pushing the gate open with her shoulder. Joe reined her to the left, turning her around so she was standing next to the gate on the other side, this time facing the opposite way. He bumped her with his right heel again and she sidestepped once more, pushing the gate closed and standing quietly while Joe relocked it.

Turning the horse east, he squeezed with both calves and she broke into a slow jog, following the fence in the direction of Scottsdale Road. In the distance three colorful hot air balloons rose from the desert floor, burners roaring like hoarse lions as they made their ascents. The mare trotted along the fenceline, her hooves clattering on the hard ground, small puffs of dust marking her tracks.

She came around a clump of chaparral and slowed abruptly, ears pricked forward. On the other side of the wire stood a small herd of YJ cattle, about twenty head in all. They were bunched around several bales of hay, recently dropped. Joe pulled up. Graying wisps on the ground told him this was a regular feeding spot. He knew Hal wouldn't feed in this pasture unless the other water tank wasn't working.

I bet the float went out again. Joe added the chore to his mental checklist of things he had to do.

He gazed out over the terrain. At the base of the soft-coned mountains, dry arroyos and desiccated ridges clove the earth in all directions. Green lawns and golf courses may have eaten away at its edges, but here the desert was still untamed. Beautiful, Joe thought, feeling as though he were the only one in the world seeing it. Lost in the view, he didn't hear the other rider approach until Cricket lifted her head and whinnied.

Coming up behind him was the brown-skinned man Joe had seen at last night's roping. This morning he was shirtless, dressed only in running shorts and buckskin moccasins. Again he rode bareback. He jogged his bay up to Cricket and reined to a stop. The two horses touched noses. Cricket squealed and struck out with her front leg. The bay nipped at the chestnut mare's neck, ears pinned against his head.

The man murmured something in a language Joe didn't recognize. The effect on the two horses was immediate. The man's mount dropped his head and relaxed his ears. Cricket nickered low in her throat and reached over to nibble on the bay's mane.

"Michael Chiago." The man extended his hand, the fourth finger ornamented with a large gold ring, a red stone in its center.

"Joe McGuinness." Joe returned the grip and studied his

visitor.

In his early twenties, Chiago had broad cheekbones and full, flat lips. His skin was the color of café au lait, milkier than Mia's. Ebony bangs skimmed eyebrows with no arch.

"That's a nice mare." Chiago nodded at Cricket. Eyes half closed, she stood next to the bay as though they were longtime pasture buddies. He looked at the sling. "I hope it is not serious."

"I aggravated an old injury." Joe shrugged, immediately regretting it as pins of pain pricked at him. "Your bay looks good, too. Do you rope off him?"

Chiago shook his head, his long hair framing his face. "Not anymore," he said. "My work keeps me too busy."

"What exactly do you do?" Joe asked, remembering his conversation with Riley last night.

Chiago's eyes narrowed and a slight crease appeared across his brow. "My job, if you want to call it that, is to reclaim my people's land."

"Does this have something to do with the casino?" Joe asked. He didn't want to be the first to bring up what had happened at the roping.

"No, that's another issue." Chiago's already firm jaw jutted further. "This is something more fundamental. My people have been treated poorly, even for Native Americans. Because we never went to war with the United States, no reservation was established for us until recently. We used to occupy twenty-four thousand square miles, from the Mexican border to this valley. Now our pieced-together territory covers but a fraction of that area and is poorly suited for farming and ranching. The fruit of my father's efforts – a law providing for over a hundred million dollars in a cash settlement – was vetoed by President Reagan." Chiago's voice was firm, his words articulated as though he had spoken them many times before, not always to a receptive audience.

"With unemployment at sixty percent and most houses without running water or electricity, few 'O'odham stay on the rez," he continued. "Instead they live in your towns and work as farm laborers or domestics."

Chiago paused and rubbed his eyes as though he was tired. Joe felt vaguely guilty.

"The Tohono 'O'odham," Chiago continued in a more gentle tone, "is probably the poorest tribe in the Southwest. A casino, built on land the government thought fit only for Indians, would change that. Your people have blanketed the desert with your developments and are now at our borders. Our slot machines will be the closest ones to white communities in the state. We need housing, education, health care, jobs. Your money spent in our casinos is going to pay for them." Chiago gave Joe a small smile. "Sorry for the speech so early in the morning, but every person I can educate about our situation brings my people a step closer to our goal."

"What about the land you want to reclaim?" Joe asked, finding himself admiring the young man's ardor.

Chiago's face sobered again. "Some of our ancestors had no choice but to sell their property. They were poor, and you can't eat dirt. But in other instances the land was stolen: deeds forged, families threatened, sellers tricked. It is that which we seek to recover, parcel by parcel." His voice hardened. "And by more effective means than a demonstration at a local roping."

Joe shifted uncomfortably in his saddle at the change in Chiago's tone. The two men sat in silence.

"So where do you start?" Joe finally asked, his curiosity getting the better of his unease.

"The Barrett Ranch," Chiago's eyes flashed like light off a blade. "It was stolen from my family."

Joe let out a low whistle.

"Well," he said, "I don't know anything about the facts of your claim, but I know Cordelia Barrett. She'll put up one heck of a fight."

"My grandfather's grandfather was a mercenary for your government against the Apaches." Chiago roused his horse and wheeled him around without an apparent cue. He faced Joe, his face tight.

"Cordelia Barrett doesn't have anything on Geronimo. And she'll surrender, the same as he did. I promise you that." Joe felt the hairs on the back of his neck rise.

"About that hay," Chiago dipped his chin toward the clustered cattle. "Your foreman didn't put it there."

Joe frowned in bewilderment.

"A cattle thief did," Chiago tossed over his shoulder as the bay moved off, the horse breaking into a lope after a few strides.

"Wait!" Joe called, "What do you mean –"

But the other horse and rider were already small in the distance.

Chapter 7

Just before nine o'clock Joe stood in the hall next to Gertrude's desk, waiting to meet with Harrington about one of his research memoranda and mulling over his encounter with Chiago earlier that morning. He cradled his elbow in his other hand, trying to take the weight off his injured shoulder while regretting his decision to forego using the sling at work.

Gertrude organized papers and ignored him. A black knit dress with silver buttons and a silver mesh belt hugged her tall body, thin save for a small potbelly. A wide silver necklace rested on her collarbones. Joe thought she looked like an oboe. She stuck an arrow-shaped orange Post-It imprinted with the words "Sign Here" on the bottom of a document and set it on the corner of her desk. Looking at it, Joe had an idea.

"Gertrude, I mean, Miss Slivens," he began, "would you by chance know what the initials D. W. in Mr. Harrington's name stand for?"

Gertrude paused and looked at him silently for a moment, then went back to sorting telephone messages, forcefully impaling them on various brass spindles. Joe was glad he wasn't one of those slips of paper.

He was thinking about Chiago again when someone bumped into him from behind. He turned to see Sydney Gardner walking away from him.

"Sorry," she mumbled without stopping, her eyes downcast.

Her hair was pinned haphazardly on top of her head, with broad streaks of ash showing through the blond, and the shoulders of her suit looked too big for her. Before Joe could say anything, she turned into her office and shut the door. At the same time, Gertrude's intercom buzzed, stopping her in mid-stab.

"Yes, sir?"

"Please send Mr. McGuinness in," crackled the box.

Joe walked into the office and gave himself up to the man-eating green chair. Harrington sat behind his desk, Joe's memorandum in front of him. As the older lawyer started to speak, an unexpected image flashed through Joe's mind: Mia smiling at him while petting Cricket's nose. He willed himself to concentrate on Harrington's words.

"With respect to the beneficiary's rights –"

Joe remembered the mole next to Mia's lower lip. He pictured himself touching it with his index finger, then touching her lips, then kissing her. He swallowed noisily, the image catching him by surprise.

"Mr. McGuinness, do you have a question?" Harrington frowned at the interruption.

"No, sir." Joe forced himself to stare intently at his copy of his memorandum, but the print swam before his eyes. "M," "I," and "A" were the only readable letters on the page. Harrington resumed his monologue, Joe helplessly deaf to it. Finally, "all in all, this was quite satisfactory" sounded faintly in his ears, and Harrington got to his feet.

I hope he didn't just give me a new assignment. Joe banished Mia from his mind as he hoisted himself out of the chair and returned to his office.

Shutting the door behind him, he sat at his desk. Notes for his next research project were stacked in the middle of his blotter. He tried to read through them, but the letters were still a jumble. He took out his client directory, finding the entry for Cordelia Barrett. He read the telephone number after her name.

Mia. He had to see her again. He was reaching for the phone when the cold hand of guilt clutched his heart. Recognizing his Irish legacy, he tried to mentally absolve himself. *I'm not what Amber wants. She'd be unhappy married to me. I'll never have enough money, enough style, or be enough fun.*

Joe had heard these complaints from Amber more than a time or two. Thinking back over the last few months, Joe became annoyed with himself. *Why don't I ever say no to her?*

Actually, it wasn't a matter of saying no. Amber never asked questions. She talked, planned, decided, and assumed his silence meant assent. Which, he thought culpably, isn't too big a leap to make.

In a flash Joe realized what he liked so much about Mia. He had known her for less than two days, but the difference was like silk and steel. She was the antithesis of Amber – a partner, not an autocrat. Mia listened to what he was saying, and asked questions that showed she cared about his responses. He had told her more about why he loved cowboying in the short time they spent together than he ever shared with Amber. And, unlike Amber, she made him feel as though she accepted – even liked – him for who he was. He looked out the window toward the north. Despite her beauty, it wasn't the way she looked so much as the way she treated him that made him wish he were back in the Barrett kitchen with her again.

But he had made a commitment to Amber. *Maybe I'm not trying hard enough to make our relationship work,* he lectured himself. He looked at his watch and reached for the phone, hoping to catch her at the gym before her next class began.

His fingers punched the buttons. She answered.

"Mia?" he stammered, caught unawares by what his fingers had unconsciously done.

"Who is this?"

"Uh, Joe, Joe McGuinness."

"Hello, Joe." Her warm greeting sent his blood racing. He took a deep breath and reached up to wipe his damp forehead with the back of his hand before responding.

"Would you like to have dinner tonight?"

"Yes."

"That's great! I'll pick you up at six. Okay?"

"I'm looking forward to it."

"Me, too. Six o'clock, then."

"Thank you, Joe."

He held the phone to his ear, smiling for several seconds

before its buzzing alerted him she had hung up.

He set the receiver in its cradle and picked up the top document from the stack of notes in front of him when he heard shouting on the other side of his thick-planked door. Stepping to the doorway of his office, he saw Sonny Barrett striding around the corner of the hallway, a wad of papers in one fist.

The receptionist trailed him, her hands fluttering like dry leaves.

"I'm sorry, sir, but you're not allowed back here."

"Get Harrington out here now!" he bellowed as he approached the senior partner's office, sounding to Joe's ears as angry as a bronc on his first jump out of the chute. Sonny's blond hair was slicked back and curled around the bottom of his ears. Forearms the size of hams bulged out of rolled up sleeves, and his pants stretched tight over hard buttocks and thighs thick from pumping iron. His nose had been shaped more by other fists than genetics, and blue eyes the same shade as his mother's burned with fury.

Gertrude, moving faster than Joe thought possible, positioned herself in front of her boss's door with arms folded and feet planted. Sonny jolted to a halt, his crimson face inches from her pale one. The receptionist hovered helplessly.

"Out of my way," he snarled.

Gertrude stiffened her spine, bringing her eyes almost level with his. Before Joe could find out if her devotion to her employer extended beyond barricade to trading blows, the door behind her opened.

"Good morning, Sonny," Harrington said, his voice low and modulated. He gave a slight nod to Gertrude, who retreated behind her desk, then turned to face Sonny, his hands clasped behind his back.

"You betrayed me, Harrington," Sonny roared, waving the crumpled papers. "I'll sue you and this whole goddamned firm for malpractice. That bitch is takin' what's mine! It's, it's – whatcha call it – undue influence!" The cords in his neck bulged above his collar and his jaw flushed wine red.

"Hey Joe." Riley's voice in Joe's ear distracted him. "Thanks for the card." Riley pressed a piece of plastic into his hand. Joe moved closer to the doorjamb of his office and Riley stepped behind him, looking down the hall over Joe's good shoulder.

"I don't blame Sonny. I'd be pissed, too," said Riley.

"What happened?" Joe asked out of the corner of his mouth, sliding the access card into his wallet while Sonny continued to rant at Harrington, who listened apparently unfazed. Joe couldn't see any flinch in the older lawyer.

"She changed her will," Riley whispered back. "Sonny still inherits, but now he gets mostly land – the ranch rather than money. And even then he can't sell or mortgage it for a certain number of years after Cordelia dies." Riley paused and lowered his voice further. "And that means no immediate funds and no way to raise them for a race car team. I guess if Sonny wants to compete, he's going to have to scrounge sponsors like everybody else."

Joe wasn't surprised Riley knew the terms of what was supposed to be a confidential document. His computer skills were no match for the firm's aging system.

"This ain't right! She's not thinking straight!" Sonny yelled, twisting the documents in his fleshy hands.

Joe thought he detected pleading behind the wrath. Harrington responded in a quiet voice, Joe catching snatches of what he said. He heard, "She's as sound in mind as you or I ... These are her wishes ... I suggest you speak with her."

"Damn straight I'm gonna talk to her about it!" Sonny smacked his hand on Gertrude's desktop, sending the vase in the corner crashing to the wooden floor. Gertrude half-jumped out of her chair but didn't say anything. Looking at the bright petals tangled in a pool of water and glass shards, Riley puckered his lips.

"He always did have a temper." Joe had heard stories during his summer at the ranch about Sonny's explosive disposition.

Joe glanced at his friend. "Do you ever worry about being cut out of the will?" he asked, his curiosity getting the better of his usual reluctance to pry.

Riley shook his head. "I'm not in it – never have been." He patted his chest. "You're looking at a trust fund baby. I think Cordelia put up the money as a concession to the fact that Grandfather didn't know about me and to appease her conscience. He probably wouldn't have disinherited Mom if he had known."

"Does she have other relatives?"

"Nope. Sonny and I are it. The last of our line, so to speak." Riley watched his cousin for a moment before suddenly clapping his friend on the back. Joe stifled a yelp of pain at the jostling of his injured joint.

"Oops, sorry, pal. How about lunch at Ciao Mein?"

Their most frequented downtown restaurant combined two of Joe's favorite foods, Chinese and Italian, in ways that sounded peculiar on the menu but always tasted good.

"I'll meet you there at twelve," Joe said through clenched teeth, massaging his shoulder.

Harrington put his arm around Sonny while continuing to talk to him, his words or the shattered vase apparently having a subduing effect for the moment.

"I know she'll be back to change this." Sonny's remark registered a few notches lower than his tirade.

"Who is that?" Stephen Merchant's voice startled Joe. He hadn't heard him approach their vantage point.

"Cordelia Barrett's son," Joe answered.

"Really? I could swear I saw him and another fellow, big guy dressed like a cowboy, when I was at Woolcott & Jones last week. Looked as though they were coming out of a meeting with John Eaton, the zoning lawyer over there."

Merchant asked Riley about an assignment while Joe thought about what the senior lawyer had said. He knew Woolcott & Jones, the largest firm in Phoenix, specialized in complicated lawsuits and transactions. Its reputation allowed it to choose its clients and require a non-refundable five-figure retainer up front. With a preponderance of its associates former Supreme Court clerks and law review staff, the firm rarely got involved in the more ordinary aspects of legal practice. Merchant must be mistaken, Joe concluded. Sonny wouldn't have any legal business that would interest Woolcott attorneys.

"I'll lay out those documents in the rear conference room right now," Riley said to Merchant, throwing a wink at Joe before walking away.

As Joe and Merchant watched, Harrington gently guided Sonny toward the reception area. The young man's face was still contorted in anger, but he allowed himself to be propelled down the hall. Just before they reached the entrance to the firm's foyer, he jerked his arm from Harrington's grasp.

"I am not going to let this happen," he said vehemently. Joe heard the steel in his voice. "You can tell my mother that." He ripped the papers he had been holding into pieces, letting them fall to the floor like confetti, and stalked out.

Harrington looked around at the small crowd that had gathered. "I suggest everyone go back to work." He stooped to collect the white squares that littered the carpet. Trudy narrowly missed treading on his fingers as she walked briskly out of her office, a folder in her hand. She made a beeline for Merchant.

"The president of Lone Mountain Development is on the line," she told Merchant. "I briefed him on the outcome of the Planning Commission meeting, but he wants to talk to you. I thought you'd better see these first."

She handed the senior lawyer the folder she was carrying. While Merchant flipped through its pages, she leaned against the partition in front of Lydia's desk and crossed her arms. Today's T-shirt was white with orange writing. "Lithium: Use It or Lose It" marched across her chest in block letters next to a sketch of the face from Edvard Munch's *The Scream*.

"Question of the day, Joe: What's the definition of a paralegal?" She cracked her gum.

Joe shook his head. He knew better than to hazard a guess on that one. "Got me, Trudy."

Still reading from the file, Merchant started to walk toward his office.

"Someone who does a lawyer's work for a secretary's salary," Trudy threw the answer over her shoulder as she followed him.

The phone in Joe's office rang. As Lydia wasn't back from wherever she had gone to, Joe pressed the button for his line and answered it at her desk.

"Do you have a minute?" Jerry Dan asked, his tone less ebullient than usual.

"Sure," Joe said. "What's up?"

"Come to my office, and I'll tell you."

Joe sat in one of Jerry Dan's client chairs, brown saddle leather wrapped around nail-studded wood. On the wall facing him hung part of Jerry Dan's collection of guns from the Old West. According to the plaque underneath the weapons, Joe was looking at an 1866 Winchester rifle and an 1876 Peacemaker Colt revolver from the Philadelphia Centennial Exposition, complete with gold and silver scrollwork and ivory grips. On the credenza below, next to a framed snapshot of his parents, was an autographed photo of Roy Rogers and Dale Evans astride Trigger and Buttermilk. Jerry Dan had told Joe if Leonard Slye from Cincinnati and Frances Butts, a Chicago nightclub singer, could become Roy and Dale, then he still had hope someday he'd become a cowboy, too.

"Forrest is driving me crazy," Jerry Dan began, frowning so much his glasses slid down his nose. He pushed them back up with his finger and kept talking. "The guy is a dictator, and a bad one at that. He steals the credit for my ideas and charges me with his mistakes. And his capacity for holding a grudge would shame the Hatfields and McCoys." Jerry Dan lowered his voice to an agitated whisper. "I also heard him talking on the phone to an interior designer about redecorating Barclay's office."

"He's going to be the new senior litigation partner?" Joe asked, aghast.

"I don't know how the partners' search is going, but I'm telling you, if they give it to Forrest, I'm looking for a new job."

As Jerry Dan listed his grievances in detail, Joe thought about his own options. With his résumé, Jerry Dan could go anywhere. Joe's options were much more limited. A horrible possibility jumped into his mind. If Jerry Dan left, he was the associate most likely to be assigned to Forrest. And he'd thought his so-called legal career couldn't get any worse! His stomach started to ache.

"So after he told the client it was my research and not his error at trial that was the reason the appeal was denied, I decided to do it." Jerry Dan waited for Joe's response.

Joe shifted his attention back to his friend. "Do what?"

"You know how hot he is on having gone to Harvard? Well, the next issue of the alumni magazine should be pretty interesting. I snitched the update form off his desk, filled it out, and sent it in. His former classmates will soon be reading about his third divorce, malpractice suit, and recent visit to Betty Ford."

"What happens when he reads it, too?' asked Joe, amazed at

Jerry Dan's nerve.

"Trudy sorts the mail, so I asked her to pull his copy. I bet you he never sees it, and if he does, he has no reason to think I had anything to do with it."

Joe shook his head in pretended dismay. "You used to be so nice, Jerry Dan."

Jerry Dan's face became serious. "I do good work, Joe. He shouldn't have blamed me for his bad lawyering."

Joe looked at his watch. "I have to go. I'm meeting Riley for lunch. Want to come?"

Jerry Dan waved him out. "Nah. I have to start work on my next case. Another loser dumped on me by you-know-who. At least it involves cowboys. In fact, it's one of the hands from the Barrett Ranch."

"What's the short version?" Joe favored his right arm as he pushed himself out of his chair.

"Assault and battery. He got into an argument and roped a fellow at Cactus Sam's." From his summer spent at the ranch, Joe knew fights at Cactus Sam's, a cowboy bar south of town, were an almost every weekend occurrence.

"That doesn't sound like something the DA would prosecute," Joe said. The district attorney's views on wasting taxpayer dollars on brawls between "rednecks and brushhounds" were well publicized, especially around election time.

"I don't believe it was the roping that prompted the charge. I think it was the dallying 'round his trailer hitch and the driving down the street that did it."

Joe smiled. "Jerry Dan, for once, I'm glad it's you and not me."

He was halfway down the hall before he couldn't hear Jerry Dan's theatrical moans anymore.

Joe slid into the booth across from Riley, who was perusing the menu.

"Sesame chicken pizza or won ton minestrone?"

"Make it two of the soup, and I'll split a small pizza with you," Joe replied.

After the waiter took their orders and brought a pot of tea, Joe pulled his chopsticks from their paper wrapper.

"Roping starts at eight." Riley poured himself a cup of the pale amber liquid.

Joe twirled one of the wooden sticks between his fingers. "I can't practice tonight."

"Your shoulder still bad? Well, you won't miss much. Shorty's steers have been around the arena more than a few times and I hear he's raising his fee. Still, I expect near a dozen guys will show up. There'll be someone to partner with." Shorty Johnson, whose acreage abutted the western boundary of Los Caballos Park, made cattle available for roping on certain evenings during the week. Twenty to thirty-five dollars a team member usually bought five or six runs.

"I'm still sore, but that's not the reason." Joe concentrated on unfolding his napkin. "I'm seeing Mia."

Riley raised one eyebrow. "What about Amber?"

Joe stiffened. "This isn't a date. Mia and I are just friends." Who exactly am I trying to convince? he silently asked himself.

Riley took a slow sip of his tea, gazing at Joe for a long moment over the rim of his cup. "So where are you guys going to go?" he finally asked.

"I asked her to dinner, which reminds me. I need a suggestion for someplace nice." Joe flashed Riley a grin. "I wish I'd asked her to the movies. The Clint Eastwood festival is still on."

"I don't know," Riley drawled. "Sounds like a date to me."

Their conversation was interrupted by the arrival of their food, and Joe excused himself to go to the restroom. His way to the back of the restaurant blocked by the dessert cart, he detoured past the booths in the far corner. In the one most removed from the entrance, Joe saw Trudy and Forrest, seated side by side. They were talking intently, heads close together, Trudy's hand resting on her companion's coat sleeve. The senior lawyer's red-rimmed watery gray eyes topped by full eyebrows and thin lips pressed into a down-turned mouth reminded Joe of a Dickens character. His hair, worn slicked back from his chiseled face, looked too black for a man past fifty. Six feet tall, he hid an extra thirty pounds with military bearing. Even in the desert summer, he wore matching vests under his custom-made suits, always accented with a Harvard tie.

As Joe approached their table there was a break in the conversation, and Forrest looked up into Joe's surprised stare. He scowled and cut his eyes away, pulling his arm out from under Trudy's. By then she had noticed Joe, too, and smiled broadly, her expression reminiscent of Farley's when he'd managed to steal a few licks from Joe's bowl of ice cream.

Doesn't look like they want company. Joe redirected his course away from the couple.

On his way back to his table, Joe noted the booth was empty. He told Riley what he had seen.

"A secret affair!" Riley exclaimed gleefully, slurping his soup.

"I don't really see the two of them as a couple, but Trudy has been in a good mood lately," Joe said.

"How can you tell?"

"She actually said, 'Good morning' to me without adding the words 'capitalist slave' or 'money-grubbing shyster.'"

Both started to laugh, Riley's spasms becoming a coughing fit. After a few more comments about the unlikely pair, the meal passed in relative silence, Riley forsaking his usual lunchtime gossip and small talk and Joe preoccupied with thoughts of Mia.

A lone pink slip hung from Joe's telephone message spindle when he got back from lunch. Printed on it in Lydia's neat writing were Amber's name and the words "Please pick me up at seven."

Joe smacked the heel of his hand against his forehead. He had forgotten about the party he was supposed to take Amber to that evening.

He picked up the phone and dialed.

"Amber, it's me."

"Hi, hon. I was hoping you'd call. What do you think – my red dress or the blue tonight?"

"That's what I'm calling about. I can't go."

"What do you mean you can't go?" He could feel the Arctic freeze in her voice.

"Uh, it's work. I'm sorry."

"Joseph McGuinness, it's rotten enough you're standing me up at the last minute. You don't have to lie about why. You and I both know you're going roping tonight!" There was the sound of plastic hitting plastic, followed by a dial tone.

Joe recradled his phone, ashamed of lying to Amber. *In more ways than one.* He pulled his in-basket toward him, hoping work would take his mind off his less than admirable behavior. On top of the pile, clipped to a memo from Trudy, was a small card. "Arizona Bar Association" was embossed across the top, with his name and "Member #57158" printed underneath.

He ran a finger across its plastic face, his brain registering the meaning of the number. Tens of thousands attorneys were admitted in Arizona. His disappointment with his job situation returned full force. Most had been at it longer, and none had fewer opportunities to try cases than he did. But at least he was an official lawyer now.

He read Trudy's memo. "Here's your bar card. Remember local court rules require your membership number to be typed next to your name on all pleadings submitted to state court."

Joe slipped the card into his wallet, then balled up the memo and threw it into his trashcan.

Nothing I have to worry about.

Harrington signed all the probate pleadings. Other than that, only the firm's trial lawyers filed papers in court.

Chapter 8

To Joe, the rest of the afternoon crawled as slowly as the days did before Christmas when he was eight years old. The grandfather clock in the reception area was just striking five as he punched the button for the elevator, whistling tunelessly under his breath. Within minutes, driver's visor flipped down, he was following traffic north onto Scottsdale Road. To his left the sun hesitated above the horizon, streaking the sky with a horizontal rainbow of yellows, reds, and purples. He accelerated once he was north of town, slowing only when a roadrunner broke cover and darted in front of him.

Joe braked to a stop in front of his adobe, dust swirling around his tires. Farley was waiting for him on the front door mat, tail whipping from side to side impatiently. The hairs of his coat were fluffed out against the twilight chill, making him look more like a porcupine than a cat.

"Drat." Joe reached for his jacket in the back seat. "I forgot about the cookies!"

Farley pushed at the door with a paw while Joe fumbled for his key.

"Don't worry, I remembered."

Farley looked up at him, eyes narrowed.

"Okay, okay, it slipped my mind." He finally unlocked the door.

Throwing his jacket across a chair back, he crossed the room. Almost tripping over Farley, who was bounding in the same direction, Joe grabbed a package of dough from the refrigerator.

One hand pulled out the cookie sheet and a large knife from the drawer next to the sink while the other twisted the oven dial to 350 degrees. Farley stayed underfoot, pressing against Joe's calves and making small yowly sounds. Joe quickly tore open the chilled raisin-studded log and chopped it into pieces. Popping a few into his mouth despite Farley's glare, he spread them over the sheet. He set the timer and opened the oven door, quickly sliding the pan onto the top rack.

Farley stationed himself in front of the oven window as though it were a television set, ears perked attentively.

"Let me know when they're ready," Joe told him as he walked toward his bedroom, his fingers tugging at his tie.

Twenty minutes later, the house smelled of burned dough. Joe gave himself a last look in the wavy mirror behind his closet door, so old that the silver was flaking from its back. He saw his crooked nose, broken in a fall from a horse but not properly set. He moved his gaze down the mirror to his yellow long sleeved shirt, khaki pants and polished boots. He ran his fingers through his mess of hair one last time and reached for his battered leather jacket.

Joe placed the plate of cookies on the floor. "Up to you to hold the fort, Farley."

The cat didn't raise his head from his dish. His jaws sounded like a nutcracker as they crushed the black-bottomed chunks.

Joe gunned his car down the YJ drive and turned right. Shadows had crept up the rocky ridges, obscuring the taupe and tan earth and the brush that covered it like green gauze. He turned on the radio. "Thank heavens for Dale Evans" sang the Dixie Chicks, and Joe hummed along with one of Jerry Dan's favorite songs.

He turned left and drove under the Barrett Ranch sign. His foot faltered on the gas pedal as the gravel drive leveled out in front of the big house, its outline fading into the blackening sky.

Should I really be doing this? Joe parked. The car's engine rattled twice before it fell silent, and he opened the door.

The evening air, tinged with coolness, brushed past his cheeks. The warm starry night had no clouds to dim the quarter moon. He heard the yip of a far away coyote and the sound of scrabbling small paws under a bush next to the house. Joe swung his legs out from under the steering wheel and walked up the front steps. A shadow moved on the porch. He walked closer and squinted into the dusk.

"Hi." Mia stepped into the halo cast by the overhead light.

She was dressed in a simple black sheath, her legs bare in low-heeled pumps. Her hair was twisted up onto her head, held by two silver-topped ebony sticks. Joe imagined pulling the sticks out, first one and then the other, and watching the heavy dark mass cascade down her back.

"Hi," Joe said, his voice husky. "You look great."

Mia walked toward him, the soft fabric pulling against the curve of her hips.

"Shall we?" She took his arm.

He could feel her smooth heated skin through his shirt. They walked down the steps to the Blind Buck where Joe stopped abruptly, looking at his car as though seeing it for the first time. Torn upholstery, duct-taped windows, rust-streaked paint; Amber had catalogued its failings on many occasions, always insisting they drive her red Miata with its "CRUNCH" personalized plates whenever they went out.

"Are you sure you want to go in this?" he asked, embarrassed.

Mia regarded him. "Do you really care what kind of car you drive?" she asked.

Joe thought for a moment. "No, I guess not." Before he could reach for the handle, she opened the passenger door.

"Neither do I."

Ahead the lights of the town winked at them, appearing and disappearing as the car tracked the dips in the road. The dark of the desert pressed against their windows. A bat swooped to snatch a bug caught in their high beams.

"So where are we going?"

"I made reservations at La Ristra," Joe replied. Named after the strings of dried red chilies that hung from many Arizona portales, the nouveau Southwestern restaurant and its innovative chef were garnering national attention. Joe had never eaten there, but Riley assured him it had the white tablecloths, four forks at each place setting, and snooty service necessary to a first date "and first non-dates, too."

"Wow," Mia said.

"Is that okay?" Joe asked nervously.

She twisted toward him, the movement stretching her dress tight against the curve of her breast. Joe caught himself staring and forced his eyes back onto the road.

"Do you like Clint Eastwood movies?"

Joe couldn't suppress a grin. "Are you kidding? I'm his biggest fan."

"Well, *Pale Rider* is playing tonight. If we hurry, we can catch the early show."

Joe glanced at her eyes, sparkling with merriment. *She didn't care about a fancy meal in a ritzy place. His kind of gal.*

"Perfect."

They joined the line in front of the theater. Pinnacle Peak had only one cinema, but its big screen, plush chairs that rocked, great popcorn and homemade ice cream made mall theaters seem second rate. Mia shivered slightly in the fall night air. In the desert, October's evenings were usually twenty-five degrees cooler than its days. Joe draped his jacket over her bare shoulders.

Mia pulled the jacket lapels together and turned her face up to his. The flecks of gilt in her velvet brown eyes shimmered.

"Tell me what it's like to be a cowboy," she said.

"Well, ma'am, sometimes it's branding and sometimes it's roping," Joe drawled in his best John Wayne imitation, "but mostly it's sweating and getting dirty and fixing stuff that's broken and pushing cows from one place to another."

Mia's full lips curved into a smile. "And how do you make sure the cows go where they're supposed to?"

"Cow psychology ain't all that complicated, ma'am," Joe struggled to keep his accent. "If cattle are looking in a certain direction, they're probably heading that way." He paused, deadpan. "Unless, of course, something happens to change their minds."

Mia's smile became a laugh, her head tipping back so he could see where the top of her smooth throat met the line of her jaw. Joe imagined tracing his finger along the line.

He cleared his throat, still flustered by the image his mind conjured up. "I did promise you dinner, but I don't think we'll be able to get into La Ristra now. How about we go to Danny's after the film?"

"That would be nice. I haven't seen *Tío Daniel* in ages."

"I'll go call him to let him know we're coming and cancel our other reservations."

Joe threaded his way through the line to the pay phone near the ticket booth. As he was finishing his calls, a black BMW convertible pulled into the valet parking lane. Joe caught a glimpse of familiar blond curls on the passenger side. He walked up to the man and woman as they joined the "Reserved Seating" queue.

"Hello, Amber," Joe said.

The blonde whirled, her red dress flaring out at the hem.

"Joe!" Amber's eyes were made even more round by surprise. "What are you doing here?"

"Looks like the same thing you are. Going to the movies."

For just a moment Joe felt a pang of guilt. Then he regarded the man standing next to Amber. In his early twenties, he was dressed casually in the manner of one who believes that in a Western town, it is the European who scores. An Egyptian cotton shirt without a collar was loosely tucked into pleated linen pants, and his ankles were bare above black loafers. Tortoise shell glasses Joe didn't think were imitation hugged his head, their extremely dark lenses reflecting the blinking marquee lights as he surveyed the people around him. Joe thought he looked like a mannequin in one of the men's stores where Riley shopped, beyond cool but lifeless. Joe saw his gaze linger on a willowy redhead in tight jeans and wondered if Amber noticed, too.

"This is Pierre." Amber hugged the arm of her companion. "Pierre, this is Joe, an old friend from school."

"Hi," Joe said, not missing the "old friend from school" part of the introduction.

The man nodded in Joe's direction, ignoring his outstretched hand. Joe was surprised at his lack of emotion – no jealousy, no anger, no sense of loss. Indifference was as close as he could come to describing what he was feeling, perhaps tinged with regret. At what, he wasn't sure.

"Look, Joe," Amber said, leaving Pierre to his surveillance of other theatergoers and dropping her voice to a defensive whisper. "I was gonna talk to you about this tonight but you canceled. You know things between us haven't been working out. Your job, playing cowboy, San Diego – "

"You're right, Amber." Joe interrupted quietly.

"I am?"

"Yes, you are." Joe watched Pierre who was still scanning the crowd like a Secret Service agent during a presidential speech. "I hope you're happy. Really I do."

"Um, thanks." Her guarded smile and pinched brows revealed a lot. "Same to you, too."

Joe gave her a quick kiss on the cheek. "Now if you'll excuse me, I have to get back to my date."

"Your da –"

The doors opened and the throng surged forward. Pierre clamped his hand onto Amber's wrist and pulled her along with him. Joe got a last glimpse of astonished china blue eyes before he turned and walked back along the line to Mia, taking her elbow as they moved slowly forward.

She studied his face. "Everything okay?" she asked.

Joe looked down, seeing the fringe of a shadow cast by her thick black lashes onto the curve of her mocha cheek.

"Everything is very okay. I just said good-bye to someone I'll tell you about over dinner."

Two hours later, in agreement that Bruce, Jean Claude, and even Arnold couldn't begin to compare to Clint, Mia and Joe pulled into Danny's parking lot. They were greeted at the door by their host, his teeth flashing in a wide smile. Mia was welcomed like a lost daughter.

"So you are here for a meal," Danny declared after he hugged Mia a third time.

"Absolutely," Joe said.

Danny seated them with a flourish and returned shortly with two bottles of Corona beer, ice melting from their necks, and the first in a procession of delicacies, most of which Joe had never seen listed on the menu. Small plates of *cerviche* were followed by warm tortilla strips wrapped around dry shredded beef, *mole* ladled over bowls of pork, rice, and vegetables, and a platter of smoky *frijoles* with grilled mahi-mahi. After the fifth course made its appearance, Joe began to wonder if the parade of edibles would ever end.

"It's all been delicious, Danny, but really, this is enough," he said when the rotund proprietor stopped by to refill their water glasses.

Danny looked at him, astonished. "But you said you came for a meal, no?"

Mia swallowed her smile with a mouthful of *menudo*.

"No, I mean yes." Joe felt the front of his stomach press against his belt buckle. More dishes came until Joe lost count.

In between bites, he and Mia talked. At least Joe talked and Mia listened. He told her about his mom and her café, about roping with Clem, about Atticus and Harrington and life on the YJ, about Riley and Jerry Dan and Amber, things he never imagined discussing with anyone, especially someone he just met.

She took it all in, chin resting on the back of her tapered fingers. She volunteered little about herself and sidestepped some of his questions. Remembering what Danny told him about her family situation, Joe didn't push. At times he thought she seemed a bit distant, even preoccupied, and he feared he was boring her. But whenever he hesitated she encouraged him to continue, her luminous eyes glowing at him.

Joe was relieved to see the arrival of dessert in the form of small cups of *flan*, pale yellow custard topped with a dusting of cinnamon. He had to threaten never to return before Danny would let him settle the bill and leave a generous gratuity.

Danny walked with them to the *entrada*, where he waited with Mia while Joe brought his car around. Cold without his jacket, which he insisted Mia wear, Joe jogged across the empty parking lot. As he opened the Blind Buck's door, its hinge squeaking in protest, what sounded like a hollow clatter drummed behind the building. He paused, listening. The murmur of Mia's voice mixed with the desert night sounds. An unseen owl hooted from the rafters. He thought he could still hear the same three-beat rhythm, now farther away.

Ghost Indians, he smiled to himself as he pulled the car forward. *And after only one cerveza.*

Danny helped Mia into the car before walking around to the driver's side. "*José,* I almost forgot." He bent down so his face was level with the open window. "Please tell *Señor* Hal I have asked all the *vaqueros.* No one has seen his cattle."

"Thanks, Danny, I will. And thank you again for a wonderful meal." Mia waved as Joe pulled away.

They rode without speaking, Joe focusing on the yellow lines in the middle of the road while Mia toyed with a loose strip of upholstery. He steered onto Ironwood, the road to the Barrett Ranch. The car bounced through a rut he didn't see until it was too late.

"Sorry!" he exclaimed, breaking the silence as their heads grazed the car roof.

Joe followed the drive to the left. His headlights swept over the shrubs in front of the house. A pair of yellow eyes looked back at them, unblinking in the arc of the high beams. A low-slung sports car was parked to one side. Joe pulled up next to it and got out to open the door for Mia. The sharp tang of horse manure filled his nostrils.

"Careful," Mia cautioned, stepping gingerly in the now moonless dark. "The cowboys ride through here and sometimes the stablehands are a bit lazy with their shovels."

Hands outstretched while their eyes adjusted to the lack of light, they skirted the other automobile, careful to avoid its flared fenders.

"This is some car," Joe remarked.

"It's Sonny's new one."

"Does he live here now?" Joe asked, surprised. Several months ago Riley drove him through the neighborhood at the base of El Piniculo, pointing out the red-tiled Spanish colonial that was Sonny's.

"No, but he still has a room, and sometimes if it's too late to drive back, he'll spend the night."

The cold momentarily forgotten, they leaned against the hitching rail next to the steps, heads tilted back to gaze at the millions of stars smeared overhead. Joe remembered a photo from an art history textbook of Van Gogh's famous painting.

That guy would have loved Arizona's sky, he thought.

"Look, a falling one!" Mia pointed. "Quick, make a wish."

Joe shut his eyes and wished, wondering what Mia would ask for. Opening his eyes, he strained to see her face, but it was hidden by the night.

"Would you like to come in for some coffee?" He heard the rustle of leather as she pulled his jacket closer around her.

"Coffee would be great," Joe said, caught unawares by the hammering of his heart.

"We'll have to be quiet. It looks as though everyone is asleep."

The ranch house loomed in front of them, all its windows black. Holding hands for balance, they cautiously climbed the steps, feeling their way with their toes.

Mia unlocked the door and fumbled for the light switch. A lamp clicked on, its feeble glow illuminating its corner of the room. Joe could see the silhouettes of oversized chairs, their cushions bearing the impressions of past occupants. Charred logs were stacked in the rock fireplace, and smoke tinged the air.

"I wonder why it's so cold in here," Mia whispered. A shiver rippled through her thin frame.

"Little late in the year for air conditioning." Joe rubbed his arms.

"Wait here in the *sala*. I'll be right back." Treading lightly, she disappeared down the unlit hallway.

Joe was about to sit down when a scream split the silence, piercing him through to the marrow of his spine.

Chapter 9

Joe sprinted out of the *sala*, catching the sharp corner of the stone-topped coffee table with the front of his shin. Oblivious of the pain, he pounded down the corridor where Mia had walked moments before. Outlined by the light from the kitchen, he could see her huddled in the doorway at the hallway's end.

Her screams had subsided into a high-pitched wail. Sliding to a stop, he knelt next to her, his hands hovering over her bowed back. He wanted to touch her, but hesitated. Her arms were wrapped around her knees, with her face hidden between them. The bones of her shoulders trembled as she rocked back and forth.

"No," he could hear her wail between her sobs, "*Madre de Dios,* no."

"Mia, what's wrong?" He looked around frantically for the cause of her terror. Then he saw it.

The bright puddle of crimson spread across the kitchen floor. Its tendrils snaked across the tiled surface, pooling around a wooden chair leg and the shoes of the chair's occupant.

Joe froze, staring helplessly. Mia, her body still swaying, was silent save for an occasional whimper. The only other sound in the room was a rhythmic plink. It got louder and louder in Joe's ears, battering at his mind until it prodded him to move, to silence the relentless clock. He brought his feet under him and straightened his legs. He paused doubled over, his hands braced against his knees.

Do not pass out, he told himself. Don't.

He made himself raise his eyes, realizing as he did there was no ticking timepiece. It was the drip of blood from the tabletop onto the tile that rang in his ears. Its sweet smell left a coppery taste on his tongue and raised the bile in his throat, almost driving him to the floor again. He forced his stomach to settle, then stood up to his full height, sucking in a sharp breath and letting it out with a shudder at the gruesome scene.

For a moment he couldn't grasp what he saw. His eyes must be seeing something else and his brain was simply misinterpreting the information. But then the rest of his senses kicked in, and he knew what was before him was real.

Cordelia Barrett lay crumpled and small across the top of the table where Joe and Mia had drunk lemonade. Several sheets of white paper were in front of her. Her mouth was half-open and her arms outstretched as though she were reaching for something to hold on to. Her blue eyes, now dim, gazed up at Joe. A burgundy clot of blood pooled from beneath her chest on the table.

Sonny lay sprawled in the chair opposite, his back to Joe. As Joe moved closer, he recognized the clothes as the same ones Sonny had been wearing that morning. A small gun lay in his loosely curled hand. Blood stained the side of his shirt where a jagged hole had been torn, while more had leaked into his lap and ran down his pant leg before spilling onto the floor. Joe stared at the gore that had seeped into the grout between the floor tiles, his mind incongruously wondering how long it would be before the stain would fade. His memory of it never would.

Although his brain was numbed by shock, Joe knew the two in the kitchen were past his or anyone else's assistance. Slowly he began to back out of the room, fleetingly wishing as he did so the scene would reverse itself, that time would move backward along with his feet. As he retreated, he had the feeling he was leaving something behind, an unknowingness, even innocence that could never be regained.

A strangled moan came from the doorway. *Mia!* A feeling close to relief at having a more compelling point of concentration infused him, propelling his feet out of the room.

He crouched beside her. Grasping her shoulders, he carefully lifted her to her feet and cradled her head against his chest, the palm of his hand keeping her face averted from the bodies. He half-walked, half-dragged her to the front *portale*, where he leaned against the railing and gulped the raw night air, willing the cold to purge the coppery stink from his nostrils. He guided her down the steps and toward his car. By the time Joe had maneuvered the passenger door open, tears were starting to leak from her eyes again.

"I'll be right back. I'm going to call the police. Stay here," he said, his mouth pressed against her ear. He carefully lowered her into the seat and shut the door.

Slowly, Joe turned to face the house, drawing in his breath.

What I wouldn't give for a cell phone now.

He forced his feet up the steps and through the doorway to the phone on the foyer table. A shiver coursed through him as he tapped out the numbers. Suddenly freezing, he rubbed his arms and shifted his feet while telling the dispatcher about the bodies. His teeth chattered as he described how to get to the ranch and agreed to wait for the patrolmen to arrive. His stiff fingers dropped the receiver back into its cradle, and feeling the clutch of a coldness deeper than the chill coming through the open front door, he bolted for the outside, not stopping until he was sitting next to Mia with the car doors locked.

Joe glanced at Mia. Her brown eyes stared back at him without focusing. He knew what she was seeing. Her fingers were pressed against her mouth as though to keep herself from screaming. Joe reached up, gently encircled her wristbones with his hands and pulled them down to her lap. He held on, murmuring words meant to soothe, and waited.

Joe didn't know how long it took for the first patrolmen to arrive, but before their brown-and-gold striped white sedan had braked to a stop, he was out of his car and jogging toward the cruiser.

Two young-faced officers stepped out of the patrol car. One had thinning black hair and an apologetic air. The other was six feet four inches of officiousness and nervous energy in a pressed tan uniform. The patches on their sleeves featured a gold six-pointed knob-tipped star patterned after the badges Old West marshals had worn.

"You call this in?" the tall one asked. His voice rang loudly in the desert stillness.

Joe nodded. "Mrs. Barrett and Sonny –"

"Where are they?" the same officer interrupted impatiently. The white piece of plastic over his pocket read "D. Frampton."

"In the kitchen. It's at the end of the hallway, almost a straight line from the front door."

"Anyone else in the house?" Frampton's partner spoke for the first time. He stood a few feet away, and the light was too poor for Joe to read his nametag.

"I don't know. As soon as we found them we got out, and I called 911."

"We?" Frampton spoke again.

Joe gestured toward Blind Buck. "I was taking my friend home. She lives here. She is – was – Mrs. Barrett's assistant."

Frampton flicked his eyes toward the car before redirecting them back onto Joe. "We'll need your statements after the scene is secured. Please wait in your car for now," he said crisply, turning away as though he had already forgotten Joe was there. He strode toward the house with the other patrolman, who was speaking into a handheld radio.

Joe walked back to the Blind Buck and peered inside. The peripheral glow from the patrol car's searchlight faintly illuminated the vehicle's interior. He could see Mia, her eyes closed, slumped in the corner where the seat met the door. Not wanting to rouse her, he leaned against the car door and watched.

"Police," yelled Frampton from outside the front door, his gun drawn. "Anyone home?"

He and his partner disappeared inside the house. Minutes later, another patrol car and a light-colored van pulled up and parked, their headlights trained on the front of the house, and disgorged their occupants. An ambulance arrived without siren or flashing lights. The first pair of patrolmen reappeared and spoke to the man from the van, now zipping up a white jumpsuit with "Pinnacle Peak Crime Lab" embroidered across its back. Joe knew Pinnacle Peak's core of wealthy homeowners and associated large tax base kept the coffers of law enforcement full. Despite its small size and apparent lack of need, the town had its own police force, as well as a full-time coroner, crime scene team, and major crimes detective.

Frampton and his partner walked across the driveway to where Joe waited.

"Why don't you tell me what happened here tonight?" Frampton asked, slipping a small notebook out of his pocket. His partner opened the door to Joe's car and spoke in low tones to Mia.

After Joe described what he had seen in the house, Frampton asked questions – identity of other relatives, details of the setting, other queries Joe forgot almost as soon as he answered them. He was finishing his account for a second time when a white Ford Explorer pulled up next to the other cars. Its driver, a man in a dark suit and tie, got out. He wore his white-blond hair in a military haircut, cropped close enough to show the shape of his skull.

The second pair of officers and the new arrival walked up to the *portale*. One of the officers gestured toward the Blind Buck as he spoke. As the man in the suit pulled on latex gloves, they all went inside.

"That will be all for now." Frampton snapped shut the cover of his notebook. His partner had already finished interviewing Mia.

"May we go?" Joe asked.

"I'm afraid you'll have to wait until Detective Dresden okays it," Frampton replied, nodding toward the Explorer.

Joe didn't ask when that might be. It seemed inappropriate to worry about time when Mrs. Barrett and Sonny would never be in a hurry again. He doubted Frampton could tell him anyway.

Left standing alone again by the tall patrolman, Joe opened the door of his car and climbed into the driver's seat. He bumped his swollen shin but ignored the pain, his only thoughts of how to console Mia.

She still sat in the corner of the front seat. A few wisps of ebony hair hung down in front of her drawn face and her eyes were closed again. She didn't stir at his arrival. He reached for her hand, letting his fingers lightly close around hers. She responded with a faint pressure. Joe tipped his head back against the tattered seat, his eyelids drooping as an unexpected wave of fatigue washed over him.

An unknown number of hours later the sound of car doors opening jolted Joe out of his doze in time for him to see two gurneys, each loaded with a large dark green bag, being carried down the steps and trundled into the ambulance, which then left as darkly and silently as it had come. Joe's eyes followed its taillights until they disappeared around the corner.

The man from the Explorer reappeared and spoke to Frampton, who nodded and walked over to the driver's side of the Blind Buck. Joe cranked down his window.

"You can go now," Frampton said.

It had been too long a night for Joe to leave without some explanation as to what had happened. "Did Sonny shoot Mrs. Barrett? I saw a gun in his hand."

The policeman ignored the question. "Where can you be contacted tomorrow in the event there are further questions?"

Joe opened his wallet and pulled out a business card, realizing it was the first one he had ever given out. Not the occasion he had anticipated, he thought ruefully before re-centering his mind on the events at hand.

"And you, ma'am?" Frampton looked past Joe at Mia.

"Ma'am?" he repeated a little louder.

Mia blinked as though wakened from deep slumber, but Joe didn't think she had been asleep.

"I'll be at my aunt's. The other policeman has her number. He said he would call her," she answered weakly.

"Thank you." Frampton pivoted on his heel.

"What about –" Joe trailed off when he realized he was talking to the patrolman's retreating back.

A shadow moved near the car. Mia let out a small cry and fumbled for the door handle. Joe turned on his headlights. Caught in their beams was a small, barrel-shaped woman, an orange-patterned blanket wrapped around her like a shawl. Her skin was the color of dried figs, and just as wrinkled. Steel gray hair flowed over her shoulders.

The older woman embraced Mia, murmuring in Spanish while her hands cupped the younger woman's face. Joe got out of the car and took a few steps toward them. Mia turned her head at the sound of his boots on the gravel.

"Joe, I ..."

Her face was chalky with exhaustion. Joe reached for one of her hands and tenderly squeezed it.

"Shhh," he said. "Go with your aunt now. We'll talk later."

The ghost of a grateful smile stole across her face before she allowed herself to be led toward the employee housing behind the ranch house. Joe climbed back into his car and sat without moving, his forehead resting against the cool arc of the steering wheel. After a moment he straightened up, started the engine, and steered down the drive.

Heading home, he couldn't stop his mind from trying to regain a sense of place and order by cataloging all that had remained unchanged. The halogen barnyard lights glowing like lighthouses in a dark desert sea, the humps of scrub and cactus lining the roadside, a yellow-eyed coyote trotting across the pavement – all were noted as affidavits life went on. He reached for the radio but pulled his hand back, continuing toward the YJ in silence. In his heart he knew no matter what he did, things would be forever askew.

Chapter 10

Thursday, October 17

Too many years of getting up early kept Joe from sleeping late, even though his head had hit the pillow only four hours earlier. He stretched and rubbed his eyes, feeling a lump of warmth next to him he knew was Farley. The cat was nestled under Joe's ribs, a paw curled over his eyes as though to shield them from the morning light. He had been effusive, even anxious, in his greeting when Joe had walked in a little past two, and had stuck to him like Velcro while he peeled off his clothes and crawled into bed.

Joe sat up and swung his legs over the edge of the mattress, rubbing his eyes again. The events of the prior evening seemed weirdly distant, and he felt lethargic and thickheaded as he pushed himself to his feet and walked into the kitchen to make coffee. With a huge yawn, Farley padded after him.

Joe's gaze strayed to the phone. He hadn't thought to get the name of Mia's aunt, let alone her telephone number. Mia – she was the only person he wanted to talk to that morning.

After the coffee had brewed, Joe and Farley breakfasted in silence, the cat finishing first as always. But rather than making his usual break for the cat door after he had swallowed his last bite, Farley instead chose to loiter in the kitchen. Following a thorough coat licking, he gazed around the room, spying the pile of clothes Joe had stepped out of a few hours earlier. He circled it warily, back arched and tail puffed up like a bottlebrush. With a quick look at Joe, he hooked a sock with his paw, batting it stiff-legged across the stone floor before abandoning it near the door. Circling round Joe's chair, he approached the sock again, belly low to the ground, stalking his prey. Once within range, he pounced, flipping the sock into the air then dashing away in pretend terror when it landed next to him.

Joe picked at his cereal, inattentive to Farley's antics. After fifteen minutes he carried his still mostly full bowl to the sink and dumped the uneaten meal down the disposal, glum at the prospect of going to work. He knew what the topic of the day would be.

The thought brought an infusion of guilt. *Riley!* For the first time since last night's grisly discovery he thought of his friend. He rubbed the stubble that had sprouted on his jaw, knowing he should see him. His eyes strayed to the phone again. He didn't want to leave without talking to Mia first. As though reading his mind, the instrument sounded its familiar ring.

"Hello?"

"Joe, is that you?"

Joe tipped the top of the phone away from his ear. Danny didn't believe telephones worked unless he shouted into them.

"Morning, Danny." Joe steeled himself for questions about what had happened at the Barrett Ranch. Danny was too well tied into the community gossip network not to know what had occurred by now.

"It's Mia. You have to do something." Danny's voice boomed into the room.

"Mia? What's wrong?"

The paper towel fluttered to the floor, forgotten. Joe gripped the receiver, his knuckles white.

"They've arrested her. The police came and got her this morning."

"Arrested her! What for?" Joe was shouting as loudly as Danny was.

"They said she killed the Barretts."

Stunned, Joe steadied himself against the counter. The phone slipped from his fingers and clattered to the floor. They had arrested Mia? His thoughts whirled. It's a mistake. An awful, terrible mistake. He had to get to the police to explain. Right now.

"Joe, Joe, are you there?" The sound boomed from the floor.

Joe bent over and snatched up the now cracked handset.

"Danny, I've got to go."

Thinking he'd better look presentable to talk to the police, Joe showered and dressed. In his haste he nicked himself twice on the chin with his razor. Farley watched with wide eyes, taking care to keep his tail out of the way of Joe's hurrying feet.

On the drive downtown Joe mentally reviewed what he knew about criminal law and procedure, which wasn't much: scattered recollections from the first year of law school and two days of the bar review course. He did know if Mia had been picked up, a warrant had been issued, which wouldn't have happened unless the police and the judge who signed it had had evidence there was probable cause to believe she had committed the crimes.

At least that was how it was supposed to work, he thought grimly. All through law school he had believed justice had replaced the law of the pack. But now he wasn't sure the prey hadn't been chosen and the circle was closing in.

He turned right onto Ocotillo, bypassing the entrance to his firm's garage, and looked for a parking space in the next block. The arresting officers would have brought Mia to the police station to be searched, fingerprinted, and photographed before putting her in a holding cell pending arraignment, the point where the legal system took over from the police. He chewed at his lip at the thought of Mia locked up.

Finding an empty space in front of the post office, Joe jumped out, barely taking time to wrench his key out of the ignition. The police station bordered the town square. It sat on the southwest corner, with the post office to its east and the courthouse to its north. On the other side of the courthouse was city hall, which housed the mayor's office and council chambers.

Joe dashed toward the small white-lighted "POLICE" sign jutting over the sidewalk. Originally the territory's – later the state's – courthouse, the building boasted a two story Western-style false facade, tall narrow windows, wooden siding, and carved balcony railings. An old hitching rail still stood next to the entrance, though it had been decades since lawmen had tied their mounts up in front instead of parking their patrol cars around back.

He sprinted up the building's steps two at a time, the stone worn to a dip in the middle from a near century of use by mostly boot-clad feet. He paused on the landing to catch his breath in the shade of the large cottonwood tree that stood alone on the lawn between the building and the street.

Forcing his lungs to slow, he surveyed the leafed giant, incongruous among the more recent plantings. His gaze drifted to the place where the tree's biggest branch split off from the main trunk. There the bark was worn away, leaving the wood underneath polished smooth and gray. The state historian's talk the day of his swearing-in to the bar came to mind, and he realized what he was looking at. White and Indian, cattle thieves and crooked speculators; all had swung from the town's infamous "Tree of Justice."

His stomach abruptly convulsed and he groped for the stair rail, fighting a surge of nausea. Murder was still a capital offense in Arizona, the electric chair having replaced the hangman's noose.

Wanting to banish the tree from his sight and his thoughts, Joe forced himself to swallow hard, then pushed through the double doors into a blast of air conditioning. He was in a waiting room, surrounded by a grouping of low light-colored tables and comfortable-looking chairs upholstered in mauve and teal.

A coffee machine burbled in the corner next to an organ pipe cactus in a large ceramic pot. Facing him was a long counter made out of blond wood that fenced off an open area beyond. A trim Hispanic woman stood behind the counter. Beyond her, other women typed and filed papers and answered phones. Doors, some open to show small offices, lined the back wall. Sunlight streamed in through clerestory windows, highlighting wafting dust motes. To his right there was a bulletin board with "WANTED" lettered across its top, empty except for two information sheets on missing children.

The woman behind the counter smiled at him, showing two dimples carved into her round cheeks. "May I help you?"

"I'm here to see Mia, I mean Miguela Santi –" He stumbled to a stop and tried again. "The woman who was arrested this morning."

Comprehension dawned in the woman's eyes. "Are you an

attorney?"

Joe nodded. She pushed a clipboard toward him.

"Sign in, please."

Joe printed his name. She took the clipboard away and consulted with one of the workers behind her. She returned to the counter, a wrinkle creasing her forehead.

"This suspect is already represented by counsel from the public defender's office."

"I'm not here to represent her. I'd just like to talk to her."

The frown stayed put. "Are you family?"

"No," Joe answered.

"Then I'm sorry, but you can't see her." The woman didn't sound sorry at all to Joe. "She's consulting with her ..." She paused, allowing him time to mentally insert the word *real*. "... attorney. Her arraignment is this morning."

This morning? Joe was taken aback. He remembered learning at bar review that the district attorney had twenty-four hours to file his case after an arrest, forty-eight to schedule an arraignment. What was the hurry? he asked himself, even though he knew the answer. The prosecutor's office was sure of its evidence. He had to talk to someone before this whole thing went too far.

"I'd like to speak with the officer in charge of the investigation." Joe figured this was his last resort.

She started shaking her head before he finished speaking. "I'm afraid that won't be possible, either."

Joe thought quickly. "I was with Mia, Miguela, when she found the bodies. I have some new information that relates to the case." He tried to squelch the tremor in his voice.

She cocked her head and looked at him for a moment, then told him to have a seat before walking to the back of the room. He sat on the edge of the nearest chair, his fingers running up and down its wooden arms while he wracked his brain for some new fact to tell the police. After five minutes, all he could come up with was Mia's innocence. It was obvious they didn't know about that.

The woman returned, her face expressionless. Joe waited for her to speak. His heart pounded.

The woman reached under the counter to press the release for the swing door. "The detective can see you now."

She led Joe into one of the offices along the back wall. Without another word, she ushered him into the small space and left, shutting the door behind her.

He was alone in the room. The desk was made out of the same blond wood as the counter, empty except for a stack of travel brochures, the top one featuring a chalet nestled among snow-capped peaks. The two chairs were upholstered in the same mauve and teal shades as the reception area. Tacked up on the wall were posters of European ski resorts.

Joe examined the poster closest to him. A girl in a red ski suit with a blond ponytail, her teeth impossibly white, had been caught by the photographer in mid-air between moguls. Tall evergreens stood guard at the edge of the run like sentinels, and the sky was a deep blue. Joe closed his eyes and let himself imagine he was on the mountain slope with her. The snow crunched under his feet and his breath made tiny clouds in the cold air. Just for a moment he was thousands of miles away from the police station, Pinnacle Peak, the desert.

The sound of the door opening yanked him back to reality. The man Joe had seen get out of the white Explorer last night walked into the room carrying a black binder under his arm. He had a weightlifter's frame, softened around the edges, and his pale face was tinged with sunburn, his nose already peeling. The creases in his pants were pressed to a knife's edge, and his suit jacket fit him like a uniform. Joe guessed he was in his forties, but his smooth face and intact hairline made it hard to tell. Except for the pouched crescents under his eyes, he looked none the worse for wear after what Joe knew had to have been a long night. Washed out blue eyes met Joe's, and he held out his hand.

"I'm Detective Karl Dresden," he said in a guttural voice. His grip was dry and firm.

"Joe McGuinness."

Dresden nodded at the poster Joe had been looking at. "Have you ever been?"

"Uh, no," Joe replied, unsure whether he was referring to skiing or Europe.

Dresden looked at the poster, his manner softening. "I have always wanted to live in the mountains and learn to ski." His tone became brisk again. "But the altitude is bad for my wife's heart problems, and she does not like the cold anyway."

Dresden moved around to the other side of his desk and sat down, setting the binder in front of him.

"Mr. Dresden –"

"Detective, please, not 'Mister'," the lawman corrected.

And never Karl, Joe thought before beginning again.

"Detective Dresden, I understand you are investigating the Barrett deaths."

The detective leaned forward in his chair.

"Murders," he said. "I'm investigating the Barrett murders."

Joe took a deep breath. "Well, I wanted you to know there's been a terrible mistake. Mia didn't have anything to do with what happened."

"And how do you know this?" Dresden asked.

"Sonny, that is, Mrs. Barrett's son, came to my law firm early yesterday. He was furious his mother had rewritten her will, basically making him land-rich but cash-poor."

Joe wished the detective would take out a notebook and start writing things down, but Dresden merely continued to look at him.

"And?" the detective prompted.

"And Sonny was desperate for money for a car racing team. He swore he was going to get his mother to change her will back."

Joe hesitated. He felt funny telling the detective how he thought the murders had happened, but it was the only idea he had come up with.

"The way I see it, they got into an argument at the ranch house. Sonny threatened his mother with a gun, finally pulling the trigger in a fit of rage."

"How do you explain his death?" The detective's face remained impassive.

"After he killed his mother, he was overwhelmed with remorse, so he shot himself."

Joe looked at the older man, waiting for his reaction. Dresden pulled a pair of half-glasses and a snowy handkerchief out of an inside pocket. He held the glasses up to the light, first polishing one lens, then the other. Just as Joe thought he couldn't stand the silence any longer, Dresden opened the black binder in front of him and scanned the first page.

"Interesting theory," he said.

Joe's face brightened with hope.

"Totally unsupported by the facts, but interesting."

Joe let out a small moan, but Dresden didn't seem to notice. Instead, the detective turned to the next page of the binder.

"The chief decided to release this information to the press, so I am not telling you anything you won't be able to read in today's newspaper." Dresden began to read out loud, ticking items off with his finger as he went along.

"Sonny's left-handed, but the gun was found in his right hand. There was no powder residue on his palms or fingers, which should have been there had he fired a weapon. Further, according to our very preliminary autopsy, the entry angle of the bullet makes it highly unlikely his wound was self-inflicted. Also, there were several sheets of paper on the kitchen table. They weren't splattered with blood, which they would be if they had been put there before the shootings, and not after. This places someone in addition to the victims at the scene."

Dresden looked up from the binder, sat back in his chair, and folded his arms across his chest.

"That is why your theory isn't supported by the facts, Mr. McGuinness. Mr. Barrett didn't kill his mother or himself. Someone tried, rather amateurishly, to frame him."

"But Mia couldn't have been involved with any frame-up!" Joe exclaimed, unable to contain himself.

"Why not?" Dresden asked evenly.

"Because I was with her last night."

Dresden scrutinized Joe with renewed interest. "So you are the man with whom Ms. Ortiz spent her evening." He took a legal pad and mechanical pencil out of a desk drawer.

"This is fortunate. I wanted to speak with you today. Thank you for saving me the trouble of coming to you."

He clicked his pencil and wrote Joe's name and the date on the top page of the pad.

"I know you went over what happened last night with the officers at the scene, but I would appreciate it if you'd repeat it for me."

Joe started what was dismayingly becoming a familiar recitation.

Thirty minutes later he abruptly stopped talking in mid-sentence.

"Detective, I've answered all your questions and told you what happened two going on three times. I see why you believe someone tried to make it look as though Sonny committed a murder/suicide. But what I don't understand is why you think Mia did it."

Dresden doodled some circles on his pad, then looked at Joe.

"Mr. McGuinness, I appreciate this is difficult for you. But Ms. Ortiz wasn't arrested on a whim. As a lawyer, you know that. I'm the detective assigned to investigate major crimes in Pinnacle Peak. When a major crime occurs, I do my job. I detect. Part of that is examining the scene. Our search of the ranch house yielded several items of physical evidence that implicated Ms. Ortiz in the murders."

"Physical evidence? What physical evidence?" Joe asked.

"Mr. McGuinness, there are things I can tell you, things I will not tell you, and things I would like to tell you but cannot. You should also know I have the greatest respect for the partners of your law firm, both living and recently deceased. They have been of great help to this department on more than one occasion."

Briefly Joe wondered which partner had done what for the police.

"All I want – " he began.

Dresden held up his hand, but it was the look on his face that made Joe clamp his jaws together.

"It is because of this respect and obligation I am willing to continue our conversation, albeit on a *hypothetical* level." The detective's gaze, his pupil's dark pinpricks in a sea of cold blue, bore into Joe's. "Although I may appear to be stating things as fact, I am simply making conjectures, presenting a supposed situation for discussion. Do you understand what I am saying?"

Struggling to curb his impatience, Joe nodded. While preserving his deniability, Dresden was going to reveal the evidence against Mia. *So tell me.*

The detective spoke briskly and without looking at any notes. "We found a blouse with blood on the edge of its hem in the bottom of Ms. Ortiz' clothes hamper. Ms. Ortiz admitted the blouse was hers. The blood is the same type as Mrs. Barrett's. Analysis of whether it is in fact Mrs. Barrett's blood will take a few days."

"So what?" Joe cut in. "Even if it is Mrs. Barrett's blood, the real killer could have planted it there."

The detective appeared not to have heard him. "We also found a shoe print in the pool of blood under Sonny. It was matched to a pair of black sandals in Ms. Ortiz' closet." The detective put his elbows on the desk and rested his chin on top of his clasped hands.

"Of course, you realize, Mr. McGuinness, this evidence has not yet been analyzed at the lab."

"I understand."

"The way I would interpret such a situation," he said, "is that Ms. Ortiz knew she had gotten blood on her blouse so she hid it, planning to dispose of it later." Dresden unlaced his fingers and spread his hands, palms turned up.

"What she didn't know was she had stepped into the blood on the floor. You see, in our hypothetical the samples we scraped from the bottom of her shoe tested out as Sonny's blood type." The older man looked almost ruefully at Joe.

"She could have stepped into the blood when she discovered the bodies." Joe ran his hand through his hair. "And gotten blood on the blouse when she put the shoes into her closet before she went to her aunt's for the night."

The detective pressed his lips together and shook his head. "Both you and she have stated she didn't get farther than the kitchen doorway. You must also assume the shoes we found weren't the same ones she was wearing last night on her date with you." Dresden set his pencil down. "She went straight to her aunt's without returning to the Barrett house. After you and she departed, we sealed off the house. She couldn't have gotten in if she had wanted to."

"But –"

The detective again stopped him with a raised hand. "Another thing I do as part of my job, Mr. McGuinness, is to look for opportunity. Let's continue constructing our hypothetical. We questioned the residents of the ranch and no one heard a car other than yours that evening. It apparently has quite a distinctive muffler, or lack thereof.

"As the house is several miles from the road, it's very unlikely someone would walk in, so it stands to reason the killer was already on the premises. The coroner puts the Barretts' death at between six and ten o'clock. The air conditioning had been turned up, making it hard to be more exact. Ms. Ortiz doesn't have an alibi for the early part of the evening. She claims she was in her room getting ready for her date with you, and she didn't see Mrs. Barrett, Sonny, or anyone else for that matter before she left. You told me she was waiting for you on the porch, from where you both proceeded directly to your car and drove away. Under such facts, Mrs. Barrett and Sonny could have already been dead in the kitchen when you arrived to pick her up."

"But it doesn't make sense," Joe said, a little less zealous than before. "What reason would Mia have to murder Sonny and Mrs. Barrett?"

"I'd say she had about three million of them." Dresden thumbed through the binder. "These are the papers that were on the kitchen table," he said after locating the object of his search, apparently abandoning the hypothetical ploy. "A confirmed copy of the latest version of Mrs. Barrett's will. In it she leaves two-thirds of her estate – mostly the ranch and other property – to Sonny. The remainder, largely cash and securities, goes to Miguela Santiago Ortiz."

Dresden rubbed his hand over his face, for the first time looking tired. "We know about her little brother, Mr. McGuinness. He needs another operation, maybe two. There's no health insurance, and the mother barely makes enough to cover food and rent."

Joe slumped in his chair, his shoulders rounded in defeat. Could he have misjudged Mia so completely? Dresden closed the binder and clasped his hands on top of it.

"You said yourself Sonny was ranting to anyone who would listen about the new will. Perhaps Mia overheard him, or he told her in anger. In any event, she decided she needed the money now, or wanted to make sure Cordelia couldn't change her mind again. So she killed them, tried to make it look like a murder/suicide, and left with you." He lifted his shoulders and spread his arms wide. "You tell me how it happened otherwise."

Joe dug his nails into his palms as a surge of frustration tinged with anger washed over him. Deep down, his mind agreed with everything Dresden had said. Intellectually, he knew the detective's conclusions were justified, but his heart still told him differently. *Mia wasn't guilty.*

Further arguments at this point would be useless. He needed Dresden to believe he agreed with him, that he'd stay out of things. Otherwise he wouldn't have a chance to uncover the facts that would prove Mia's innocence. He unclenched his fists.

"I see your point, Detective," he said, his jaw stiff.

Dresden's voice softened. "Mr. McGuinness, I've been a cop for more than twenty years. Most murders are committed by a family member or a friend, with money or love as the motive. Ninety-nine out of a hundred times, if the evidence points to a suspect who falls into one of those categories, I don't need to look further." He paused. "But there's always that one exception. So if there's evidence, real evidence, out there, I want to know about it." He pointed a blunt finger at Joe. "But I don't want you looking for it. That's my job. Agreed?"

Joe hesitated. This was exactly the promise he had no intention of making.

"I understand what you're saying, Detective," he said carefully.

It wasn't exactly a commitment not to interfere, but it apparently satisfied Detective Dresden. He pushed his chair away from the desk.

"Now, if there's nothing else –" the detective said, getting to his feet.

"May I see her?"

Dresden looked at his watch. "Court convenes in twenty minutes. You can have ten."

Joe followed Dresden through the reception area and down the hallway to the holding cells. They passed through a metal detector into a small lobby. A man in a uniform sat behind a battered desk, reading the paper. Two metal doors were set into the wall behind him. The floor was scarred with scuffmarks and the once yellow walls were now dark with grime. A fluorescent bulb hummed overhead and the air smelled stale. Either the interior decorator for the rest of the police station hadn't made it into here yet or ambiance for inmates was a low budget priority, Joe thought.

"Morning, Braxton. Mr. McGuinness is here to see Ms. Ortiz. He's a lawyer."

Joe tried not to show his surprise. He thought "let's talk about a hypothetical" was as far as Dresden would bend the rules.

"Her other one's still in there. He might as well join the party." The man jerked a thumb toward the door on his right, barely lifting his eyes from the sports page.

Dresden gave Joe a long look, then walked back down the corridor.

What was that about? Joe watched the detective's back disappear around the corner.

A lock clicked behind him. Joe turned in time to see a petite woman shutting the door indicated by the guard. In her early twenties, she wore a navy suit and matching low heels with bows on their tops. The seams of the suit puckered, and the material was shiny. A gold locket lay on top of her faded pink shirt, which was buttoned to the collar.

Although the legs visible beneath the skirt were slim and shapely, it was the face that drew Joe's gaze. Eyes slightly too close together and a nose and mouth twisted and flattened as though perpetually pressed against glass gave her the look of a sneering prizefighter. Mousy-brown hair that appeared to have received only seconds of attention that morning was pushed away from her face by a wide navy band.

"Who are you?" the woman asked. Her flat voice betrayed no accent.

"I'm Joe McGuinness, a friend of Mia's."

One corner of the sneer twisted up, producing a crooked smile that was curiously engaging.

"Joe! Mia has told me about you. I was hoping we'd have a

chance to talk." She shook his hand vigorously. "I'm Veronica Schwartz, from the public defender's office. You can call me Ronnie."

"How is she?"

"Bearing up as well as can be expected."

"I don't know that much about criminal law. What happens exactly at the arraignment?" Joe was embarrassed at his ignorance, but Ronnie didn't seem to care.

"That's right, you're in private practice." She tapped her forefinger on her chest. Joe noticed the nail had been chewed to the quick. "That's where I plan to be in six months. Five years here is enough."

She shifted her briefcase to her other hand.

"I joined the PD out of law school because I wanted to keep innocent poor people out of jail. I've learned if most people get to the point of being arrested, poor or not, they're probably guilty, if not of the crime they're charged with, then of something else."

Joe felt a knot in his stomach. *This was Mia's lawyer?*

"Now don't get me wrong," Ronnie said, holding up a hand like a traffic warden. "I've fought for each of my clients every step of the way, and I'll do the same for Mia. I'm just talking about the way the system works. That's why I wanted to talk to you."

She threw a quick glance toward the guard, then lowered her voice.

"I don't know if you're up to speed on the evidence the prosecutor has so far, but it's pretty incriminating. He's got enough for murder one if he wants. We'll find out what he's going for at the arraignment this morning." She moved closer to him. "Mia sees you as a friend. I tried to talk to her, but I wasn't getting through. Maybe you can."

"Talk to her about what?" Joe asked.

"Taking a plea. Manslaughter's a possibility. She could be out in five."

Joe stepped back, aghast. "That's ridiculous!"

The guard looked up. Joe gave him a curt nod and waited until he returned to his paper.

"She didn't do it!" he whispered furiously, struggling to keep his voice down.

Ronnie grabbed his jacket lapel and pulled his face within inches of hers.

"At this point I don't care if she did or she didn't." Her brown eyes bored into his and her teeth were almost clenched. "We've got a leading citizen of the town and her son murdered, and the evidence makes it look damn certain Mia's responsible. Without anything else, I'm not going to risk sending her on a one way visit to Old Sparky down in Florence. How about it, Joe – would you?"

Joe stared at her, suddenly dry-mouthed. His inability to speak didn't matter; there was nothing he could say.

She awkwardly smoothed down the front of his coat and stepped away from him.

"To answer your earlier question, besides finding out what the charge is, Mia will enter a plea of not guilty, of course."

Ronnie had no hint in her voice that she had just talked about Mia being sent to the electric chair. "A date will be set for the preliminary hearing, and don't even think about bail."

"How long before trial?"

"With the usual motions from us, I'd guess ten months, maybe a year."

Joe's heart sank at the thought of Mia in jail that long. Then he caught himself. *There are worse places for her to be. Like Death Row.*

Ronnie glanced at the watch on her wrist. "I've got to get ready for court." She looked at him with sympathetic eyes. "Think about what I said."

The click of her heels reverberated down the corridor as Joe gripped the metal doorknob and asked the guard to buzz him in.

He opened the door tentatively. Mia sat at a small wooden table, its top a mosaic of scratches and burn marks from cigarettes. She looked small in an old sweatshirt several sizes too big.

"Joe!" she exclaimed as soon as she saw him.

As his heart threw itself against his ribs, Joe walked across the small space and sat on the other side of the table from her, reaching his arms out to take her hands in his. He was surprised at how cold they felt. Up close, he could see her skin had a waxen pallor, and her eyes had dulled to a muddy bronze. The scar on her forehead seemed more pronounced. She looked at him, a sad smile tugging at her mouth.

"Some second date, huh?"

"Are you okay?"

She pushed her hair back behind her ears. Her eyes filled with tears. "I didn't kill them, Joe." Her words came out a whisper.

He squeezed her hands. "I know you didn't. And I'm going to make sure the police know it, too. Now let's get to work. We've only got a few minutes. I need to ask you some questions."

"Okay." She wiped her eyes with the back of her sleeve.

"Did Ronnie tell you about the evidence they found at the house?"

She nodded.

"The white blouse stained with blood in the bottom of your clothes hamper. Do you have any –"

"I told Ronnie I've never worn that blouse!" Mia interrupted. "It was a Christmas present from my Aunt Flora. It's two sizes too big. It hung in the back of my closet. I never got around to giving it away."

"What about the black sandal?"

"If I were going to commit one murder, let alone two, those would be the last shoes I'd wear!" she exclaimed. "They have four inch heels. I can barely walk in them. They were part of my outfit when I was a bridesmaid in my cousin's wedding."

Joe tried to think of a better way to phrase his most difficult query, but couldn't. "What about the money?"

"I didn't know about the will, Joe. I didn't even have a clue." She gripped his hands so tightly his finger bones ground together.

"Has there been trouble recently between you and either of the Barretts? Arguments? Bad feelings?"

"No! Never!" Mia shook her head adamantly, then looked at him through wet lashes. "You must believe me. I would never do such a terrible thing."

Joe looked into the still beautiful face. "I believe you."

Knuckles sounded on the door and Officer Frampton walked in. "Time's up."

He walked to Mia's side, unhooking the handcuffs from his belt. She slipped her hands from Joe's and pushed up her sleeves, exposing slender wrists.

"You don't need to use those," Joe protested, but Frampton

ignored him.

The cuffs secured, the policeman grasped Mia's upper arm and steered her through the door. Her eyes caught Joe's for a moment and then she was gone.

Is this the only way he'd ever see her again – behind locked doors in windowless rooms? Joe's mind flipped through the events of the last twelve hours.

Dresden wasn't going to help her. Neither was Ronnie Schwartz. That left him.

He retraced the route he and Dresden had taken from the reception area. The way out seemed longer than the way in.

Chapter 11

Joe arrived at the firm a little after ten. He nodded without speaking to Lydia and walked into his office, shutting the door behind him. He sat at his desk and started to flip through the papers in his overflowing in-basket. Thirty seconds later he pushed the pile away.

"I can't do this now," he muttered, unable to keep his mind away from Mia. *Time to start keeping my promise.*

She said she didn't know about the will. Was there anyone else who could confirm that? *Of course,* he thought, striking his palm against his desktop. Proof could be as close as two doors away.

He stuck his head out of his office and looked down the hall. Harrington was bidding good-bye to a bent-over woman with a hump on her back. Gertrude stood next to her at near attention, ready to lead the client back to the lobby.

My chance, thought Joe. He took half a step back from his doorway and stayed there, watching. Next door he could hear Sydney on the telephone.

"I want to kill the bitch, I really do!" she said in an agitated whisper.

Joe tuned out the rest of her conversation, presumably talk about a pending case. I'll never use that verb lightly again, he vowed.

He watched as the elderly woman slowly shuffled toward the main doors with Gertrude at her elbow, then slipped out of his office and walked quickly toward Harrington's now closed door. His hand was raised to knock when a voice stopped him.

"Mr. McGuinness!" Joe lowered his hand and turned.

"Miss Slivens," Joe's voice cracked, "It's really important that I speak to Mr. Harrington."

She considered him for a moment, then reached for her phone.

"Mr. Harrington, Mr. McGuinness is here. May he come in?" She paused to listen.

"No, I don't think it's something that can wait," she said firmly. Gertrude hung up the phone and nodded briskly at him.

"Thank you," Joe whispered, but her gray curls were already bent over her typing.

Joe pushed open the heavy door. Harrington looked at him, eyebrows raised quizzically.

"Yes?"

Joe avoided the green chair and remained standing.

"Mr. Harrington, it's about the Barretts."

Harrington's face creased into a look of sympathy.

"Oh, of course. I understand from the police you were there. If there's –"

"No, it's not that," Joe interrupted. "It's Mia. The police think she's guilty, and her lawyer wants to plead her out. I know she didn't do it, but I have to figure out how to convince them." Joe paused, spent after the rush of words.

"And Mia is –"

"Mrs. Barrett's assistant. I was taking her home last night when we, that is, she –" Joe stopped talking and jammed his hands into his jacket pockets. "She didn't kill them!" he burst out. "And I'm the only one who wants to prove it!"

A look of comprehension flickered in Harrington's eyes as he scanned Joe's face, now twisted in misery.

"How can I help you, Mr. McGuinness?"

"It's about the will," Joe said. "Does Mia really inherit?"

Harrington cleared his throat. "As you know, Mr. McGuinness, communications between an attorney and his client are privileged. As a member of this firm, that privilege extends to you. I will tell you what Mrs. Barrett and I discussed, but you cannot repeat it to anyone else, not even Mia. Do you understand?"

Joe nodded.

"Cordelia had come to regard Miguela, Mia, as you call her, as a daughter. She knew about her brother Jaime's accident and helped the family out from time to time. During our last meeting she instructed me to redraw her will to include a substantial bequest to Mia and to modify the terms of Sonny's legacy." The senior attorney paused and met Joe's eyes.

"To be frank, I tried to discourage her. Not with respect to the provisions for Mia but the restrictions on Sonny's use of the ranch. Perhaps imprudently, I asked her whether she really wanted to control her son's life from the grave. She remained adamant. So I acceded to my client's wishes and drafted up the new instrument."

"Did Mia know about the new will?"

"I do not know. Mrs. Barrett did not indicate her intentions in this regard. She did, however, request a copy of the revised document. That was what was in the envelope you delivered. I presume she intended to put it in her safe deposit box, as was her practice. We, of course, keep the original here. Perhaps she made another copy and gave it to Sonny, or he came across the one you delivered to the ranch house. As you may have observed, he had a copy of the will with him when he came to the firm yesterday. Whether he or Cordelia informed Mia of the new terms or she found out about them on her own, I do not know."

Joe tried to contain his despair. *So Mia could have known about the new will. He had given it to her himself.*

The white haired lawyer swiveled in his chair and looked out the window. "Mr. McGuinness, no lawyer of this firm should interfere with an ongoing police investigation." Harrington stared through the glass. "But we do have certain duties as executors of the estate." He pivoted his chair back around, facing Joe again.

"Part of those responsibilities is the inventory and collection of the deceased's belongings."

Joe's stomach churned at the thought of going back to the Barrett house. He was too close to all of this.

"I have already made arrangements for the ranch property," Harrington continued.

The surge in his stomach abated.

"But there remains Mrs. Barrett's safe deposit box. This

morning I had delivered to the bank the power of attorney authorizing the firm to take charge of the contents."

Harrington unlocked a drawer in the credenza behind him and drew out an envelope. "Here is the key and the bank name and address. Bring any documents back to the office with you but leave any valuables – jewelry, negotiable instruments – in the box for now."

The older lawyer turned toward the window again, his fingers steepled under his chin. Joe silently left the office.

A short while later Joe was on the sidewalk, a file folder to carry papers back to the office tucked under his arm. Mexican birds of paradise nodded their red and yellow heads in the heat, leaves splayed like fingers. The light was so brilliant it hurt to look at the sky. Squinting, Joe patted his pocket for his sunglasses, remembering they had melted into a useless shape when he had left them on his dashboard a few days earlier. He hadn't had time to replace them yet.

He cut diagonally across the park, keeping his eyes away from the police station. He wondered where Mia was, and quelled the urge to try to see her again. Head down, engrossed in thoughts of Mia, he didn't see the approaching pedestrian. Their shoulders brushed against each other.

"Sorry," he said without breaking stride.

"Mr. McGuinness?"

His roughly spoken name brought him up short. Dresden. Emotion replacing restraint at the sight of the officer, Joe unleashed his pent-up thoughts.

"Detective, your physical evidence doesn't add up," he began without preamble, spitting his words into the hot air around them.

"Ah, yes, our hypothetical," Dresden said coolly, looking unperturbed by neither the temperature nor Joe's assertion.

"The blouse with the blood was one she never wore. An aunt had bought it for her and it was too big."

"Perhaps she had slipped it over the clothes she was wearing to protect them while she was applying her make up." Dresden stood comfortably, his weight balanced over the balls of his feet. "Or to protect them from splatters of blood."

Joe raked a hand through his hair and tried again. "Then why didn't she hide this so-called evidence? Putting it in a clothes bin is ridiculous."

"Maybe she didn't think she had enough time, or maybe she thought it would be best to get rid of it later. Sometimes the decisions of a panicked killer aren't the best ones."

Dresden slipped off his glasses, cradling them in his palm. His pale blue eyes looked almost colorless in the harsh light.

"What about the shoes, Detective? It makes no sense. Who commits murder in high heeled sandals?"

A small crease marred the smooth forehead. "You had a date that evening, correct?" Dresden's words became clipped with impatience. "A perfect occasion for pretty footwear. She was walking through the main house to wait for her escort, you, when she heard an argument in the kitchen. She moved closer, in time to hear Mrs. Barrett's capitulation to Sonny's pleas to change her will, leaving him everything again. Because of panic or greed – Who knows the reason? – she killed them both, then changed her shoes." He shrugged his well-tailored shoulders. "Perhaps they were bloody, perhaps she didn't feel like being pretty anymore that night."

"But she says she didn't know about the will." A trickle of moisture ran down Joe's back, more from fear for Mia than the heat.

"No?" Dresden lifted one blond eyebrow. "You said yourself you delivered the document to Ms. Ortiz, not Mrs. Barrett, despite the instructions of your employer." The detective fixed him with an unblinking stare.

Like a rattlesnake about to strike. Joe glared back at him.

"Mr. McGuinness, I have been in law enforcement almost as many years as you have been alive," Dresden said. "I can smell guilt, and I can smell innocence." The detective tapped the side of his nose. "Right now, Ms. Ortiz reeks of guilt. I am not without sympathy for you. But sometimes the obvious answer is the correct one. I suggest you accept what has happened and get on with your life."

With a nod of dismissal, Dresden turned in the direction of the police station. Joe watched him go, lifting his gaze from the retreating policeman to the cottonwood tree beyond, its branches scratching against the sky.

Muscles twitching with frustration, Joe walked toward the bank again, his pace soon quickening into a run. Arms pumping, leather soles slapping against the concrete, he slammed his body against the revolving doors, gasping for breath on the other side under curious tellers' stares. Refrigerated air chilled the sweat on his forehead, and his shirt hung damply under his arms. Hugging his sore shoulder, which burned with pain, Joe half-ran, half-walked across the lobby to the customer service desk.

Moments later, a small woman in a blue dress showed him into a mahogany paneled cubicle and brought in Cordelia's box. Joe raised the lid. On top was an envelope with the firm's name on it. A roll of velvet lay underneath. Joe picked up the soft fabric and a glittering diamond choker fell onto the counter.

"Yikes!" Joe carefully rewrapped the jewelry. Besides the envelope, the only other documents in the box that weren't stock certificates were a packet of letters held together with a frayed ribbon.

He picked up the envelope that had been on top. After a moment's hesitancy, he undid the flap and pulled out the papers inside. It was a copy of Cordelia's will, dated three days ago. He hurriedly scanned its provisions. It was all there: the bequest to Mia, the restrictions imposed on Sonny's sale or mortgaging of the ranch.

He reread the ban on developing the acreage. What if the restriction had made someone else other than Sonny furious? Joe tried to remember what Stephen Merchant had said about seeing Sonny with the Woolcott & Jones real estate lawyer. Who was the "cowboy" who had been there, too? Joe slammed down the lid of the box and pushed the button for the attendant.

Back at his desk, Joe capped and uncapped his pen while he waited for the receptionist to transfer his call.

"John Eaton." The mellifluous and low-pitched voice was certainly well-suited for assuaging anti-development neighbors and persuading city council members.

"Mr. Eaton, this is Joe McGuinness at Barclay, Harrington &

Merchant." Joe spoke firmly, knowing he needed to project confidence at all costs.

"Mr. McGuinness, what can I do for you?"

"I assume you've heard about what happened to Cordelia Barrett and her son."

"Mmmm, yes. I saw the headlines this morning. Terrible tragedy."

"Yes, it was. In any event, we're executors of the estates." Joe involuntarily crossed his fingers, partly for luck and partly because of the deception he was perpetrating. "I just wanted to confirm the proposed development hadn't yet been finalized."

"No, it wasn't. The Planning and Zoning presentation is ready, but we hadn't yet obtained Mrs. Barrett's signature."

"I didn't think you were representing Mrs. Barrett." Joe hoped his wild guess wouldn't blow up in his face.

"We weren't. Sonny was our client. His mother's involvement was limited to transferring a portion of the ranch into his name, which would then become his capital contribution to the partnership." He chuckled. "You'd be surprised how much acreage five star resorts require."

The Barrett Ranch a resort? Joe now understood Cordelia's insistence on development restrictions.

"Who were Sonny's other partners?"

When Eaton didn't immediately respond, Joe realized his mistake. If Joe truly knew about the deal, he'd certainly know who was a party to it. He tried to salvage his ruse.

"I mean, had a definite decision been made?" he added hastily, glad Eaton couldn't see the flush creeping across his cheeks. "I want to avoid any unexpected claims down the road."

"Of course. Although Sonny talked about bringing in others, there ended up being only one. Let me give you his phone number."

Joe heard papers rustle. Eaton came back on the line.

"My paralegal must have the file. I'll have my secretary call you. You know, he may even be in the book."

Joe held his breath.

"His name is Charles Healy."

Chapter 12

S taring at but not really seeing the painting on the wall in front of him, Joe pressed his fingertips to his temples. *Chuck Healy was Sonny's partner?* A resort built on a parcel carved out of the Barrett place and the Rocking H would rival La Hacienda in size and most likely reap the partners profits in the eight, not seven, figure range.

But why the murders? Joe frowned in concentration. The money involved gave Healy motive enough to kill Cordelia if she were blocking the project. And Sonny? Perhaps he caught Healy in the act, perhaps he told Healy about the will, and the rancher thought he'd take his chances on picking up the acreage once the Barretts were gone and the remaining heir was the only suspect. Mia made an easy scapegoat for other reasons. Healy might have figured no one would care if another poor Mexican went to prison or worse. It could have been personal, too. Healy may not have taken her rejection as he well as he had seemed to Tuesday night.

In four strides Joe was out the door.

"Lydia, I've got to go out — don't know when I'll be back," he called over his shoulder as he jogged to the elevators.

North of town, the Blind Buck sped into and out of the low spots in Scottsdale Road, Joe heedless to the risk of bottoming out. Each depression was marked with a large yellow diamond sign bearing the warning "DO NOT ENTER WHEN FLOODED." The desert didn't get much rain, but when the moisture came, it arrived in a deluge, heaviest in late summer. Joe had seen water from these monsoons fill the arroyos channeled into the hillsides and cascade toward flat land without regard to pavement in its path. He marveled that despite the signs and common sense, people still tried to drive across the torrents every year, resulting in the occasional drownings and many more fines under the town's "idiot motorist law" when they had to be rescued.

He turned left instead of right onto Old Adobe Road. The steering wheel jerked in his hands, as though the car was telling him he had gone the wrong way.

"We're not going home just yet," Joe said, zigzagging around the deeper ruts in the unpaved road.

He passed a fatigued collection of doublewide trailers set at haphazard angles amid the cholla and palo verde. Most were missing metal skirts at the bottom, and mangy dogs lolled in the shade under the dilapidated boxes. One trailer had been cut in half, the open end patched with sheet metal and strips of plastic. Joe recalled Riley telling him about Tuney White, a Barrett Ranch cowboy and the trailer's owner, and his interpretation of the judge's ruling on property division in his divorce case.

Joe kept his windows rolled up against the powder-fine dust churned up by his tires. It was unseasonably hot for October. The sun burned down, transmuting the desert's subtle hues into a blinding glare. Five miles beyond the asphalt, the car bucked over a shiny cattle guard. Suspended overhead from two poles was "Rocking H Ranch" spelled out in script. Beneath the letters hung a black metal silhouette of a roper and calf.

Behind wire fences clumps of cattle chewed their cud in the heat. A lone horseman stood in the field to the south. His horse snatched a mouthful of grass while he scribbled something on the palm of his glove. The day's cow count, Joe presumed.

Interspersed among the hides carrying the Rocking H brand were a few flanks bearing the cloverleaf mark Joe had seen on Don Rogers' horse. Joe had heard it was a practice carried over from the Old West: hands were allowed to run a certain number of their cattle with the owner's herd, acknowledgment the only retirement fund a cowboy would probably ever have was a cow. As an old cowboy had once told Joe, "Some people follow the stocks. I just brand and feed 'em."

Joe pulled into a cleared open space and parked next to an

island of prickly pair and ocotillo rimmed by a stone border. Newly leafed after last month's rains, the ocotillo looked like fuzzy pipe cleaners bent from use. The prickly pear's red fruit gleamed like polished garnets.

Getting out of the car, Joe surveyed the place. Similar to the Barrett place but smaller in scale, the Rocking H appeared to be a prosperous operation. Fences were mended, stock looked fat, and the hay barn was full. To the south, set apart from the ranch buildings, was the main house, a Spanish Mission two-story with a red-tiled roof and ornate metal balconies. A high wall broken only by a pair of tall, carved, shut-tight wooden doors, encircled the house.

A wiry man led a young horse out of the barn nearest to Joe. The colt frisked at the end of the line, skipping forward a few steps, then stopping to toss his head. The man ignored the horse's antics as he slipped a tin of Copenhagen out of his back jean pocket for a pinch. Noticing the car, the man altered his course to where Joe was standing. Bowed legs gave him a ragged walk. He moved like a marionette played by clumsy fingers. As he neared, Joe recognized Healy's roping partner.

"What do you want?" Rogers asked when he was within hearing distance.

The colt appeared frightened by the Blind Buck and approached on stiff legs, snorting loudly.

"I'd like to speak to Mr. Healy," Joe replied.

Rogers spat a brownish glob onto the ground between them.

"I'm his foreman. Anything you got to say to him you can say to me," he said. Joe could see flecks of tobacco between his teeth.

"I need to speak to him."

Rogers scrutinized Joe's face, then shrugged. "Suit yourself," he said curtly. "He's in the main barn." Jerking the lead, Rogers headed toward the corrals, the colt jigging in his wake.

Joe walked to the entrance of the same barn from which Rogers and the colt had emerged. A pickup truck was parked in the center section. Blackened tools, racks of horseshoes, and an anvil crowded its bed. A portable forge was on the ground next to it, hooked to a propane tank. The smell of burned hoof hung in the air. A dark horse stood quietly in cross ties, a rear ankle balanced on the horseshoer's tree trunk-thick thigh. Healy bent over next to the farrier, studying the upturned hoof.

"You're right, Jess. Go ahead and pad him," Healy said, straightening up. He looked in Joe's direction.

"Mr. Healy? It's Joe McGuinness," Joe called.

Healy walked toward him, tucking his shirt in behind the silver buckle at his waist.

Be careful, Joe warned himself. Don't spook him.

"If you're here about the missing stock, I still haven't heard anything." Healy leaned against the doorjamb and tipped his hat forward against the brightness outside. "Not a loss I'd wish on anybody, especially in this market. Price of beef's been in free fall the last five years."

"Good reason to get out of the cattle business." The words popped out before Joe could stop them. So much for the subtle approach.

"What are you talking about?" The rancher pushed his hat back to fix Joe with a hard stare.

Joe plowed ahead. "I'm here about the Barrett murders."

"Helluva thing." The rancher's eyes didn't leave Joe's. "Heard that little Mex gal did it. I knew she was a hot one."

Fury coursed through Joe, leaving his fingertips tingling.

"Mia's innocent." Joe struggled to control his temper. "But regardless, you must be relieved. Mrs. Barrett can't stop your development anymore."

Healy's lips stretched into a sardonic smile. "I don't know how you found out about that, but in case you didn't notice, Sonny isn't here anymore either. I'm back to square one on the project."

"Where were you last night?" Joe asked bluntly.

Healy's Irish ancestry betrayed him, and his cheeks burned with anger. "What the hell are you implying?" he growled, squaring off to the younger man.

Joe stood his ground. "Where were you?"

"Not that I have to answer to you, but I was at Shorty's, roping. Ask your partner, Riley. He was there, too."

Joe's hopes sank. *So it can't be Healy.* His adrenaline ebbed, replaced by fatigue and the stress of the day.

"Thank you for your time, Mr. Healy," he mumbled, walking

back to the Blind Buck on unsteady legs.

He jockeyed the car around and drove out of the yard, catching a glimpse in his rear view mirror of Don Rogers' staring at him from his perch on top of the corral fence.

Twenty minutes later Joe was slumped over a table at Danny's waiting for a late lunch. The heels of his hands pressed against his forehead. The only other customers were two former bullriders at the far end of the bar. From overhearing past conversations, Joe knew they had each given up the sport about fifty bulls too late.

"Hey Danny, Steve here is trying to give me some advice on a new truck," one of them called out.

"How's it going?" Danny asked from behind the grill where he was charring green and red peppers.

"Between him trying to think of what he was going to say and me trying to remember what he just said, we're having a helluva time." Both men cackled.

"A toast to rodeo," the speaker continued, clinking his beer glass against his buddy's. "One of the few sports left where men don't wear earrings."

"What about the eartags on the steers?" his companion asked blearily, sending his friend into a paroxysm of laughter.

At the sound Joe lifted his head. His gaze roved aimlessly, finally settling on one of the tattered Western prints thumbtacked to the wall. It showed a hunched buffalo, head lowered, surrounded by wolves. I know exactly how he feels, Joe thought dispiritedly.

Danny set a bottle of Coke and a plate of soft tacos on the table. Joe pushed the Coke away. "I ordered a beer, Danny," he said irritably.

Danny pushed the Coke back. "No *cervezas, José.* It's not the time."

Joe's fist crashed onto the table, making the utensils jump. "When will the right time be, Danny? When she's on the bus to Florence?" He stared into Danny's sympathetic eyes. "What am I going to do?"

Danny sat down and grasped Joe's wrists. "I don't know, but you can't quit. You are all she has." His fingers dug into Joe's flesh.

"Listen to me. I want to repeat to you what my father used to tell me whenever I was trying to do something hard, something I was not sure I could do. He would say '*Daniel*, the chicken, she plays a part in bacon-and-eggs, but the pig, he is committed.'"

But look where the pig is the next morning, Joe thought, unsure what his friend was trying to convey to him.

"I know you, my friend," Danny explained. "You are not just involved, you are committed. You will find a way to help her." Danny got up from the table. "Now eat. You need your strength."

The front door banged open. "Joe!"

Riley strode across the room and sat in the chair Danny had vacated. "I've been looking for you, buddy. Good thing I saw the car." He twisted in his seat. "Nothing for me, Danny."

The *cantina* proprietor inclined his head and walked back behind the bar as Riley dragged his chair around the table next to Joe's. It was the first time Joe had seen his friend since the murders. The skin seemed tighter around his eyes and his tan was tinged with ash, but his manner was as breezy as always. Joe wasn't surprised. He knew Riley kept his feelings away from the light. But he also knew loss buried didn't ache any less.

"I'm sorry about your aunt and –" he began awkwardly.

"It's okay," Riley interrupted brusquely. "At least they know who did it."

Anguish tightened the muscles on Joe's face.

"Hey." Riley put his arm around his roping partner's shoulders and tipped his blond head close to Joe's dark one. "I didn't –"

"Where were you last night?" Joe blurted.

Riley pulled his arm away and stared at his friend. "Should I have my lawyer here?" His light tone sounded almost forced.

Joe rubbed his face with his hands. "I'm sorry. I didn't mean it that way. I was checking Chuck Healy's alibi. He said he was at Shorty's."

Riley waved away the apology. "Don't worry about it, amigo. Healy was there. It's hard to miss that big buckskin of his."

Joe picked up a fork and poked at his cooling food before setting it down again.

"Riley, do you know of anyone, I mean anyone, who was mad at Sonny?"

Riley shook his head. "You know we weren't that close. He didn't confide in me."

"Well, had you heard of anybody having an argument or a disagreement with him recently?"

Riley reached for the Coke bottle. He picked at the label with a fingernail.

"C'mon, Riley," Joe pressed.

"The last blow up I know about was the one he had with Mia." Riley avoided Joe's eyes. Bits of metallic paper littered the table.

"Mia? Why would he have a fight with Mia?"

Riley studied the bottle in his hand. The clatter of pots from the kitchen had momentarily stopped, and the two cowboys were silent, nursing their beers. In the corner, the refrigerator hummed, sounding overloud in the otherwise still space.

"I thought you knew," Riley at last said through barely parted lips.

"Knew what?" Joe demanded.

"About Mia and Sonny. They used to be a couple. That is, until Sonny dumped her last month."

Chapter 13

Joe was shocked. She lied to me, thrummed through his head. *No!* his heart shouted. *Riley was wrong. He had to be.* Joe pushed his tongue against the back of his teeth, the denial vibrating against his palate. Then it hit him.

Oh God, he thought. How could he have been so naive? He had wanted her to be innocent. There was a dull ache behind his eyes. He had been so blind. He had wanted her.

She lied to me. She lied to me. The words beat a tattoo across his brain.

"Riley, are you going to the office?" he asked thickly.

"Yeah. I thought we'd –"

"Please tell Lydia I won't be back today." Joe forgot to pay for his uneaten meal in his rush to his car.

He sat at the small table in a state of anger that, under his raw feelings, he knew was inappropriate. Mia sat across from him. Her hair looked dry and coarse, and her skin was taut across the sharp bones of her face.

"So you knew absolutely nothing about inheriting under the new will," Joe said for the third time in five minutes.

"I told you: Mrs. Barrett used to say she would take care of me, but I thought it was just a figure of speech. I didn't take it seriously." Mia looked at him, her eyes dark pools drawing him into their depths. "Why do you keep asking me these questions?" She cocked her head as though to be sure to hear his answer.

He steeled himself. "Were you ever involved with Sonny?"

Mia became very still, her gaze holding his like a fishhook. Seconds ticked by. As he watched, something behind her eyelids closed to him. Joe felt his heart contract.

When she spoke, her voice came without inflection. "Yes, we saw each other for a while."

"This is the man you're accused of killing!" Joe shot to his feet, his jealousy overcome by fury. He stood over her, trembling. She looked up at him without blinking.

"Why didn't you tell me?" he asked through jaw muscles so taut he had trouble forming his words.

Her lips parted slightly then pressed together again. "You and I barely know each other," she said finally, her expression unreadable. The chill in her voice nicked the edge of his heart.

"Apparently." Joe left the room.

Joe sat on the front steps of his adobe. The day was still brilliant, with just a puff of wind. While Java looked on worshipfully, Farley stretched out next to him, his throaty rumble of a purr at full throttle as Joe kneaded the ruff around his neck. Eyes closed in happiness, the cat tipped back his head so Joe could scratch under his chin, losing his balance in his bliss. He tumbled to the ground, landing in an undignified sprawl. Scrambling to his feet, he proceeded to smooth his coat with his tongue, feigning nonchalance. Joe smiled for the first time that day.

Joe patted his thigh and Java came forward for her share of attention. He scratched behind her ears and down her spine while the big dog wiggled in ecstasy.

"You're a golden retriever in a rottweiler body," he told her.

Java panted happily. After a final rub he pushed the sturdy black-and-tan body away and stood, dusting off his jeans.

"Time to see if Will Rogers was right about the world looking better from the back of a horse."

Joe guided Cricket along the familiar path. The even cadence of his horse's walk soothed the remnants of his rage, and the sun warmed the left side of his face. He felt the iciness that gripped his heart start to thaw under the kiln-like heat, leaving him feeling as empty as the acres around him.

Once past the YJ's northern fenceline, he turned east. A taupe coyote flashed through the taupe landscape, moving so lightly its tracks were the only confirmation it was earthbound.

A whistle behind him broke through his musings, and he twisted in the saddle, squinting at the approaching cloud of dust. Recognizing the rider on the loping horse, he reined Cricket to a stop. Michael Chiago came up next to him, his mount's saddleless back slick with sweat.

"Afternoon," Chiago said.

Joe nodded.

"Want company?"

"Okay." Joe squeezed his legs and Cricket resumed her walk. Chiago's bay fell into step beside the chestnut.

"I heard what happened," Chiago said after a few strides. "I'm sorry for Mia. She's a nice girl."

Joe didn't say anything. A hawk coasted overhead, tracing patterns against the washed-out sky. Pebbles falling off a near-by low rock marked a chuckwalla's scuttle for cover, his sunbathing interrupted.

A thought struck Joe. Chiago had been quite adamant, even vehement, about his people's claim to the Barrett Ranch.

"Michael, where were you last night?" Joe broke the silence, half-disgusted with himself for asking the question but unable not to.

"Do you accuse me of murder?" Carbon-hard eyes studied Joe from under blunt-cut black hair.

"I know you're the man in charge of war, and you think the Barrett Ranch belongs to your people," Joe countered.

Michael Chiago laughed, his teeth startling white in the coppery planes of his face. "You think we're going to come swarming over the hill shooting arrows from our bows? Even Injuns are savvy to modern methods, my friend."

"What are you talking about?" Joe asked, too worn out to think.

"Lawsuits, of course. These days we collect attorney's fees instead of scalps. In any event, if I had killed the Barretts, I wouldn't be here now."

"Why not?"

"The Tohono 'O'odham believe that to kill someone infects you with a type of bad magic. A man who has taken another's life must stay alone in the desert for sixteen days, purifying himself through fasting, dancing, and other rituals. Even if I do not always subscribe to all the old ways, I could not insult my father or the rest of my community by failing to do these things."

"I'm sorry," Joe rebuked himself for his accusation. *Let this thing go.*

"Don't be con –" Chiago reined his horse to an abrupt stop. "Look at this." Curious white cattle faces stared back at them.

"What is it?" Joe asked, surveying the thirty-odd Herefords on the other side of the fence. They were younger animals, the source of steaks and other choice and prime cuts for restaurants and supermarkets.

Michael Chiago dismounted and examined the barbed wire. The small herd pushed forward restlessly, lowing and scraping at the ground, which was littered with hay remnants. Joe watched Chiago unhook the top strand of wire and pull it back.

"Pretty easy for cows to go missing if there's a hole in the fence." Chiago refastened the wire, grabbed a handful of black mane and swung up onto his horse's back.

"Rustlers dump hay on the other side of a fence in an area that's isolated but still accessible by truck," he continued. "The cows get accustomed to the sound of the engine and come when they hear it. After a few visits they leave the feed in the truck and open the gate they've made in the fence. The cattle load themselves and the rustlers drive them away."

Chiago nodded at the milling animals. "Looks as though these guys are hungry. The thieves are probably due back fairly soon."

"What about the brand?" Joe asked, indicating the "YJ" mark on the jostling hips. "Wouldn't the inspector catch it at the slaughterhouse?" He knew meat's origin as well as quality was confirmed when it entered the processing plant.

"They might be butchering for their own use, or trucking to a slaughterhouse that is less than careful about checking brands."

Joe remembered Hal telling him thirty-five million cattle had gone to slaughter last year. That was a lot of animals for anyone to keep track of.

"Well, thanks," Joe said. The unbidden return of his distress about Mia muffled his gratitude. "I'd better get back and tell Hal." He pressed his heels into Cricket's side, circling the mare around until the two horses stood head to tail, their riders facing each other.

"Don't be afraid to follow the truth, Joe, wherever it may lead," Chiago said quietly.

"Is that advice from a famous elder of your tribe?" Joe asked.

"Nope. Yours." Chiago clucked to his horse, and the bay started forward at a trot, weaving around the cholla. Joe turned to watch him go.

"Thomas Jefferson" floated back to him as Chiago rode into the shrub-choked wash.

Chapter 14

Friday, October 18

Joe poked his access card into the reader while stifling a yawn. While tossing and turning the night before, he'd reminded himself the last thing he needed to do now was lose his job. Prompted by the assignments piling up on his desk and fueled by two cups of coffee, he made it to the office an hour early.

The door clicked open. He walked through the reception area and turned right, almost breaking through a strip of yellow "Crime Scene" tape suspended across the hallway. He turned around to see Forrest Whitford being herded under protest into the main conference room by a uniformed officer.

"If you'll step into here, please," the officer said, waving Joe forward.

Two men in jumpsuits wheeled a gurney around the opposite corner. A large dark green plastic bag was balanced on top. Joe's stomach roiled.

If I never see another one of these again it won't be too soon, he thought.

"I can't get this zipper up," one of the men said.

"Here, I've got something to cover her," the other replied. "Hold up a minute." They stopped, pinning Joe between their cargo and the taped off hallway. He couldn't help but look.

It was Trudy. Disheveled hair and exaggerated pink circles on wedding gown white cheeks made her look like a discarded doll.

He could see the blue veins running down the underside of one arm. Joe caught a glimpse of her T-shirt before the drape settled over her. "Denial is Not a River in Egypt" it proclaimed, underlined with a brown-red smear Joe belatedly realized was blood.

Once the gurney was out of the way, the patrolman ushered Joe into the conference room where the other early morning arrivals were already assembled. Lydia looked at him with concern.

"Joe, are you all right?" she asked. "You seem a little pale."

"I'm okay," he said, willing his breakfast to stay put. "What happened?"

"Poor Trudy. Sydney found her in the file room this morning, caught between the racks. No one knows much more than that."

Joe grimaced. Like most law firms, BH&M had more paper than space to keep it. In an effort to win the storage war, the firm had invested in a motorized shelving system. Four rows of gray metal shelves ran floor to ceiling, mounted on metal tracks. One row was against the far wall, with the other three pushed up next to each other on the opposite side, leaving a three and a half foot aisle in between. Joe knew every shelf was filled to capacity with red file folders full of documents. He figured each eight-row tier of shelving held more than a thousand pounds of paper.

Only two banks of shelves could be accessed at a time: those bordering the aisle. The shelves moved laterally so the corridor could be created where it was needed. Pushing a button and twisting the dial on the panel by the door moved the chosen shelf in the designated direction, stopping it when it was within an inch of its neighbor.

But how could Trudy have been caught? Joe tried to quash his mental picture of her slim body being crushed between two slabs of paper and metal. He knew there was a safety override. Anything more than trivial weight on the floor between two racks prevented them from closing. Further lurid imaginings were interrupted by Forrest's increasingly loud argument with the patrolman.

"My pretrial conference starts in ninety minutes. The case file is in my office. If you won't let me get it, then send one of your people. Because of this –" Forrest spit the words out through clenched teeth, "this incident, I have to make my appearance by telephone. But I can't make my argument without that file!" He glared at the stoic officer.

Joe listened, stunned, remembering the scene he'd witnessed between the paralegal and the lawyer at the restaurant. Trudy was dead, and Forrest's overriding concern was a court date?

But Mia's in jail for a double murder reminded the tiny voice from the rear of his brain. And your big worry this morning was keeping your job.

"It's not the same thing." He felt the beginnings of a headache.

"Pardon?" Lydia asked.

"Just thinking out loud." Joe's pain intensified. "You know, Lydia, you were right. I don't feel very well. Do you think he'll let me go to the washroom?"

Lydia spoke to the officer, who beckoned Joe through the door, heightening Forrest's aggravation.

Alone in the tiled space, Joe splashed cold water onto his face, then pressed a damp paper towel to his forehead. He looked at himself in the mirror.

"It's not the same at all," he said to his reflection.

On his way back to the conference room, he stopped at the water fountain in the lobby.

"The second to last door on the right. It's on my credenza," he heard Forrest say, followed by the sound of a door closing and footsteps retreating down the wood-planked hallway. Dabbing at the water drops on his chin with his sleeve, Joe walked into the reception area, unnoticed and alone.

Acting without thinking, he bypassed the closed double doors and turned left, following the hallway around the corner. The door to the file room was open. Joe looked in and inhaled sharply. A spill of crimson liquid, its edges smudged with footprints, spread across the vinyl tiles. His heart fluttered and his legs started to tremble. It was the Barrett kitchen all over again.

The remembered queasiness returned with a vengeance. His balance momentarily abandoning him, he stumbled forward into the room, grabbing one of the file racks for support. Lowering himself to a squat, he dropped his head between his knees, trying to keep the heaves at bay. A corner of white on the floor under the bottom shelf edged into the periphery of his blurred vision. He semiconsciously reached for it, seeking a focus point away from the gore.

It was an envelope addressed to Trudy, in care of the firm. He stared at the writing on its face while he pressed his forehead against the cool metal siding, waiting for the roaring in his ears to subside and his stomach to settle.

"Hey, what are you doing in here? This is a crime scene. Out, now!"

The cop hoisted him to his feet. In his haste to comply, Joe stuffed the found envelope into his pocket and allowed himself to be led back to the conference room, where Riley had just arrived.

"What a day to be late! What's going on?" Riley guided Joe to a pair of empty chairs on the far side of the table.

Joe explained what had happened before the events of the morning and his lack of sleep overwhelmed him. Succumbing to exhaustion and the pain that was beginning to radiate from his temples, he pillowed his head on folded arms and tuned out Forrest's complaints about false imprisonment, not speaking to anyone else until Harrington called for the group's attention almost an hour later.

"Ladies and gentlemen," the senior partner began, the furrows bracketing his mouth looking deeper than usual, "as you may know, a terrible tragedy has occurred. The firm will be closed for the rest of the day. I understand Officer Frampton has made arrangements to speak with several of you." Joe started at the name. "Please meet him in the small conference room off the reception area. The police have asked that the rest of you leave the premises immediately so they can continue with their work. Officer Young will retrieve any personal items you need. Thank you." Forrest bolted through the door, the rest of the room's occupants following more slowly.

"Mr. McGuinness?" Harrington raised his voice over the group's subdued murmur. Joe looked up. "Would you stay a moment, please?"

Riley threw him a questioning look. Joe shrugged, his mind too battered by recent events and lack of sleep to have any idea what Harrington wanted.

After the last person left, Harrington shut the door.

"Mr. McGuinness, what I'm about to tell you must be kept confidential."

Joe nodded reluctantly. Lately, knowing things that were supposed to be secret only seemed to bring him trouble.

"The police explained to me that Ms. Cummings was found trapped between two of the filing racks." The older lawyer removed his glasses and massaged the bridge of his nose. Slipping the glasses back on, he looked at Joe. "She died from a puncture wound. Apparently a letter opener had been left on one of the shelves. It pierced her chest cavity when the racks came together."

Joe shuddered. "What about the pressure pads?"

As had been explained his first week at the firm, sensors were embedded in the file room floor. If more than fifty pounds of weight were detected, the moving rack automatically stopped approximately two feet from the ones on either side of it.

"The police surmised she cued the racks to close, then attempted to take down a file from a rack moving toward another, stepping onto its bottom shelf so as not to trigger the pads. Something happened to delay her – perhaps her clothing caught on a shelf –and the racks closed, with the letter opener –" Harrington left the sentence unfinished. Joe winced at the image of Trudy's frantic scramble to free herself. She must have been in excruciating pain.

Harrington cleared his throat. "A substance believed to be cocaine was found in her jacket pocket. Dealer weight was the term the officer used."

Another reason the accident could have happened, Joe thought.

"I've already spoken to her parents," Harrington continued. "They are flying in from out of the country. They have asked if we would collect her personal things that are here and deliver them to her apartment. Apparently she lives, was living, with a young man. The police informed me you can have access to her office tomorrow."

"Certainly, sir." My role at the firm, he thought. Call Joe when you want dead people's stuff picked up.

Jerry Dan met up with Joe in the parking garage.

"I overheard one of the forensic guys talking," Jerry Dan stage-whispered over the roof of the Blind Buck. "He said they're not so sure Trudy's death was an accident. Someone could have stabbed Trudy and then closed the files on her afterward."

"Mmmm," Joe replied, trying to fit his car key into the slot in the door. His head was throbbing too much for him to cope with one of Jerry Dan's outlandish theories.

"He said the button that moves the shelves didn't have any fingerprints on it," Jerry Dan pressed. "Not even Trudy's."

The pounding of Joe's pulse in his ears grew louder and more insistent as he paused to study his friend.

Jerry Dan solemnly returned his gaze. "Makes you wonder about Atticus, doesn't it?"

Joe broke his key off in the lock.

Chapter 15

The locksmith took two hours and fifty-two dollars, including a ten-dollar charge for the out-of-date key blank. Joe drove home with gritted teeth and a hand raised against the glare. The headache that had been threatening all day had finally arrived full force. Leaving his clothes where they dropped on the floor, he swallowed three aspirin and collapsed onto his bed, not waking until the late afternoon.

Lying on his back with his hands folded behind his head, he stared up at the ceiling, still exhausted.

I need more than sleep, he decided, rolling over to check the clock on his nightstand. Deciding it wasn't too late, he pulled on a pair of jeans and jogged down to the barn.

"Hiya, girl. Bet you didn't expect to see me again so soon."

Joe pulled a carrot out of his back pocket and broke it in half. Cricket's ears pricked up at the sound and she moved forward eagerly. Velvet lips tickled his palm.

"How about a quick ride?" He stroked the arch of her neck.

The chestnut, still chewing, bumped him with her nose.

Joe tacked up the mare quickly, then gathered the reins and stepped into the stirrup. He figured he could make it out and back on the trail that looped around the county land northwest of the ranch and still beat the sun to the horizon.

The horse stretched out her neck as she walked along the well-worn track. Joe made himself comfortable in the saddle and let his mind empty.

Tall ocotillos stretched their thin arms upward, stark against a western sky already fading into yellow where it met the land, a harbinger of the spectrum of color it would later smear around the descending orb. Shadows lengthened, and the small desert noises hushed as the creatures of the day retired to safe havens in advance of nocturnal predators. The heat had begun to dissipate. Soon the night's chill would set in.

Cricket jogged around the collection of boulders that marked the halfway point. Some towered over the top of Joe's head. Once she was headed back the way she had come, the mare accelerated her pace, impatient to return to her flake of alfalfa and warm stall.

A loud crack ruptured the stillness, and the cantle of Joe's saddle jolted forward.

Cricket humped her back and bucked, startled by the impact. Joe grabbed for the saddlehorn and hung on. When the mare's four feet landed on the ground again, he pulled on one rein and spun the spooked horse around, spurring her toward the protection of the rocks.

Pulling up behind a boulder outcropping, he dismounted and peered cautiously around a jagged granite edge, scanning the landscape. He had recognized the sound of a rifle shot, having heard it many times before, especially around calving season. Joe had never seen coyotes eat anything but rabbit, but many cowboys used their rifles on them anyway.

A horse and rider galloped north in the distance, squirts of dust marking their course. Joe strained to see in the failing light.

"Damn!" he exclaimed in frustration. The rider was too far away to identify. The pair swung eastward behind a screen of palo verdes. Joe tracked them with his eyes. There was a flash of brown and black where the trees thinned before they plunged into a wash and were lost to view.

Joe stepped back and spoke soothingly to the still trembling mare while he thoughtfully fingered the crease left in the back of his saddle by the bullet.

The horse he'd seen was a bay. Like the one Michael Chiago rode.

Chapter 16

Saturday, October 19

Joe got off the elevator, carrying a cup of coffee with a bagel balanced on the lid in one hand and a cardboard carton in the other. He figured if he worked the whole weekend he might be caught up by Monday. He hadn't told Hal or Riley or anybody else about what had happened in the desert yesterday afternoon. What was there to tell? he had asked himself after he fed and watered Cricket and sat down to a dinner of microwaved chili. He didn't know who had shot at him, not for sure anyway. And it could have been an accident, he had rationalized while rinsing off his dishes; merely a cowboy aiming for a coyote. Resolving to worry only about hanging onto his job, Joe had set the alarm for five and crawled under the covers.

The door to the reception area was propped open, the firm branding iron jammed under the handle, not unusual for a Saturday. It was the lawyers' solution to restroom and water fountain access without having to use the card reader. What surprised Joe was that someone had beat him to the office. He checked his watch. It wasn't even seven o'clock.

He walked to his office, set his coffee on his desk, and looked at his in-basket while chewing on his bagel. Lydia had put the overflow next to it, making a pile almost as tall as the original. He thought again about his plan for catching up. Make that a week from Monday, he mentally corrected.

The document on top of the stack closest to him was several inches thick. "The Stefanopolos Family Trust" read the cover sheet. Joe groaned. Translating the testamentary desires of the Stefanopolos clan patriarch into binding legalese had been his most difficult assignment to date from Harrington. I'll collect Trudy's stuff first, he decided. Carrying the box he'd brought from home, he walked down the hall, pushed open the door, and stared.

Her office looked as though it had been turned upside down and shaken. Papers were strewn across the floor, two drawers from the credenza overturned on top of them. The plants from the windowsill had been dumped out of their pots, their exposed roots making them look bare and defenseless. A chair lay on its back. A T-shirt dangled from one of its legs. He righted the chair and picked up the shirt. "Let's Put the 'Fun' Back in Dysfunctional" was printed across its front.

His stomach tightened. *What had someone been looking for?* He shook his head, embarrassed at his momentary panic. You're getting paranoid, he chided himself. Obviously the police searched her office as part of their investigation.

"I just didn't think they'd make such a mess," he muttered, getting down on his hands and knees to sort through the clutter. Working his way around the room, Joe stacked firm documents on top of the credenza and put Trudy's personal items into the box. Twenty minutes later, he crawled into the well of her desk to retrieve the last of the loose papers.

"Ouch!" He banged his head on the bottom of the middle drawer. Looking up to check his headroom, he saw what appeared to be a sheet of brown paper taped to the wood. He reached up and pulled it down. It was a sealed envelope.

Carefully backing out from under the desk, he turned it over. Nothing was written on either side. Joe sat back on his heels, ran his car key under the envelope's flap, and dumped out the contents: two folded pieces of paper, a book of matches, and a bankbook.

First he examined the matchbook. "Club Diana" was embossed across the front in gold script. On the back was a Phoenix address. Joe had never heard of the place.

Opening the bankbook, he saw Trudy had set up the account

at the beginning of the month. He flipped the page to check the deposit record and let out a low whistle. The opening balance was a hundred dollars. Ten thousand more had been added a week ago. He turned to the next page and scanned the figures. Withdrawals totaled about thirty-five hundred dollars. Maybe the stories about Trudy's salary had been true, Joe mused. A piece of paper fluttered out from between the pages, and he picked it up. Dated yesterday, it was a deposit slip. The amount on the last line was also ten thousand. Was Trudy expecting another paycheck so soon?

He smoothed out the two pieces of paper that had also been in the envelope. One was the first page of a motion to dismiss a complaint and request for sanctions brought by defendant CelGen against KB Enterprises. "Atticus Barclay 22410 and Forrest Whitford 44548" was typed in the upper left corner, identifying them as the BH&M lawyers representing CelGen. Joe didn't know anything about KB Enterprises.

The other document appeared to be the top half of a letter from Cordelia Barrett to her bank. Printed on stationery engraved with her name and Pinnacle Peak address, it had been ripped in half across the salutation. The bank's name and address in the upper left corner and "Dear Mr. –" was all that was left.

He set the bankbook aside, intending to ask Harrington what to do with it, and slipped the papers and matchbook back into the envelope. Did it go to the police or her parents? Probably not the police. Despite Jerry Dan's view, Trudy's death was accidental, and although the bankbook might be some evidence on the drug charge, the other things he had found certainly were not.

But something stopped him from dropping the envelope into the carton with the rest of her things. He knew doing that was the equivalent of throwing it away. He thought about Trudy. She had hidden the items for a reason. Out of a sense of obligation to her, he'd make an effort to find out why.

Taking the firm directory out of the bottom drawer of her desk, he flipped through the pages and called the telephone number after Trudy's name.

"Lo," answered a deep voice, thick with sleep.

"Good morning. My name's Joe McGuinness and I'm a lawyer at the firm where Trudy worked. Am I speaking with her –" Joe hesitated. *Roommate? Boyfriend?*

"I'm Chaz, her boyfriend."

"Chaz, her parents have asked me to take her personal things from the firm to your place so they can get them when they pick up the rest of her stuff. Would now be a convenient time for me to come over?"

"Might as well," Chaz said. He confirmed the address Joe read to him from the directory and hung up.

Joe pulled up in front of an older apartment building. A nondescript flat-topped oblong two stories high, it was sheathed in coral stucco, the west-facing walls faded to light pink. Scraggly stunted bushes whose only flowers were discarded fast food wrappers stood in the narrow band of dirt between the building and the stained sidewalk.

He got out of Blind Buck, which didn't look out of place in the neighborhood, and walked into the building's courtyard. Strands of bougainvillea waved dispiritedly over the top of the chain link fence surrounding a drained swimming pool, the fuchsia blooms clashing with the orange blossoms of the Indian paintbrush and the red berries of the pyracantha growing next to them. The white tiles along the pool's rim were streaked with brown and green, and the plaster interior was veined with cracks. A pile of dried leaves had collected in the deep end. On the far side of the yard, green globes of citrus dangled from densely leafed orange trees with gnarled whitewashed trunks.

Joe climbed chipped concrete stairs to the second floor and walked down the breezeway until he was standing in front of the door with the right number on it. He propped the screen open with his elbow and rapped the knocker twice.

A young man dressed in a T-shirt printed with the name of what Joe presumed to be a musical group opened the door. His multicolored hair stood out in tufts as though he had just gotten out of bed, although Joe suspected it looked that way all the time. Red-streaked eyes looked out of a pale lean face. Joe tried not to stare at the ring through his eyebrow.

"Chaz?" Joe asked.

"That's me. Come on in."

"Thanks." Joe set his cardboard carton down and looked around the room. Across from the sagging couch and stained coffee table were a new-looking thirty-two inch Sony television and a high-end stereo system that included a pair of speakers four feet tall. Joe was impressed. His electronic possessions were limited to a twelve-inch portable TV and a Discman.

Chaz walked over to the pile of T-shirts stacked on one end of the sofa. On top was a green one Joe didn't remember seeing before. "Only Idiots Read T-shirt Slogans" it said.

"I thought I'd pick out something for her to wear, you know, for when they put her in –" Chaz choked on the words.

"I'm sorry," Joe said.

Chaz swiped at his eyes with the back of his hand. "What do you think?" he asked, holding up two shirts. "Born Again Pagan" was printed in white on hot pink; white writing on a blue background proclaimed "God Grades On A Curve."

Joe thought of how the firm would seem just a little more ordinary without Trudy's ever-changing T-shirts and hair color or her tart comments on the legal world.

"Actually," Joe said, surprised at the catch in his throat, "I think either would be fine."

"Yeah, I thought her parents would like something religious. I'll give 'em both and let them choose." He clutched the T-shirts to his chest, his eyes filling again. "She was a good person, you know. What they said about her dealing drugs was a lie."

"What do you mean?" Joe asked.

"Trudy wasn't like that. She didn't even use. Said it was bad for her vocal chords. And there's no way she would deal."

Joe nodded without saying anything.

"Look, just because we don't dress the same as you doesn't mean we're druggies," Chaz burst out.

Joe felt old, despite the fact there wasn't that much difference in his and Chaz's age. He remembered friends from high school making a similar speech to their parents.

"I mean it," Chaz went on. "We were saving money so our band could cut a demo record and go to LA."

"Looks like you were spending some of it, too." Joe glanced at the big TV.

Chaz shook his head emphatically. "I'm telling ya, Trudy wasn't dealing. This stuff came from her bonuses."

"Bonuses?" Joe asked.

"Yeah. She said all of you guys thought she was hot, that she practically did her boss's job for him."

Joe slipped the bankbook out of his pocket. "This was in her office." He handed it to Chaz who looked at the cover and flipped through the pages.

"Oh, wow." His jaw sagged open when he saw the account balance.

"You seem surprised," Joe said.

"Are you kidding? I thought she had gotten an extra grand, maybe two. With money like this we could have gone to LA, cut a demo, and maybe had enough left over for a used van, too."

"Was she expecting another bonus?" Joe asked, thinking of the deposit slip.

"She didn't say anything," Chaz replied. "But that don't mean much." He swept a hand toward the electronics equipment. "I didn't know this stuff was coming until it showed up."

On impulse, Joe took out the rest of the things that had been in the brown envelope and showed them to Chaz. "I found these with the bankbook. Do they mean anything to you?"

Chaz examined the letter fragment and legal pleading. "Nope." He looked at the matchbook. Recognition flickered across his face.

"Trudy and I went there to see the Idiot Savants a coupla weeks ago, you know, that new band from Portland. She saw one of your lawyers there and got all excited."

"Who did she see?"

"I think she said her name was Cindy or something like that."

"Sydney, maybe?"

"Yeah, that's it." He handed back the papers.

Joe picked up the bankbook. "I have to keep this until I know whose it is."

Chaz shrugged. The animation that had appeared when he talked about his plans with Trudy had vanished.

"I really am sorry."

"Thanks." Chaz blinked rapidly, trying to keep the tears at

bay.

Joe walked to the door.

"Are you planning to check out that club?" Chaz asked.

"I was thinking about it. Why?" Joe replied.

"I don't think it'd be your scene."

Joe opened his mouth to protest. He wasn't as old or out of it as Chaz thought.

"It's a lez bar, man," Chaz continued. "You know, dykes. But the music's decent."

Joe swallowed his lecture, mumbled, "Thanks again," and left. The screen door banged behind him.

Chapter 17

Sunday, October 20

The alarm woke Joe at five on Sunday morning. He had forgotten to turn it off. Returning to the firm after leaving Chaz' apartment, he had worked through the backlog of papers on his desk until late in the evening. Too tired to wait for even a microwave dinner to heat, he had shucked off his clothes and crawled under the comforter, asleep before he could turn off the bedside lamp.

Shuffling out to the kitchen in search of a simple breakfast, he saw through still heavy-lidded eyes the message light on his answering machine blinking in two beat intervals. The first caller was Riley.

"Hi, bro' – what's going on? Merchant has had me closeted on this CelGen deal. Let's catch lunch or a ride. I want to know what you've been up to. Call me."

The second message was from Jerry Dan.

"Joe, I tried to catch you at the office." His voice radiated concern. "I hope you're okay. If there's anything I can do –" Jerry Dan paused too long and the machine had cut him off.

Deciding to talk to his friends when he was more awake, Joe chewed on a granola bar and looked longingly at his bed. But the thought of his still full in-basket propelled him into the shower, out of the house, and behind the wheel of his car. He was so fatigued he felt as if he were sleepwalking.

Working without a break, he put the last of his dictation

tapes on Lydia's desk in the early afternoon and admired his clear desktop with bleary-eyed satisfaction. All Stefanopoli bequests had been taken care of, down to the single dime Franco wanted to leave his youngest grandson "because that boy, he no can save even one."

Like George Carlin used to say, stuff, stuff, and more stuff. Joe put away the last of the files. Viewed from the perspective of Trusts and Estates law, life was simply about getting money, using some of it to buy stuff, and then figuring out to whom to leave your stuff and money because you usually died before you could use up either of them. And deciding, too, what message you wanted to send to those who were still going to be around, he mentally added, thinking of the pages of instructions in the file from Franco.

Be careful about being too critical, he warned himself. Just what had he done lately that went beyond his self-interest? This last musing prompted him to reach for the phone. Trudy's death and his load at work had taken his time but not his thoughts from Mia. He had already dialed the number twice that morning, but this time he didn't hang up after the first ring.

"Hello?"

"I'd like to speak to Mia – Miguela Ortiz, please."

"What department is she in?"

"She's in custody," Joe chewed on his lip, hating the words.

"And you are?"

"Joseph McGuinness, a lawyer." He hadn't known if prisoners were allowed to take calls from the outside other than from their counsel, and anyway it wasn't exactly a lie.

A clunk had sounded in his ear as though the receiver had been dropped onto a counter. Almost three minutes passed before the voice had come back on the line.

"She does not want to take your call."

"But –" There was a click, followed by a dial tone.

Joe set the receiver down. He couldn't really blame her for not wanting to talk to him. He'd replayed their argument over and over in his mind, and was ashamed of how he'd acted. Joe knew his accusations were ridiculous. But if Mia wouldn't talk to him, how could he ever explain? And what about his promise to prove her innocence?

Discouraged and drained, he walked out to the parking garage. The urge to sleep on the drive home was overwhelming. Cranking down the window, he tilted his head into the breeze as he forced himself to sing along with the blaring radio. He drifted across the asphalt several times, the double yellow line on the wrong side of the car before he realized it and swerved back into his lane. The last five miles he used his fingers to hold open first one eyelid, then the other. Pulling up next to his front door, he turned off the ignition, closed his eyes, and tilted his head back, gathering himself to go inside.

"Hey Joe! Wake up!" Knuckles rapped on the glass.

Joe blinked open his eyes and rubbed the back of his neck, his muscles stiff.

"Huh?"

Hal's face grinned back at him from outside the car. Joe checked his watch. Four o'clock. At least I got an hour's nap, he thought.

He got out of the car and stretched, the bones in his back cracking.

"Afternoon, Hal. How's it going?"

Java trotted over at the sound of his voice. Farley didn't stir from his patch of sun on the top step.

"You taking Cricket out?"

Joe rubbed his jaw, feeling the stubble. He hadn't done a very good job shaving that morning. "I better. She didn't get worked yesterday."

"Mind riding the north fence line?" Hal's face creased with worry. "Even though I rewired that section of fence, I'm four short on my count from two days ago."

Joe's mind flashed back to his last ride in the desert. He had already decided not to tell Hal about the shooting. There was a chance it was an accident, and the grizzled old foreman had enough on his mind with the missing stock. Still, it didn't hurt to be careful. "Can I take Java with me?" He hoped the dog would at least bark if someone got too close.

"Sure. She could use the exercise." Hal fondled the dog's ears. "Don't want you getting fat, do we girl?" Java leaned against the old cowboy's legs, squirming with happiness. Farley sat with his paws tucked under him, eyes squeezed into slits against the sun, showing no interest in the topic of exercise.

Stepping over the cat, Joe went inside to change clothes while Hal tacked up Cricket.

"Have a good ride." Hal slapped Joe on the leg once he was mounted up. Joe whistled to Java, who barked her acceptance of his invitation.

Cricket walked down the driveway toward Scottsdale Road with Java zigzagging in front, nose to the ground. A few hundred yards short of the pavement, Joe reined the mare north, picking up the track that ran outside the barbed wire fence marking the YJ eastern boundary. They stayed on the trail, paralleling the fence, cutting west and then turning north again.

Cricket tossed her head impatiently and jigged a few steps. Joe let her break into a jog. Java bounded through the brush, chasing every rabbit she could scare up. After a bit, Joe loosened the reins and Cricket broke into a lope. He kept his eyes on the strands of wire but didn't see any signs of tampering.

A yelp sounded from under a nearby creosote bush.

"Java?" Joe reined to a stop.

The dog hopped toward him, whining and favoring her hind leg. As the rottweiler got closer, Joe saw the cause of her misery. A chunk of teddy bear cholla had attached itself to her hindquarters.

Joe dismounted and called the dog over.

"Easy, girl." Holding the reins in two hands with about a foot of slack between them, he looped the leather around the chunk of cactus and gently tugged. The offending piece fell to the sand. Java licked his hand gratefully.

"Be careful," Joe admonished her, slipping his foot into the stirrup. Mounted again, he continued along the fenceline. As he approached the place where Chiago had found the hidden gate, he slowed Cricket to a walk. The glint of new wire marked where Hal had made his repairs. He pulled up and scanned the area.

What looked to be recent cattle tracks led away from the fence and through the chaparral. Making sure the dog was following, he turned Cricket off the path and followed the marks in the soft ground. A little more than a mile later the sand became hard-packed earth and rock, and the tracks disappeared. After circling for fifteen minutes, he gave up. The trail had vanished.

"Hal won't be happy about this," Joe told Cricket as he stopped in a small clearing for a final inspection of the area.

The sight of a small cottontail huddled under a prickly pear reminded him he hadn't seen Java in a while. He cupped his hand to his ear but heard only the usual small creature and bird noises. Conspicuously absent was the sound of big dog crashing through the desert.

"Java!" Joe's shout startled the bunny into flight.

No response. He stood in his stirrups, put his fingers to his mouth, and whistled.

What sounded like a muffled bark came from somewhere to his left. He rode toward the sound. Cricket picked her way carefully through the spiny underbrush.

"Java?" he called again.

A low "woof" sounded from a stand of palo verde trees. He urged Cricket closer, at last spotting Java stretched out in the meager shade offered by the thin green limbs, tongue lolling to one side.

Joe got off and walked up to the dog.

"Tuckered out, girl?" He stroked her broad head. Java panted her response. Getting his canteen out of his saddlebag, Joe set his battered Stetson upside down on the ground and poured some water into the crown. Java lapped it up, not raising her head until the last drop of moisture was gone.

"You need to recuperate for a bit," Joe admonished.

He wrapped the reins around a branch and loosened the cinch. Cricket sighed and shifted her weight to her near hip, cocking her rear ankle on the off side so the hoof rested on its front edge. Joe sat on a log next to the prone dog. He picked up a stick and scratched along her back with it.

"Feel better?"

Java rolled over, wiggling onto one side and then the other before getting up and shaking herself. A fine cloud of ash rose from her coat, making Joe sneeze.

"What did you get into, girl?" Joe poked at the ground with his stick, unearthing charred wood shards.

Campers, Joe thought with annoyance. Fires were prohibited in the area. A spark could start a conflagration that could sweep across the dry scrub in minutes. He'd tell Hal, sorry to add to the foreman's worries.

He poked at the ashes, making sure they were cold. His stick hit something hard. Reaching down, Joe picked up the piece of metal. It looked like an old misshapen horseshoe or the outline of the club from a deck of cards with its tail missing.

Joe absently turned the strip of iron over in his hand as he thought about the events of the past few weeks. Atticus' death, the Barrett murders, Amber, Mia and her arrest, Trudy's accident: a chain of events that had taken too much from him.

It wasn't fair. He'd already lost more than most. He never laid eyes on his dad, and his brother was gone almost before his memory of him formed. His mother always told him his imagination supplied more than he truly recalled. Clem passed when it was his time, but Joe hadn't been ready to let him go. He needed certain places filled: brother, father, mentor. There were too many vacancies. His life felt like a tipped chessboard, with the pieces sliding off the edge and him helpless to catch them.

He traced patterns in the soil with the shard of iron. A hundred unseen insects hummed overhead. What if his disequilibrium sprang from an internal source? Had his losses so eroded his self-confidence that he had begun embracing things because they were available and not because they were right for him? He thought of Amber again. Yes, he admitted to himself, a big part of why I wanted her was because she wanted me. So am I making the same mistake by staying at the firm?

Java pushed her nose into his hand, its cold dampness interrupting his thoughts. He looked up through the slender branches and saw the light was starting to leech out of the sky.

"Ready for home?" Joe rose to his feet.

A short yip was the response. Retightening the girth, Joe pulled the reins over Cricket's head and swung into the saddle. He steered the mare toward home, the dog trotting alongside. Across the horizon, saguaros stood at attention as the sky lowered its colors in the west. Joe had felt alone many times while riding, but this was the first time he felt lonely, too.

Chapter 18

Monday, October 21

Joe recognized the tall figure walking ahead of him in the parking garage.

"Good morning, Mr. Harrington."

The older man stopped and turned toward him, the lines around his eyes made deeper by the harsh overhead lights or recent events, Joe didn't know which. With more than a little discomfort, Joe recalled the conclusion he had reached last evening as he rode Cricket back to the barn. He knew Harrington was more than good at what he did, and a lawyer interested in probate work could have no better teacher. But, as Joe had finally admitted to himself, he wasn't that lawyer. He didn't want to abandon his dream of trial work, no matter how remote its attainment seemed at the moment.

But the pursuit of his goal had to be postponed for a while longer. He had made a promise to Mia. Staying at the firm, with access to information on the Barretts and relative freedom to investigate, gave him the best opportunity to fulfill it. His conscience pricked him. Even if it made him feel as though he was there under false pretenses.

"Mr. McGuinness," Harrington greeted him with a half nod. They walked wordlessly toward the building lobby.

"I dropped off Trudy's things at her apartment this weekend," Joe offered in an attempt to fill the silence. "I also found this." He handed over the bankbook.

"Thank you." Harrington tucked the vinyl-covered rectangle into the outer pocket of his briefcase as they climbed the steps to the revolving door. At the top, the senior partner paused, his hand on the chrome push bar. The look on his face was one Joe had seen only once or twice, when the question being considered wasn't could they could do something for a client, but rather should they.

"I'm afraid there has been a disturbing development," Harrington said before pushing open the door.

The change in tone had been almost imperceptible, but Joe felt it thrum from the top of his skull to the base of his spine. He knew he didn't want to hear what Harrington was about to say.

Their wingtips echoed hollowly as they crossed the marble floor. "Detective Dresden has revised his preliminary hypothesis regarding Miss Crawford's death," Harrington said.

Joe's stomach tightened. Stopping in front of the elevator door, the older man looked at Joe with weary eyes.

"He believes the girl was murdered."

The inside of Joe's mouth went dry and his tongue felt thick and large. "Why does he think that?"

"I understand there are several reasons," Harrington replied, his usual monotone replaced by a voice that peaked and dipped with emotion. "First, it appears an accident was quite unlikely. The shelf system's safety mechanism was tested a dozen times. On each occasion it worked flawlessly. Further, the evidence technicians found no fingerprints on the letter opener handle or the button that operates the shelves, leading to the conclusion they had been wiped clean or whoever touched them wore gloves. Miss Crawford was barehanded when she was found. "

Why was there a letter opener in the file room in the first place? Joe wondered, thinking of the neatly incised envelopes attached to his daily mail. Trudy had always used the file room's electric model.

"Finally, the medical examiner found the injury site to be inconsistent with the angle or height of the shelf where the opener was found." The older lawyer grimaced as though he were in pain. "Put simply, her wound could only have been inflicted by an upward stab."

Harrington reached out and pushed the "up" button with a

bony finger, the veins on the back of his hand prominent under the translucent skin. The motor whirred and the cables clanged in the shaft as the car started to descend.

"Does he have any idea who did it?"

"That he did not share with me. He did say although the drug and alcohol scans were negative, he is not ruling out a narcotics connection in light of the quantity of cocaine found in Miss Crawford's possession and her patronage of certain nightclubs."

Joe tugged at a loose thread on his sleeve. His conscience poked him again, harder this time. Should he mention the "bonuses" Chaz had told him about? Harrington would know about the balance in her account as soon as he looked at the bankbook. The firm might have actually paid Trudy the extra money. She obviously kept Merchant's practice organized and did more than the average paralegal and secretary combined. But she also could have been selling coke without her boyfriend's knowledge. Joe didn't want to risk alienating Harrington by snooping into staff salary matters or add fuel to the idea the daughter of one of the firm's biggest clients was in fact a drug dealer.

A whoosh of air followed by the ping of an unseen bell announced the elevator's arrival. They entered the wood-paneled space, the doors closed, and the car started to rise, Joe's stomach following half a second later. His conscience's jabs changed to kicks.

There was also the matter of the envelope he had found taped under Trudy's desk. Joe knew he should take it to Dresden and tell him everything he had found out. But he also knew the envelope's contents would likely involve the firm further in Trudy's death. Great last act as an employee, he thought.

He also wasn't sure if what he knew was covered by some sort of employee confidentiality. By talking to the police, he could be putting his job and maybe his law license at risk as well. He glanced at Harrington, noting the drawn features and slight slump of the usually military-square shoulders. I'll wait a little longer, he decided.

The bell sounded again and the doors slid open, revealing "Barclay, Harrington & Merchant" spelled out in chrome on the opposite wall. Joe stepped back to let Harrington exit before him. The senior lawyer paused on the car's threshold.

"Thank you for your help, Mr. McGuinness," he said. "Atticus would have –" The lawyer stopped himself. "Your assistance and discretion have been appreciated."

"Any time, sir." Joe swallowed the revelation of his decision to defect that teetered on the tip of his tongue. I'll tell him soon, he mentally promised as he walked toward his office. *Just a few more days.*

"Assuming I ever get out of the office," he groaned under his breath as he surveyed his desktop a moment later. Someone from Word Processing had stacked the hard copy of his weekend dictation in the middle of his blotter, on top of his earlier versions. The pile had fallen over, mixing pages of the latest printouts with prior drafts. In took him fifteen minutes of comparing document code numbers to segregate out the correct papers for proofreading.

He put the last of the corrected documents onto Lydia's desk several hours later. Dropping off the final memo, he noticed Sydney's door was open. He walked over to the doorway and looked in. Sydney stared out the window, her glasses resting on top of the open casebook in the middle of her desk. He rapped his knuckles softly against the wood.

"Got a minute?"

She gave him a wan smile. Her makeup only partly hid the circles under her eyes. "Sure."

"How's it going?" Joe wondered how to broach the subject of the matchbook and Chaz' disclosure.

"Things are in upheaval around here, aren't they?" Sydney fingered the edge of a page.

"I meant with you. Are you okay?"

"I'm fine." She pushed the book away and folded her hands in front of her. Joe saw the polish on her nails was chipped. Steeling himself, he walked into the room uninvited and stood in front of her desk.

"Sydney, where were you Thursday night?" Joe watched her face.

Her brow knitted as she thought back to last week, then gasped as she realized what he was asking. Her knuckles whitened as she squeezed her hands together.

"I didn't –" she began, then fell silent.

"Sydney, please tell me." Joe felt a tug of guilt. His words were soft and coaxing, like a friend's. Which he knew he wasn't.

"Home. Alone." She slid her eyes away from his. The lie hovered between them.

He hesitated, thinking of the misery he was about to inflict. But then an image of the file room floor flashed before him and he put his compassion away.

"Can you verify that?" he pressed. "Did you talk to anyone on the phone? Watch television?" He felt like a bully.

Two bright spots of color appeared in Sydney's ashen cheeks and she straightened in her chair.

"You have no business accusing –"

Her assertive posture collapsed in sagging defeat as quickly as it had appeared, and she slumped forward, covering her face with her hands.

"This is a nightmare," she said in a voice muffled by tears.

Joe quietly closed her office door. He shifted his weight uncomfortably from one foot to another while she cried. Minutes passed before she wiped her eyes with a tissue and raised her head, meeting his gaze straight on.

"I was at Club Diana the night Trudy was killed." Sydney tilted up her chin. "I went home to my lover's house afterward." She took a deep, shuddering breath. "And yes, I'm gay."

She ran her hand through her hair. "God, I can't tell you how long I've waited to say that to someone here." Tears glistened underneath her lashes. "I just didn't think it would be like this."

"Trudy knew," Joe prompted gently.

Sydney's eyes hardened. "Oh yes, that little bitch knew. But I didn't tell her. She saw me at the club and figured it out. Then she blackmailed me."

Joe blinked in astonishment.

"She even had the gall to describe herself as a reasonable businesswoman.'" Sydney's laugh was devoid of humor. "I had to make only one payment, and she'd keep my secret safe."

"What did you do?" Joe asked.

"I paid her ten thousand dollars a week and a half ago and

TWIST PHELAN

have been living in hell ever since."

"Because she wanted more?"

Sydney's lips twisted into a bitter smile, and she shook her head. "That wasn't it. Trudy actually kept her end of the bargain. No 'knowing' looks in the hallway, no other demands, nothing. But the anticipation ate me up. I was waiting for the other shoe to drop. I mean, have you ever heard of a blackmailer who stops at one installment?"

Joe mutely shook his head. Sydney's brown eyes were sad.

"I may have wanted her dead, but I didn't kill her." Her chest heaved with a sigh. "I know you have to tell that detective about this. Maybe it's all for the best."

Joe gave in to his intuition. "Sydney, I'm not going to say anything to the police or anyone else, at least for now and maybe not ever. I'm sorry if I hurt you. Thanks for telling me about Trudy." As he slipped out of the room, she was lifting the phone out of its cradle.

He retreated to his office, shutting the door behind him. So that's where Trudy's "bonus" had come from, he thought as he paced across his carpet. He knew in his gut Sydney had been telling the truth when she said she hadn't killed Trudy. All that he'd accomplish by talking to the police now would be the exposure of her private life. He couldn't go to Dresden without the answer to the question he started with. If Sydney hadn't killed Trudy, who had?

His intercom buzzed.

"Joe?" Lydia's call crackled through the speaker box.

"Yes?"

"I didn't find the Schneider project on any of these tapes."

Errol Schneider's tax research! He had forgotten all about it. "Not even started, Lydia," he admitted. "I'll be in the library."

He picked up a legal pad off his desk and searched his coat pockets for a pen. His fingers touched a square of paper, and he pulled it out and examined it. It was the envelope he had picked up in the file room the morning Trudy's body had been found. Sent to her by the Arizona Bar Association, it had already been opened. He looked inside. There was no letter, just a check made out to the firm for $225, with "overpayment of bar dues" printed in the memo space in the lower left corner. He walked out to Lydia's station.

"Lydia, could you send this to Accounting or whoever is in charge of bar dues now?" he asked, handing her the envelope with the check inside and filching a pen from the container on her desk. He gave her a rueful smile. "You know where I'll be for the next few hours."

She held up her fingers and wriggled them. "My computer and I will be waiting."

Thirty minutes later he was immersed in the tax digests when Forrest walked into the library. Pulling an evidence treatise down from one of the shelves, he stood next to the table where Joe was working, scanning the index in the back.

This was the first time Joe had seen him since the morning after Trudy's murder. He covertly stared at him, thinking back to what he'd seen at Ciao Mein. He scrutinized the chiseled face for signs of grief without success. *Jerry Dan's right. The man's got the feelings of a machine.*

Forrest glanced down, his eyes meeting Joe's. "Yes?" he asked brusquely.

Joe floundered for a response. "Ah, I just, ah, wanted to say I'm sorry about Trudy."

A look – panic? anger? – flitted across the lawyer's face, momentarily stripping him of his usual haughty demeanor. A stain of red crept across the skin above his starched white collar.

"Yes, well, thank you," he muttered through tight lips. Abandoning the book he had been reading, he strode from the room.

Great. Now he thinks I was goading him about his affair with Trudy. He tapped his pen on his pad in self-annoyance. *Think you can get through the rest of the day without annoying any other senior lawyers?* He reached for the next volume, committing himself to dictating a first draft before breaking for lunch as penance.

Several hours later, Joe's stomach growled loud enough for Lydia to hear as he handed her the tape with the Schneider memorandum.

"Forget to eat again?" she asked.

"Not exactly."

"It's two-thirty."

"Already? I'm going to make the drive up to Danny's. Bring you something?"

"How about Peking duck *mu shu* with bamboo shoots and plum sauce?"

"I'll see if Danny has added it to the menu," Joe grinned and headed for the elevators.

Joe straddled a barstool, the only customer in the *cantina*.

"*José*. Good to see you. *Qué hubo?*" Danny exuded cheerfulness as he set a glass of Coke down on the counter.

How's it going? Joe repeated to himself. *I've poked into another murder that is none of my business, upset two of the senior partners at my firm, and withheld evidence from the police.*

"Okay." He took a big swallow of cola and bit down on an ice cube, its coldness making his teeth ache.

"And with Mia?" Danny's face became serious.

Another situation I'm handling well, Joe thought. *She won't take my calls or see me, and I still don't have a clue who killed the Barretts.* "Fine." He pasted what he hoped was a confident look on his face.

"*Bueno.*" Danny beamed at him as he refilled his glass. "I knew you would be able to help."

Joe ordered a burrito, and Danny disappeared into the kitchen. He reemerged a few minutes later, trailing the smell of fresh chopped onions and several sheets of paper in his hand.

"*José*, I have a small favor to ask. What happened to the Barretts, it made me think. You never know when God will call you. So I made a will. But because it is written in English, I wanted you to make sure there are no mistakes."

"Danny, I would have drafted a will for you." Joe recognized the fill-in-the-blanks form sold by stationery stores.

"I no want to trouble you," Danny called over his shoulder as he went back to assemble Joe's meal. He returned with a shallow dish laden with rice, fragrant *frijoles*, and a plump burrito, setting it on the counter with a flourish. "Be careful, the plate is hot."

"Thanks. It looks great." Joe reached for his fork. He read

through the form as he ate, careful not to dribble sauce on the pages. Danny looked on with the approval associated with grandmothers who liked to watch their family members eat.

"Everything looks okay to me." He turned over the last page. "All you have to do is sign it in front of two witnesses and make a copy."

"What is the copy for?" Danny squinted at the glass he was polishing.

"The original is what gets submitted to the court. It should be stored in a safe place. I could hold it for you at my office if you like. The copy you keep with your important papers –" Joe stopped in mid-sentence and stared at the document he had just read.

"Oh my God."

"*José*, is there something wrong?" Danny's thick brows pushed together in concern.

Joe jumped off the stool, tipping over his Coke with his elbow.

"I think there's something very wrong." He fumbled bills out of his wallet and grabbed his jacket. "Sorry, Danny, but I have to go."

"Go, go. I will take care of this." Danny waved him out while he mopped up the spill with his bar rag.

"Thanks." Joe grabbed his jacket and sprinted for the parking lot.

Chapter 19

Joe stood at the counter devastated. "I just need to see it for a moment!"

The blond woman behind the sign reading "Evidence" was unmoved. "And I told you unless the investigating officer or one of the lawyers on the case signs for it, you can't." She tugged at her too small uniform for emphasis.

"But the prosecutor and Detective Dresden aren't here!" Joe exclaimed in exasperation.

"I'm sorry, sir." The woman moved away from the counter.

"Wait! Can I get permission by telephone?" Joe implored.

"That you may, sir." She indicated the phone on the counter with a languid wave.

Joe snatched up the instrument.

"What's Detective Dresden's number?"

"I'm not allowed to give out that information, sir."

Swallowing his frustration with great effort, Joe laid down the receiver with exaggerated care. His eyes roved the police station while he tried to figure out what to do next. A door clicked open down the hall, and a familiar-looking figure started in the direction of the reception area. His shoes pounded out a staccato rhythm on the linoleum as he gave chase, and he windmilled his arms to stop himself from colliding into her.

"Katie!" Joe hadn't seen her since she had left the firm.

Katie Hewson looked up from the papers she was reading.

"Do you work here now?" Joe asked, his hope buoyed by the case file in her plump hand.

She nodded, the rolls of flesh on her neck moving independently of her chin. "I'm an assistant city prosecutor."

"Hey, that's great." Joe couldn't think of anything else to say except to ask for what he needed. "Do you think it would be possible for you to do me a small favor?"

Her lumpish face was impassive. "What did you have in mind?"

"I'm trying to look at a piece of evidence in a criminal case."

"Is this something you're working on for the firm?"

"Sort of," Joe hedged.

Her pudgy features pushed into a smile. "I might be able to get you access –"

Joe's heart leapt. She inclined her head toward him and dropped her voice to a whisper.

"But I'd sooner rot in Hell than help anybody from BH&M," she rasped, her cheeks coloring. "You know what the market for second year lawyers is like this time of year?"

Saliva sprayed from the angry red gash that was her mouth. "This was the only job I could find, prosecuting drunk drivers and dog bites for fifteen hundred dollars a month!" She glared at him in fury, her eyes narrowed.

Joe recoiled, stunned. The hatred in her words reverberated deep in his gut. He watched dumbly as her wide, shapeless body lumbered away from him.

"Joe! What are you doing here? Visiting hours aren't until this afternoon."

Relief coursed through him, dispelling Katie's venom. Joe whirled to face Mia's lawyer. Ruffles edged the high collar of her blouse, almost brushing the bottom of her earlobes. Her suit, made from material that looked machine washable, was beige, a shade that sallowed her skin and deadened her already drab hair. But her brown eyes were warm and the smile she gave him over the stack of papers clutched to her chest was genuine.

"Ronnie, I need your help." He seized her wrist and half-dragged her toward the counter down the hall. "I have to see the evidence file in Mia's case."

Ronnie pulled her arm from his grasp, halting their progress. "Hold on a minute! Do you mind telling me what's going on?"

Joe gripped the sides of her shoulders. "It's vitally important I look at the stuff the police found at the scene the night the Barretts were murdered."

Ronnie studied his face. "Okay," she said after a moment. "But you owe me."

"Anything." Joe hurried her forward again.

"Lunch with Jerry Dan Kovacs."

Joe shot her a look.

She colored slightly. "I think he's kinda cute."

"Done."

Joe flagged down the blond woman. Fifteen minutes later, he and Ronnie were ensconced in a small cubicle, its only furnishings two chairs and a table. A cardboard carton was between them, its seal having been broken by the evidence clerk.

Joe opened the box. Gingerly setting aside the blood-splattered clothing sealed in glassine bags, he pulled out the copy of Cordelia's will that had been found on the kitchen table that night. Each page was encased in plastic. He skimmed the text with confusion.

"What is it?" Ronnie demanded.

"I'm not sure," Joe admitted. "Can I get a copy of this?"

While Ronnie left to find the clerk, Joe tore a sheet off his pad and started scribbling rapidly. He was folding the paper into thirds when Ronnie returned with the copies.

"One last request," Joe said. "Can you give this to Mia?" He thrust the note into her hand.

"I'm here to serve," Ronnie replied with a wry grin.

"Keep your fingers crossed." He hugged the surprised girl, then glanced at his watch.

"Oh my gosh, I've got to see if Lydia can stay late." He fished a quarter out of his pocket.

"Pay phone's outside the front door."

"Thanks again." Joe broke into a run down the hallway, the copies rolled up in his hand.

"Don't forget about Jerry Dan!" Ronnie called after him before signaling to the clerk the box contents were ready to be inventoried and sealed again.

Joe waved as he turned the corner.

The firm had emptied for the day by the time Joe burst from the elevator and sprinted to his office. Lydia was waiting for him at her computer. Grabbing onto the partition in front of her desk, he pressed his hand against the stitch in his side and gulped air into his lungs.

"Thanks for staying," he gasped.

"You look as though you've just run for your life," Lydia observed dryly.

"Mia's more than mine, I hope."

His breathing still ragged, he unrolled the copy of Cordelia's will he had brought from the police station. Lydia looked at it, delicate eyebrows arched.

"Back in a minute," he said.

Ducking into his office, he searched through the case folders on the back of his credenza. Finding the two items he was looking for, he carried them to Lydia's desk. One was the copy of the will he had found in Cordelia's safe deposit box. The other was a manila envelope. He unfastened its clasp and turned it upside down. Out spilled the pieces of the document Sonny had torn up the day he'd come to the firm, later collected by Harrington and deposited in the file.

"Lydia, could you put this back together while I get one last thing?"

"All the king's horses and all the king's men." She reached for the first fragment as Joe started down the hall.

After a quick check to make sure he was alone, Joe approached the file cabinets that lined the wall in back of Gertrude's desk. He felt around behind them until his fingers found the magnetized metal box he had seen Harrington make use of one Saturday. Opening it, he took out the key that was inside and unlocked the first cabinet. Pulling out the drawer marked "A-F," he flipped through the "Bs" until he found a folder printed with Cordelia Barrett's name.

Inside was the original of her will. He removed the document, pushed the drawer shut, put the key back, and returned to his secretary's desk. He laid the original will next to the three copies, including the one Lydia had just finished piecing together.

"Okay," he said, "let's see what we have."

As Lydia watched, Joe compared the four documents, word for word. It wasn't until the last page that he found the discrepancies.

"Yes!" he exclaimed. "That's it!" He looked at his secretary, struggling to contain his excitement.

"Lydia, when the firm does a will for a client, we keep the original and they get a copy, right?" he asked.

"That's correct," she said.

"So here is the original from our files and the copy I delivered to Cordelia that I found in her safe deposit box."

Lydia nodded.

"We also have two more wills, the one Sonny ripped up and the one found at the murder scene." He indicated the document she had reassembled and the copy from the police file. "So where did these two extra copies come from?"

"Mrs. Barrett made them from her copy before she put it into her safe deposit box?"

"Not exactly. She or someone else made only one copy." Joe pointed at the numbers at the bottom of the four documents. "Look at the word processing codes. The copy from her safe deposit box and the one Sonny had have the same numbers as the original. That means they were made from the original or from Mrs. Barrett's copy of the original."

"I'm following you, I think." Lydia frowned in concentration.

"Now look at the word processing code on the will that was on the Barrett kitchen table."

"It's different!" Lydia exclaimed.

"And the witness names aren't the same as the ones on the original, either."

Comprehension flooded her face. "That means –"

"Exactly. Look at the numbers. The original was printed out October 14. The one the police found was run off two days later. Can you check the records for the times?"

Lydia moved her mouse and her computer screen came to life. She tapped the keys and brought up the word processing directory.

"The original will was printed out Monday at 4:17 p.m.," she announced after scrutinizing the entries.

"How about other one?" Joe forced himself to keep calm.

She scrolled through the listings. "Here it is. October 16 at 3:34 a.m."

She scrutinized the code numbers of the will from the murder scene. "Did you see this?" She pointed to a number in the string. "Another document was printed out at the same time."

"Really?" Joe couldn't contain his surprise. "Can you call it up?"

Lydia's fingers danced across the keyboard. "It'll be out in a minute." She nodded at the printer on top of the file cabinet behind her. The lights on the front of the machine flashed and its motor started to whine.

"Only one more question," Joe said, his eyes meeting hers. "Can you tell me who was in the office Wednesday morning?"

Lydia started typing without a word. Joe didn't ask how she was able to access supposedly restricted files.

The printer's whine changed to a chatter and the first sheet began to emerge from the slot on top. Joe stood up to read it. "Revocation of Trust" was all he glimpsed before Lydia's gasp pulled him back to her screen.

"Well?" Joe prompted. "Who was here?"

She looked at him with a strange expression. "You were."

Joe fought the nausea rising in his throat. He knew who the murderer was.

Chapter 20

After sending his bewildered secretary home with assurances he would explain everything later, Joe refiled the original of Cordelia's will and slipped the copies and the document Lydia had printed into an envelope and dropped it into his bottom desk drawer. He sorted through the papers on top of his desk, hunting for Dresden's business card. He knew he had taken things too far by himself. A loose scrap fluttered to the floor and he picked it up. "Practice at your place tonight, pardner. See you at 7:30" was scrawled in Riley's handwriting.

Finally locating the card in the back of his Rolodex, he called the number printed on it. Whoever answered told him Dresden wasn't in and transferred him to the detective's voicemail. Joe left a message, depressed the buttons on the top of the phone, and started to tap in a sequence he knew by heart. His eyes fell on Riley's note, and he paused, receiver in his hand. He hung up the phone.

After shucking his suit for jeans and boots, Joe walked out his front door to find Cricket already saddled and tied to the hitching rail. The sun had set an hour earlier, its exit marked by streaks of coral cloud against sky the color of bleached denim. Velvety dark had descended, broken only by the ovals of near daylight brightness cast by the barn and arena lights. Clouds of bugs swarmed around the halogen fixtures.

"Over here, bro'," Riley called, riding Sultan out from the shadows. "Thought you might be late, so I tacked up your horse."

"Thanks." Joe zipped up his jacket as he walked across the illuminated yard, his boot heels crunching on the gravel.

Untying the chestnut, he checked her cinch, slung his rope over the saddle horn, and mounted up. The two horses walked side by side toward the arena. The odor of the brush released by the day's heat still lingered, pungent and sweet.

"Hope this is okay with you," Riley began, "but I asked Bill Hutchison to partner with me tomorrow night. When you missed practice these last few times I figured your shoulder was still giving you problems, so –"

"Fine by me." Joe pulled in front of the arena gate.

"Gate stuck again? I'll get it." Riley started to dismount ...

"I know, Riley."

Riley lowered himself back into the seat of his saddle and cocked his head. "Know what?"

"I know about the will."

Riley's laugh was quick and too loud. "Cordelia's? I told you, I'm not in it."

"I'm talking about the copy you printed off the firm computer." Joe struggled to maintain his composure. "The one that was on the kitchen table."

Sultan tossed his head and Riley fingered the reins, eyes averted from Joe's. "How'd you find out?" he finally asked, his voice sounding far away.

"The word processing numbers and the access card records," Joe said, his anguish now plain. "I also know Cordelia revoked your trust."

Riley's shock of blond hair gleamed in the garish light. "Congratulations. All that detective had was the trust revocation."

Which Harrington had to have known about, too, Joe realized. "You know the police would have found out you borrowed my card," he pressed.

"So? I printed out some documents. Big deal. Twenty people saw me roping at Shorty's when Sonny and Cordelia were killed."

"And you assumed no one would tell Dresden about your night rides on Sultan."

Riley stroked the powerful neck. "Ah, my cat-eyed steed," he said, sounding almost bemused.

Joe forced himself to ask. "Why'd you do it, Riley?"

Riley toyed with a lock of Sultan's mane while he stared into the night at something only he could see. The pitiless lights overhead threw the planes of his face into stark relief, obscuring his eyes in pools of shadow. When he began to speak, Joe had to strain to hear him.

"Tuesday morning Cordelia told me what she'd done," he said in a near whisper. "At first I didn't believe her, but when I checked on the firm's computer, sure enough, she'd screwed me coming and going. Not only was I being cut off, but the ranch – *my* ranch – was going to Sonny and everything else to that spic girl." Riley's bitterness was almost palpable.

"I printed out the documents and carried them around with me all day, even took them to Shorty's. I thought roping would take my mind off things but it didn't. I ended up riding Sultan over to the ranch after the first round."

Joe remembered the fresh manure in front of the house.

"Cordelia was in the kitchen. Sonny was there, too. I started to talk, yell, actually. I told Cordelia it wasn't fair to cut me out, that the ranch would have been at least half mine if Grandfather had lived. I said I was the only one who really cared about the place. Sonny wanted to carve it up into a resort and Mia was just kissing up to an old lady so her brother would be taken care of." Riley's words trembled with remembered anger.

"Cordelia didn't even blink. She said the ranch was Sonny's and Sonny's alone, and Mia deserved what she was giving her. I asked her what the hell I was supposed to live on, seeing as how she'd revoked my trust. Cold as ice, she looked at me and said, 'I believe you still have a car, a house, and a job, which is more than you deserve. Most people who commit forgery end up in prison.'" Riley gave a small shrug. "I guess Trudy told her," he said, tiredness edging his voice.

Joe was confused. "What forgery? What does Trudy have to do with this?"

Riley flashed him a lopsided smile. "A while ago I signed Cordelia's name on a letter to the bank authorizing the withdrawal of capital from my trust account."

"Oh Riley," Joe said softly.

"I needed the money." Riley's already prominent lower lip pushed out further. "And I figured she'd leave me something in the end and it could all be balanced out then. But Trudy found out about it somehow. She even showed me a copy of the letter I'd written. I was so mad I ripped most of it out of her hand. She smirked and said she didn't need the paper – she'd just tell Cordelia directly unless I paid her ten thousand dollars. I told her she had a better chance of getting milk from a bull than a dime from me, 'cause if I had the money to pay her off I wouldn't need to tap my trust in the first place."

Riley blinked rapidly and his voice became ragged. "Anyway, when Cordelia made that crack about prison, I lost it. I was standing next to the cabinet where the ranch firearms are kept."

He stared down at his hands. "The next thing I remember is feeling the gun recoil."

Riley raised his head and met Joe's eyes, his jawbone flexing under his thin skin. "When I realized they were dead, I saw my chance to make the ranch mine. Afterwards, I rode back to Shorty's."

Those were Sultan's hoofbeats he had heard behind Danny's, Joe realized.

"But why Mia?"

"It made sense. The new will gave her a motive. If the police didn't buy the murder/suicide, they'd look to her."

"So you killed Trudy for revenge?"

"Trudy? I didn't have anything to do with that."

Joe's disbelief showed on his face. Riley's gaze didn't waver.

"Not that it much matters at this point, but I wasn't the one who killed her. Why would I? She'd already caused all the damage she could."

Riley gathered up his reins. "I gotta go." He wheeled Sultan around and started back toward the barn.

"Wait! We can sort this out," Joe called, cueing Cricket to follow.

"I don't think so." Riley twisted around in the saddle to keep his eyes on Joe. "Stay there," he commanded. Sultan's hooves clopped loudly on the packed earth.

"But –" Joe pulled up at the sight of the gun resting on Riley's cantle. He moved his mouth but no words came out, his voice lost to shock. "Where'd you get that?" he at last rasped.

"It was Cordelia's. I know it's not worth anything over distance, but at least it'll make sure you stay put." He was right. Joe had seen Riley shoot enough times to know he rarely missed at close range.

"Riley, don't," Joe pleaded.

Riley waved the gun in an expansive gesture. "What choice do I have, Joe? Build up my biceps or become a jailhouse lawyer while I wait for my turn in the chair down at Florence? I don't think so."

"But a good criminal attorney –"

"Would say I'm crazy?" Riley interrupted. He bared his teeth in a rictus grin, eerily resembling the Jack o' lanterns that had begun to appear on *portales* around town. "Remember that old English murder case from Crim Law? The defendant was 'exonerated because the balance of his mind was disturbed.' What a great concept. Unfortunately, I don't think I would qualify, unless it's unbalanced to want what should have been yours." He choked back what sounded like a sob. "The ranch – a family ..." His voice trailed away.

"But *we're* family, Riley," Joe's eyes filled. "Remember what you told me after you saved me from the bull? You said we were brothers, that we'd always be there for each other."

Riley was blunt. "So, brother, now it's your turn."

Joe's heart lurched. There it was. A second chance. An opportunity to make up for Patrick. Its seductiveness was near overwhelming, but his conscience didn't hesitate. With the taste of self-loathing in his mouth, Joe inched his right hand toward his rope.

Riley barked out a laugh. "So much for fraternal allegiance." His voice hardened. "Don't try it, Joe." He raised the gun. "This thing may be a peashooter, but we both know it spits bullets farther than you can throw, especially with that shoulder."

Joe shook out a loop. The gun's barrel tilted back slightly as Riley cocked the hammer. The tension stretched between them like a strand of newly strung wire.

"I'll kill you," Riley said in a flat voice.

After a moment's hesitation, Joe let his hand fall back onto his thigh. Riley clucked to Sultan and the big gelding quickened his walk. Keeping the gun aimed at Joe's midsection, he halted Sultan next to Joe's car.

"Keys in the ignition?"

Joe nodded.

"I'll trade you." Riley patted the big horse's shoulder. "It's a good deal. This fella's worth ten Blind Bucks. But if I'm going to make the border tonight –" Riley shifted his weight and began to dismount.

The lariat whistled once, then sailed across the stableyard as Riley swung his leg over the gelding's back. Joe followed the rope with his gaze, willing its flight with his heart, while fire burned through his shoulder and down to his fingertips.

The loop floated over Riley's head, settling around his waist. Through a haze of pain, Joe pulled it tight and dalleyed his end as Cricket backed rapidly. Elbows pinned to his sides, Riley was jerked from the saddle, landing with a thud on the hard ground.

Stepping off the chestnut mare, Joe ran toward the prostrate figure, one hand on the taut rope. The air seemed to thicken, slowing his movements. Riley struggled to his knees, coughing. Joe saw the dull gleam of metal still in his hand.

"Drop it, Riley!" he yelled, willing his leaden legs to move faster. The toe of his boot caught on a clump of earth, and he nearly fell. Dimly he heard a car's tires on the gravel drive.

Riley lifted the gun. Their eyes locked for an instant, and Joe was jolted to the core of his soul. He was looking at someone he had never seen before. His pulse thumping in his ears, he kept running. Riley took aim.

"No, Riley, NO!" A shot cracked through the night air, and Joe felt a pain like no other.

Chapter 21

Wednesday, October 23

Joe shifted in his chair, the thick bandage that bound his elbow to his side chafing under his arm. His shoulder was killing him. His heart hurt much worse.

The horror of Riley's death wouldn't leave him. Without warning he would get a flash of Riley pushing himself to his knees against the pull of Joe's rope, and feel a jolt of helplessness, as though he were back running across the gravel drive, the loose rocks sliding under his slick boot soles. He would relive tugging on the coarse nylon, his hands shaking from the cold or the pain in his shoulder or both. He would hear again the report of the gun Riley had pressed against his temple, and would remember being overwhelmed by anguish, powerless to move or even think, until Dresden's blunt fingers grasped his shoulders and half-lifted, half-dragged him away from the ruined corpse.

"Now maybe things will get back to normal around here." Jerry Dan's boots hooked around the rungs of the visitor's chair in Joe's office.

"What about Trudy?" Joe pushed a pencil around his desktop with his free hand, his eyes never leaving the rolling cylinder.

Jerry Dan looked at his friend with sympathy. "Riley killed Trudy. He did it because she tried to blackmail him."

Joe gnawed on his lower lip. "But he said he didn't care, that the damage had already been done." The pencil careened off an untasted mug of cooling coffee.

Jerry Dan raised his shoulders and lifted his hands, palms up. "So he wasn't telling the truth. Like my mama used to say: 'Everybody has a flat side.' The police are convinced he's guilty. That's enough for me."

Joe shook his head stubbornly. "They were wrong about Mia. What if they're wrong about this? It only made sense for Riley to kill Trudy before, not after, she told Cordelia about the forged letter, assuming Cordelia didn't find out some other way."

Joe rubbed his hand across his face. His eyes felt gritty in their sockets. He'd gone too long without sufficient sleep, and the last two nights it had continued to elude him. The firm had offered him a few days off but he had demurred, preferring the activity of the office to the tomb-like solitude of his adobe. "All I'm saying is that it's not as certain as you may want to think."

"They pulled the access card records for the night Trudy was killed. She and Riley were the only ones here that late."

But Riley showed how easy it was to use someone else's card, Joe thought as Jerry Dan's chair scraped across the floor.

"How about an early dinner? I've got to come back and finish this brief I've been working on." Jerry Dan stood, leaned over the desk, his brown eyes earnest behind smudged lenses.

"Joe, I know you and Riley were close, and I'm sorry this has happened. But you need to put it behind you and get on with the rest of your life. Like patching things up with Mia, for example."

Joe's mouth twisted. "Doesn't look like that's going to work out. I've left a half dozen messages since she was released. I pretend to be her lawyer so they'll put me through, but she won't take my calls."

"Give her time." Jerry Dan walked to the door. "Coming?"

"No thanks." Joe swiveled his chair to face the window.

Jerry Dan hesitated a moment, shook his head and left.

Joe sat behind his desk and stared through the panes of glass while the firm emptied out for the evening. On the distant hillside, stucco homes lit by the setting sun glowed with pastel paint. Cars traveled in packs down the main boulevards, moving from traffic light to traffic light.

Once the noise of the office had quieted and the after-hours stillness had settled in, Joe exhaled deeply and got to his feet. He swayed a bit as he found his balance, feeling hollow to the core. He reached behind his credenza and retrieved the envelope he had tucked there. The movement sent stabs of pain down his arm, and he leaned against his desk until it passed. The omnipresent ache he remembered from the original injury had returned.

Sitting in his chair again, he unfastened the clasp and took out the photocopies he made of the items in Trudy's envelope before turning them over to Dresden yesterday morning. He looked at the ten thousand-dollar entry in the bankbook and the deposit slip made out for the same amount.

Setting them aside, he ran his fingers lightly over the image of the Club Diana matchbook, then picked up what he now knew was the top half of the letter Riley had forged. He stared at the words until they blurred before crumpling it into a ball and pushing it aside. Swiping at his eyes, he reached for the last item, the cover page of the CelGen motion. Starting with the lawyers' names at the top, he read the document line by line.

Sydney had confirmed she'd paid Trudy the same day the funds had appeared in Trudy's account. Harrington had told him the police had turned up nothing further to support their theory Trudy was dealing drugs. So if Riley wasn't going to give her any money, Joe reasoned, then Trudy had expected a second ten thousand from somebody else.

What if she had had something on Atticus? And he had died, or been killed, before he was supposed to deliver the money? Maybe a look through his case files would ... Realizing where his thoughts were taking him, he abruptly dropped the papers onto his desk.

"Enough," he muttered, leaning back in his chair and looking up at the acoustical tiles overhead.

It's not your job, he admonished himself. And nothing I do will bring Riley back. Jerry Dan's right. It's time to get back to what I'm supposed to be doing. With a sigh, he dragged his overflowing in -toward him.

Leafing through the documents, he paused at a copy of the trial brief Jerry Dan had filed in his cowboy assault case. "Thought you'd get a kick out of this" was scrawled across the top. Joe pulled it out of the stack, setting it next to the CelGen pleading page. He let his gaze flit idly from one to the other, his eyes widening when he realized what he was seeing.

"Holy shit," he breathed.

He fumbled for his bar directory and looked up the number. Phone tucked under his ear, he punched the buttons, hoping someone was still there.

"That was fast," said the cheery female voice on the other end.

"Uh, is this the Arizona Bar Association?" Joe asked.

The voice cooled into professional diction. "Yes, it is. Sorry. I thought you were someone calling me back. I'm afraid we're closed. You can call back tomorrow after nine –"

"Please, I have just one question. It will only take a moment."

A board creaked in the hall. With a furtive glance toward his open door, Joe continued more quietly.

"It's really important, just a quick check of your records," he implored, cupping his hand around the mouthpiece.

"W-e-l-l," the voice said, stretching out the word and Joe's hopes along with it. "I haven't shut down the computer yet. Go ahead. What do you want to know?"

He made his request and was put on hold. Sanitized Rolling Stones, volume too high, filled his ear. He heard a thump he didn't think was part of the song, followed by several others. He pressed his palm against the instrument's earpiece, muffling the music, and looked toward his still empty doorway.

"Hello?" he called. No one answered.

The music disappeared and the woman came back on with the answer to his question.

"Are you certain?" he asked, although he had been expecting the response. She assured him the information was correct, said "Good night," and broke the connection.

Joe replaced the receiver while trying to get his mind around what he had just confirmed.

Riley had been telling the truth.

Chapter 22

For the second time that week Joe left a message for Karl Dresden, who wasn't expected in until the next morning. Deciding to leave suspect apprehension to a professional this time, and feeling tired through to his bones, Joe draped his jacket over his injured shoulder and flipped off his light on his way out the door.

Hal was unsaddling Cricket when Joe walked into the barn. Sultan stood nearby in the crossties. Joe felt his heart constrict when he saw the big black gelding.

"Evening, Joe." Hal lifted the saddle off the mare's back.

"Hi, Hal."

Farley scampered out of the tackroom at the sound of his voice, mewing plaintively. Joe squatted and stroked him under his chin. He could feel the vibrating vocal chords beneath the thick fur.

"Miss me, guy?" Farley licked his fingers with his pink sandpaper tongue. Joe straightened up. "Thanks for taking Cricket out."

"No problem." Hal pulled the saddle blanket from the mare's back onto the saddle in his arms. As he headed for the tackroom, he gave an exaggerated shiver. "She was such an easy goer I stayed out too late. I'd forgotten how cool the desert gets this time of year once the sun goes down."

Joe followed him into the tackroom and pulled his jacket off a peg. "Here. Put this on."

"Thanks." Hal slipped his arms into the sleeves and zipped up the front. "What's this?" He pulled a small object out of one of the pockets.

"Darn, I meant to tell you," Joe said. "I found it in the remains of a campfire on the other side of the north fence, under that big stand of palo verdes. Looked as though hikers had been there."

Hal sniffed at the scrap of iron and turned it over in his hand as they walked back to the horses. Tipping his hat back on his head, he continued to study the piece of metal while Joe picked up a brush and began working on Cricket.

As he rhythmically stroked the coppery coat, Joe wondered how long was it going to be before he could throw a rope again. Long before I'll stop missing Riley, he thought with sadness. Try as he might, he'd been unable to avoid the question that had haunted him ever since he had crouched over his dying friend: If he and Riley had been real brothers, would he have let him escape, even helped him?

The chestnut mare turned her head and nuzzled his elbow, interrupting his grief. Joe rubbed behind her ears.

"Sorry, girl, but I'm fresh out of carrots."

Cricket took his sleeve in her teeth and tugged it gently in protest. Joe started to groom her legs.

"Why that sonava bitch," Hal growled suddenly, his face dark with fury.

"Who?" Joe straightened up to face the ranch foreman.

"Healy's foreman, that's who! He's a goddam –" Hal broke off, his gaze momentarily flicking to a spot behind Joe.

"I've got to call the police, son," he said briskly. "Can you finish up here?"

Before a mystified Joe could respond, the old cowboy hurried off as fast as his bowed legs could carry him.

"I don't have any carrots. Would an apple do?"

Joe slowly turned around, half-afraid he had imagined the voice. Mia stood in the barn's aisleway, a shiny red fruit cupped in her palm. She looked thinner and there was still a suggestion of shadow under her tilted eyes, but her hair had regained some of its sheen and the glow was returning to her mocha cheeks.

She walked toward him. Warmth coursed through Joe's body,

an ecstasy not too far from pain.

"I'm sorry," he said, his words carrying regret not only for his actions but for all that she had endured.

"I'm the one who should apologize."

She came nearer, close enough for him to see the bits of gold swimming in her chocolate irises and the fine dark hairs that curled around her temples. "Thank you," she whispered.

He reached out his good arm, and she stepped into it, nestling her face into his chest. They stood there without saying anything, Joe gently rocking her back and forth until the telephone in the tackroom shrilled, invading their cocoon. Reluctantly disengaging himself, Joe answered it.

"Hello?"

"Your office rang, hon." His aunt's voice came crisply over the wire. "They said you're needed back there."

Joe frowned in confusion. "Was it a Mr. Harrington who called?"

"Sorry, I didn't catch the name. Did sound like an older man, though."

"That's okay," Joe replied. "Thanks."

He hung up the phone and went back to where he had left Mia. Cricket was munching contentedly, juice dribbling down her chin, while Mia stroked her forelock.

"You won't believe this, but I have to go back to work," he sighed with exasperation. "Maybe we could see each other later?" he asked, suddenly nervous as to what her answer might be. *Was this a farewell visit?*

Mia smiled at him, giving him a glimpse of the mole at the edge of her lower lip. "Don't worry. We'll have lots of time together."

They put the horses back into their stalls and embraced once more. With Mia's words written on his heart as a promise, Joe drove down the driveway toward the main road, his eyes never leaving the rear view mirror until he couldn't see her silhouette in the barn entrance anymore.

The elevator doors opened onto the dark lobby, the only illumination coming from the small emergency light at the entrance to the fire stairs. Strange, Joe thought, recalling on his previous late nights the cleaning staff and word processors had always left a few overheads on. He inserted his access card into the reader and the main doors clicked open.

"Mr. Harrington?" he called, still breathing heavily from his dash across the parking lot. There was no response.

He walked through the reception area. The building was absolutely quiet. Even the hum of the air conditioning was missing. Kachina dolls stared sightlessly at him from behind shadowed pottery. He felt the hair stand up on his arms. The slowdown from running to walking, he told himself.

"Mr. Harrington?" he called again as he stepped into the book-lined hallway.

The senior partner's office was dark, but a dim light glowed from around the next corner. Making the turn, he saw it emanated from his office. He's waiting for me there, he thought, feeling foolish at his fears.

His office was occupied. Sitting in one of the visitor chairs, facing the door, was Forrest Whitford.

"Hello, Mr. McGuinness," he said, spearing Joe with his gaze.

Joe tried to keep the apprehension from his face.

"Please, sit down." Forrest nodded at the chair behind Joe's desk. When Joe didn't move, Forrest jumped to his feet, his anger erupting like a geyser.

"Sit in the goddamned chair," he hissed through clenched teeth, brandishing a heavy-headed stick in his right hand. Joe edged around the corner of his desk and groped for his seat, his eyes on what he recognized as the branding iron from the reception area.

Forrest stood with his legs apart in front of Joe's desk, tossing the piece of metal from one hand to the other. "It appears you have discovered my little secret." His usually pallid cheeks were flushed, and his eyes were unnaturally bright.

"I'm not sure what you're referring to, Mr. Whitford," Joe began cautiously.

"Don't lie to me," Forrest screamed, smashing the desk with the iron, splintering the wood.

Joe thought queasily about what the metal rod could do to his head. He had to diffuse Forrest's anger.

"Okay. I'm sorry. Maybe everything can be fixed. I wouldn't say anything, and you could take the exam and it would be all right." Joe's words tumbled out, his voice sounding thin and high to his ears.

"You idiot," Forrest spat. "I've been practicing law without a license for twenty-seven years. Do you think that's something that can be 'fixed' just like that?" He snapped his fingers. Joe flinched at the sound.

"With Atticus out of the way and projected revenues more than doubled because of the merger I negotiated, the partners would have had no choice but to make me head of litigation." Rage and something else glittered in Forrest's eyes. "Then that girl, that nothing of a girl with her ridiculous hair, came to see me." His voice changed to a falsetto. "Mr. Whitford, the bar association sent a refund check. Apparently the firm paid dues for one lawyer too many." A muscle jumped in his cheek, his tone low and dangerous again.

"Then she slapped a pleading onto my desk and pointed at my name at the top." His face mottled at the memory. He mimicked Trudy a second time. "Rather a high bar number for someone so long in practice, wouldn't you say?" Joe watched his fists clench and unclench. "God, I wanted to crush her throat right then and there."

Forrest began to pace in front of the desk.

"But I fooled the bitch," he said, baring his teeth in a mirthless smile. "I asked her what I had to do. 'I'll tell you at lunch,' she said. So I went to the restaurant and played along. 'Only one payment,' she promised, but I knew she was lying. People like that are parasites forever. I set up a meeting to give her the money but instead implemented a more permanent solution."

Laughter bubbled from his spittle-flecked lips. "Thank God for Merchant's developer clients – best drug connection around."

Forrest halted abruptly and turned to face Joe, the glee draining from his face.

"Now you crop up," he snarled. "Quite the hero, weren't you, figuring out the Barrett murders. Well, here's one you won't be able to solve. Your own!"

Joe realized if he was going to make a break for it, it had to be now. Abandoning his chair, he ducked his head and bolted for the door. He was barely clear of his desk when Forrest swung.

Joe felt the rush of air as the iron bar passed by his ear a split second before it connected with his collarbone. Charges of pain ran up from his shoulder, bursting like fireworks in his brain. There was a roaring in his ears, as though he could hear the hum of his blood as it coursed through his vessels. He went down, collapsing like a puppet whose strings had been cut.

Curled into a ball on the floor, Joe hazily waited for the next blow. Instead he heard a thud, followed by a vibration through the floorboards as though something heavy had dropped next to him. Hovering on the edge of his awareness was a voice he thought he knew. Fighting dizziness, he struggled to focus on the figure looming over him. Bit by bit, Jerry Dan came into view, twirling his Peacemaker like a gunslinger.

"Jerry Dan ...? What are you doing here?" The garbled words slurred from Joe's mouth.

"Rescuing you from the bad guy, amigo." Jerry Dan squatted down to help Joe sit up.

Surges of nausea rippled through Joe as he tried to feel his way back into his body, a cell at a time. Through blurred vision he made out Forrest sprawled face down on the carpet. He clutched Jerry Dan's arm.

"You didn't shoot him, did you?"

"Heck no!" Jerry Dan exclaimed, regarding his weapon fondly. "This thing hasn't spewed lead for almost a century. I conked him on the head with it when he was getting ready to take another swing at you. He'll just be out for a while."

Joe leaned back against the front of his desk. "How'd you know we were here?"

Jerry Dan pushed his glasses up onto his nose and beamed. "I was at my desk, getting ready for a think session, when all the lights went out. I heard someone walk down the hall and thought I better see what was up. After Forrest started ranting, I called the cops from my office, then snuck back with my six shooter to see if you needed help before they showed up."

His equilibrium still precarious, Joe let his chin drop onto his chest. Jerry Dan's sock-clad feet loomed into view, the right foot in red stripes and the left in blue and green argyle.

"Jerry Dan, your socks don't match," Joe said woozily before another wave of vertigo almost toppled him over.

Jerry Dan propped Joe upright again. "Another advantage of wearing boots." He grinned and wiggled his toes. "I had to take them off to sneak up on you guys. Now are you going to be okay while I hogtie this desperado before he wakes up?" He reached behind his back, pulling out a piece of rope with a small loop at the end that had been tucked into the waistband of his pants. "I even have a calf roper's pegging string," he said, holding it up triumphantly.

Despite the agony it caused him, Joe started to laugh.

Chapter 23

Saturday, October 26

Joe had been sitting on a bale of hay outside Cricket's stall when Hal arrived to exercise the chestnut mare. Even though his shoulder, newly encased in elastic and Velcro, complained with every little movement, he was determined to go for a ride. Hal was reluctant, aware of the doctor's warnings against jostling fractured collarbones. But after Joe promised to limit his excursion to a twenty-minute walk, Hal had relented and saddled the mare.

Now Joe headed north, allowing Cricket to pick her own path through the cacti. About a half mile from the barn, Michael Chiago, mounted on his bay, emerged from the entrance of a chaparral-shrouded arroyo.

A coiled lariat hung from his right shoulder. He reined his horse in next to Joe's, and the two men rode wordlessly side by side, their mounts' hooves swishing through the sand.

"I used to have a brother," Chiago said, breaking the silence.

Joe noted the "used to" but didn't say anything.

"He ridiculed our traditions, couldn't wait to move off the rez. To him, the white way was the right way." A hawk circled in the distance. Chiago followed its maneuvers with his eyes for several moments before continuing.

"He got involved with developing the casino. Made promises to some guys who were connected that he couldn't deliver on. His body was found in one of the canals."

"I'm sorry," Joe said quietly.

"There were signs he was in trouble, but I didn't want to see them. After he died, I was angry with him, and then myself, for many months. His ghost was quite persistent."

"You believe in ghosts?"

Dark deep set eyes bored into Joe's from under a fringe of ebony hair. "Don't you still feel Riley's presence?"

Joe felt the familiar ache he had had too often lately. "I catch myself looking for him before I remember he isn't here."

"That will happen less and less, until one day you won't look anymore. Then he'll be truly gone. To my people, ghosts are dead things that won't lie down. It was a long time before my brother rested in the east."

"And now?"

"Now I just miss him every day."

Chiago slung the rope off his shoulder and handed it to Joe. Instead of the usual machine-produced nylon, it had been woven by hand out of strands of horsehair.

"Here. This was his." He dug his heels into his bay's flanks and loped away before Joe could respond.

Joe, Mia, and Jerry Dan sat around the table littered with burrito remnants. A flotilla of *piñatas* dangled overhead, the breeze from the ceiling fans making the paper maché creations sway like floats in Macy's Thanksgiving Day Parade. Draped over the back of Joe's chair was the lariat Michael Chiago had given him. Joe fingered the black and white plaits.

"I can't believe you figured out Forrest wasn't licensed because the bar number on his pleadings was too high," Jerry Dan said.

"My number is fifty thousand something. If Forrest had been a lawyer for almost twenty years, his couldn't be in the forty thousands," Joe replied.

"And Trudy realized it when the bar association sent out the refund check," Jerry Dan marveled.

"The firm had overpaid its bar dues, and it was her job to find out where the mistake was," Joe said. "Forrest had managed to get hold of the cover letter. The police found it when they searched his house. But it was evident he was still looking for the check. That's why he tore Trudy's office apart." Joe shook his head. "I can't believe I was carrying the check around in my pocket the whole time."

"No wonder the guy's walls were bare." Jerry Dan scooped up some salsa with a tortilla chip and popped it into his mouth. "Why didn't he get caught before?"

"He'd always handled the bar association stuff for the firm. This year Atticus decided it took up too much lawyer time and assigned it to Trudy. By the time Forrest found out about the change, it was too late."

"I still don't understand why he just didn't take the test again," Mia said.

"He couldn't," Jerry Dan replied.

"Why not?"

"'Cause he's one of those folks who're born on third base but grow up thinking they've hit a triple. He couldn't admit he'd flunked the bar exam, even to himself." Jerry Dan picked up his glass and swirled the dregs of beer around the bottom. "So do the police think Forrest killed Atticus, too?" he asked.

Joe shook his head. "Atticus's death really was an accident."

"I can't believe it. Death by other than homicide in Pinnacle Peak." Jerry Dan wet the corner of his napkin in the dregs of his water glass and wiped hot sauce drips from his fingers.

"How did Forrest sneak into the firm that night?" Mia asked.

"He used Riley's access card. Everyone knew he kept it in his desk drawer," Joe replied. "The entry records for the night Trudy was killed show her and Riley as the only ones in the office. They also show Riley arriving at work the next morning about when I did, more than an hour before the firm opened. Riley actually got in late that day. It was Forrest using his card. Later, he put it back into Riley's drawer."

"You know, it's funny in a way," Jerry Dan said. "Riley was framing Mia while Forrest was framing him." An uncomfortable silence fell across the table. Looking chagrined at having dampened the mood, Jerry Dan cleared his throat.

"Um, Mia," he began, feigning casualness, "does your public defender have a boyfriend?"

"I didn't know you knew Ronnie, Jerry Dan," she replied, a

twinkle returning to her eyes. "Why do you ask?"

Red infused Jerry Dan's cheeks, creeping up to his hairline. "Aw, I met her at an appellate seminar. She seemed pretty nice."

Joe's face split into a broad grin. "Actually, I think I can arrange for you to have lunch with Ms. Schwartz."

Jerry Dan beamed as brightly as a paper lantern. "Really? That would be fantastic!"

He scrunched his eyebrows together. "Do you think she knows how to line dance?"

Dale Evans' voice started up from the jukebox in the corner, saving Joe and Mia from answering. Jerry Dan lip-synched along until the chorus, which he began to sing out loud.

"Happy trails to you," he crooned before stopping himself mid-refrain.

"That reminds me! You're looking at the assistant to the area chairman of the campaign to award Roy and Dale an honorary Oscar." Jerry Dan's eyebrows lifted in disbelief. "Can you believe they've never received even one?" His voice turned solemn. "And now that they're both gone –"

"It's an injustice." Joe agreed with a straight face.

"You could wear your trophy buckle to the ceremony," Mia suggested.

Jerry Dan tilted back in his chair to admire the oval of silver at his waist. Over the gold pair of team ropers were the words "Winter Series Champion." Jerry Dan's eyes met Joe's.

"Are you absolutely sure you want me to have this?"

Joe nodded emphatically. "You earned it, Jerry Dan. If you hadn't been there that night, you two could be attending my funeral instead of sitting here having another beer."

Danny walked up to their table. "Did I hear a request for *más cerveza*?"

"A small pitcher when you have a chance, please," Joe said.

Danny rested his hands on the back of Mia's chair. "I have heard about the bad lawyers, but not about *Señora* Crawford's missing cattle. *¿Qué pasó?*"

"Don Rogers, Chuck Healy's foreman, was the one who had set out the hay and made the gate Michael Chiago found," Joe said.

"After the cattle got into the habit of gathering next to the fence, he'd drive his truck in, unhook the wire, and load up a few head, taking them to a remote place to overbrand them. Then he'd turn the stock – now carrying his Cloverleaf mark – in with Rocking H cattle. Because he was in charge of the cow count, no one realized how fast his 'herd' was growing." Joe shook his head. "I found one of the iron pieces he'd used to alter the brand, but I didn't know what it was. As soon as Hal saw it, though, he figured out what had been happening."

"Look, Danny," Jerry Dan said, taking a pen from his shirt pocket and reaching for a napkin. "Here's how it worked." Tongue caught between his teeth, he drew the YJ brand:

Next to it, he sketched the piece of metal Joe had found:

"Here's the Crawford brand and here's the scrap Joe found. Look what happens when you put one on top of the other." He drew the two marks again, this time putting the fragment on top of the YJ mark.

"See?" he asked. "The YJ is turned into the Cloverleaf." Jerry Dan looked at Joe. "What I don't get is how can you tell the difference between a cow with a doctored mark and one with a genuine Cloverleaf brand. Don't they both look the same?"

"Hal and the state brand inspector went down to Crow's Landing, the slaughterhouse in Tolleson, and pulled some of Rogers' hides from his last shipment. You can tell if a brand was done all at once or added to by looking at the underside – the scar looks different when you shine a light through it."

"What a perfect crime," Jerry Dan said. "No one can tell you stole the cow unless you turn the cow inside out." He leaned toward Mia. "And if I were a cow, I would have serious objections to that," he said in a stage whisper. She rolled her eyes at him.

"So what happens to *Señor* Rogers now?" Danny asked.

"Hal told me he's going to be prosecuted for felony theft," Joe replied.

"What about shooting at you?" Mia asked with a frown.

"There's no proof it was him," Joe said with a rueful shrug of the shoulder that was still mobile. "All I saw was someone on a bay horse in the distance. The police figure he was picking up some YJ head that day and wanted to scare me away from the area."

"I can hardly wait to tell everybody back home about this!" Jerry Dan said happily. "Cattle rustling! Indian land feuds!" He grinned broadly at his friend. "And Joe gets his first trial out of it, too."

"We'll see," Joe cautioned.

"A trial?" Danny repeated.

"Tess asked me for help recovering either what her missing cows were worth or their replacement from the remainder of Rogers' herd," Joe explained. "I'm going to draft a complaint next week."

"So the police, they are pleased you are such a good crime solver?" Danny asked.

"I think Dresden's just happy it's all over," Joe replied.

"Tess already gave Joe a reward," Jerry Dan told Danny.

Joe looked embarrassed. "I didn't do all that –"

"Rogers wouldn't have been caught without your help, right?" Mia interrupted.

"But it was really Michael and Hal who –" Joe started before Danny's impatience got the better of him.

"*Amigos!* What is this reward you are speaking about?"

"Tess gave him Cricket!" Jerry Dan announced.

Despite trying, Joe couldn't suppress his smile of happiness. Danny's face crinkled with pleasure.

"That is splendid, my friend," he said. "A horse is the best partner a cowboy can have." He bowed toward Mia. "My apologies, *señorita*." Mia blushed while Danny stacked their dishes onto a tray and hoisted it to his shoulder. "Now if you'll excuse me," he said, and walked toward the kitchen, whistling.

"Please excuse me, too." Mia pushed her chair back, her cheeks still crimson. "I need to call my aunt." She walked toward the pay phone in the back.

"What happens to the Barrett Ranch now?" Jerry Dan asked once she was out of earshot. "Is it Mia's?"

Joe shook his head. "She gets the stocks and money bequeathed her under Mrs. Barrett's will. Except for Sonny, there weren't any other specific bequests. The coroner determined he was killed first, so the ranch didn't pass to his estate."

Jerry Dan wrinkled his nose. "This sounds like a law school exam question. The things you T&E lawyers have to pay attention to!"

Joe's mind flashed to the letter he had left on Harrington's desk that morning, but he didn't say anything. He would tell Jerry Dan about his decision later.

"So who gets the ranch?" Jerry Dan pressed.

"Everything but Mia's share goes to Mrs. Barrett's residual beneficiary. I don't know if they'll decide to keep operating the ranch or sell it. I'm sure Chuck Healy is already sniffing around."

"I never took T&E. A residual beneficiary is –?" Jerry Dan asked.

"The person or entity designated to get anything not otherwise willed away," Joe quoted from memory. "The unclaimed leftovers, so to speak."

"They better bring a pretty big plate to this meal," Jerry Dan observed. "Who is it?"

"The Tohono 'O'odham Indian Community. Harrington said Mrs. Barrett had found some family papers describing her grandfather's apparently less than scrupulous means of acquiring the ranch. She didn't want to disinherit Sonny, but if something happened to the both of them, she wanted the property to go back to the original owners."

"Justice is served!" Jerry Dan chortled. "Native Americans avenge white man's thievery. I bet Michael Chiago is one happy warrior."

"You can ask him yourself," Joe said. "I understand he wants to talk to the firm about doing the tribe's legal work."

"Assuming there still is a firm, given this latest round of 'personnel cuts.'"

And there's one more to come, Joe thought soberly, as he glimpsed Mia on the far side of the room. She wended her way through the tables, slipping into her chair just as the front screen door banged. A tall figure was outlined in the opening.

"Wow," Jerry Dan said under his breath. "I wouldn't have pegged him for a customer." Joe shushed him as Alistair Harrington walked toward them.

"Good afternoon Miss Ortiz, Misters McGuinness and Kovacs," the senior lawyer said once he was standing next to their table.

"Hello, sir," Joe replied.

"Mr. Harrington," Jerry Dan and Mia chimed together.

Harrington focused on Mia. "I am so sorry about the ordeal you have been through."

"Thank you," she replied. "Every day gets a little better."

Harrington nodded to Joe and Jerry Dan. "If you gentlemen have a moment, may I have a word with you?"

"Yes, sir," Joe said. Jerry Dan scavenged an extra chair from a neighboring table, brushing the tortilla crumbs off its seat.

As Harrington sat down, Mia gave Joe a quick glance and started to rise. "I should be getting back now –"

Harrington held up a hand. "Please stay. I didn't mean to exclude you."

Danny appeared with a foam-topped pitcher and refilled the empty glasses. "May I get you something, *señor?*"

"*Una cerveza, por favor,*" Harrington replied in flawlessly accented Spanish. Danny cocked an eyebrow at Joe and left to fill the order.

Harrington cleared his throat. "As members of the firm, I wanted you to know Mr. Merchant and I have finalized negotiations with the new senior litigation partner. Are you familiar with Tyler Raynes?"

Joe bit his lower lip and shook his head. "I haven't heard of him," he said as his stomach twisted.

"Her!" Jerry Dan corrected excitedly. "She's the lawyer who got that big verdict against the lawyers and accountants for that

Texas S&L. Class actions, securities fraud, wrongful death – you name it, she does it." He leaned toward Joe. "She's awesome," he muttered out of the corner of his mouth.

Harrington cleared his throat. "It is Mr. Merchant's and my hope you both will stay at the firm and assist in the rebuilding of the litigation department."

"Count me in," Jerry Dan said quickly.

Joe stared at Harrington in astonishment. *Hadn't he seen the letter?* The sight of the envelope Harrington extracted from his inner jacket pocket stilled his thoughts of rushing back to the firm and retrieving it. The ache in his stomach intensified as he recalled with painful clarity the words he had typed last night: "It is with regret I resign my position with the firm to pursue opportunities in trial work ..." So much for finally taking his future into his own hands instead of letting circumstances carry him where they may, he thought miserably.

"Mr. McGuinness, I believe you left this in my office."

Joe was frozen, unable to move.

"By mistake."

Joe reached for the envelope, his gaze never leaving Harrington's face. "Thank you."

"And?" the senior lawyer prompted.

Joe was confused. "Sorry, sir?"

"Will you also be staying?"

A grin split his face. "I'd be very pleased to, sir."

"I must admit your decision causes me a certain amount of regret." Harrington's full attention centered on Joe. "We'll miss you in the Trusts and Estates department. You did good work."

Joe flushed. "Thank you very much, sir."

Danny set Harrington's beer on the table. Jerry Dan raised his mug. "To Harrington, Merchant & Raynes," he announced.

"The new firm's name hasn't yet been chosen," Harrington cautioned, "But I toast the sentiment." He touched the rim of his glass to Jerry Dan's.

Joe felt as though an enormous weight had been lifted off his shoulders. Feeling almost reckless, he turned to the older lawyer. "Speaking of names, sir, may I ask you a question?"

Harrington set down his glass. "Certainly."

"What do the initials D. W. stand for?"

Jerry Dan's mouth dropped open.

Harrington leaned toward the center of the table. As though drawn by magnets, Joe, Jerry Dan and Mia inclined their heads forward, too.

"I've never told anyone before," Harrington began in a conspiratorial tone. The other three waited expectantly. Harrington paused, then spoke.

"But if I ever did, it would have to be at a meeting of the Deadheads." The corners of the severe mouth twitched upward for the briefest of moments. "So don't be a stranger, Joe."

Jerry Dan's laughter rang out while Mia stifled a smile behind her hand.

Joe grinned and shook his head. "I won't, sir. I sure won't."

About the Author ...

Twist Phelan, attorney, athlete and author, has found the physical adventures she encounters as a traveler of the globe as exciting as the challenges she faced in the courtroom. She has paddled surf skis and outrigger canoes in Australia, mountain biked in Costa

Rica, competed in triathlons, skate-skied in Scandinavia, Continental Europe, and North America, played polo in South America, scaled mountains on four continents, and in less than three weeks cycled from the Pacific to the Atlantic.

To accurately portray her protagonist's hobby in *Heir Apparent*, Phelan took roping lessons and participated in a team roping event.

Climbing mountains in foreign countries or in her life comes easy for Phelan. She earned her bachelor's and law degrees from Stanford University, completing her undergraduate studies in two years. Her success as a plaintiff's trial lawyer enabled her to retire from practice in her early thirties.

Phelan's home is wherever her latest athletic endeavor takes her. But no matter where she is, part of every day is spent at her computer working on her novels.

Her passion for horses, admiration for the legal profession and love of the Sonoran desert inspired Phelan to pen a new mystery centered in the fictional desert resort town of Pinnacle Peak, Arizona.

Twist Phelan can be reached at tphelan@twistphelan.com

About SANDS Publishing ...

SANDS Publishing, LLC is an Independent Publisher of nonfiction and fiction books founded in 2001. The company objective is to provide a quality read with every book.

Books may be ordered through Baker & Taylor, directly from the company at (619) 445-4105, fax (619) 659-6017, or on the Website at www.netbookbiz.com.

SANDS is preparing to launch two new imprints.